Robert B. Parker's

...ANCE

"[Spenser is] on top of his game . . . one of the genre's most engaging heroes." —*Detroit Free Press*

"Parker hasn't lost his ear for hard-boiled dialogue." —*Playboy*

"Vintage Spenser . . . Parker's brilliance is in his simple dialogue and in Spenser. Here is a character who is fearless, honest, and clever but never preachy. He's self-deprecating, sometimes sensitive; hard-boiled but never boorish. And he doesn't take himself too seriously." —*Philadelphia Inquirer*

"Our own Dashiell Hammett . . . Spenser and his psychologist sweetheart, Susan, talk dirty, accept each other's irrationality, and have fun. So will anyone who reads this book." —*Baltimore Sun*

"Well-sketched supporting characters . . . fast-paced." —*Chicago Tribune*

"Deeply satisfying." —*Kirkus Reviews*

"The unexpectedly complex machinations of the case complement the always stellar dialogue, the palpable sense of potential violence, and the bantering relationship between Spenser and longtime lover, Susan Silverman." —*Booklist*

"His characters are realistic . . . the dialogue is crisp and often amusing . . . perfect for light summer reading." —*Fresno Bee*

"The world's most perfect private eye . . . the dialogue is as brisk and clever as always." —*Los Angeles Times Book Review*

"Vintage Parker . . . the action rings true . . . Spenser proves himself once more a modern-day knight in shining armor." —*Publishers Weekly*

CHANCE

ROBERT B. PARKER

BERKLEY BOOKS, NEW YORK

THE BERKLEY PUBLISHING GROUP
Published by the Penguin Group
Penguin Group (USA) Inc.
375 Hudson Street, New York, New York 10014, USA
Penguin Group (Canada), 90 Eglinton Avenue East, Suite 700, Toronto, Ontario M4P 2Y3, Canada
(a division of Pearson Penguin Canada Inc.)
Penguin Books Ltd., 80 Strand, London WC2R 0RL, England
Penguin Group Ireland, 25 St. Stephen's Green, Dublin 2, Ireland (a division of Penguin Books Ltd.)
Penguin Group (Australia), 250 Camberwell Road, Camberwell, Victoria 3124, Australia
(a division of Pearson Australia Group Pty. Ltd.)
Penguin Books India Pvt. Ltd., 11 Community Centre, Panchsheel Park, New Delhi—110 017, India
Penguin Group (NZ), 67 Apollo Drive, Rosedale, North Shore 0632, New Zealand
(a division of Pearson New Zealand Ltd.)
Penguin Books (South Africa) (Pty.) Ltd., 24 Sturdee Avenue, Rosebank, Johannesburg 2196,
South Africa

Penguin Books Ltd., Registered Offices: 80 Strand, London WC2R 0RL, England

CHANCE

A Berkley Book / published by arrangement with the author

PRINTING HISTORY
G. P. Putnam's Sons hardcover edition / May 1996
Berkley mass-market edition / April 1997
Berkley premium edition / April 2010

ISBN: 978-0-425-15747-3

BERKLEY®
Berkley Books are published by The Berkley Publishing Group,
a division of Penguin Group (USA) Inc.,
375 Hudson Street, New York, New York 10014.
BERKLEY® is a registered trademark of Penguin Group (USA) Inc.
The "B" design is a trademark of Penguin Group (USA) Inc.

PRINTED IN THE UNITED STATES OF AMERICA

30   29   28   27   26   25   24   23   22   21   20

JOAN:
*Every town is Paris;
every month is May.*

IT WAS ALL TO COME. THE COCKTAILS, THE CRYSTAL, THE starched white napkins, and the soft Sunday mornings with orange juice and floral print coverlets. Apple trees in spring blossom. Evenings He would come home from work with His collar open and His tie loosened and His shirt still crisp, making a nice contrast with the tan on His face and His strong hands. Nights she would lie in the hollow of His muscular arm. They would have a sports car at first and then when they had blond children with red cheeks they'd get a station wagon. She would wear linen dresses and pearls and flattering heels. Standing in the parking lot, in the summerplace night, she studied herself reflected in the dark window of the club. Her red hair was pulled back and tied with a blue ribbon. She wore a pair of white shorts, and a blue

1

sleeveless tee, and dark loafers with no socks. She had on bright lipstick and a lot of dark eye shadow, and her blusher, carefully applied, hid her freckles and almost hid the bruise where her father had hit her. She took a cigarette from her purse and lit it and put it in her mouth and looked again to see how she looked with the smoke curling up in front of her face. There were mercury vapor security lights just under the eaves of the club and their light gave the rows of parked cars an otherworldly gleam. When the club door opened she could hear the dense racket of the band and the crowd, and smell the booze and the sweet pungent marijuana smoke. She unwrapped a stick of Blackjack chewing gum and folded it into her mouth and chewed it soft. She loved the way she looked chewing gum while the cigarette bobbed in her lips and the plume of its vapor made little figures in the air.

He might be in there tonight, and He'd find her, and force His way through the crowd, moving easily as strong men do where others struggle. There would be no need to speak, she'd know Him when she saw Him and He would be the rock on which she would inarticulately found her life. He would be her strength and her joy and her life and her safety.

The door opened again and people crowded out through it.

"Here I come," she thought, and slipped into the loud and reeking room and the door closed behind her.

CHAPTER

1

I WAS BUCKS UP.

I had just collected a very large fee from a very large insurance company, which could easily afford it, for solving a very large insurance scam. I was sitting in my office on a warm fall afternoon with the window open behind me, looking at my checkbook, admiring my bank balance, and thinking about whether I should retire or buy a new gun, when an important thug named Julius Ventura came in with a sullen-looking young blond woman.

"How you doing," Ventura said.

"I'm bucks up," I said.

Ventura was one of those guys who paid so much attention to how tough he was that he didn't pay much attention to anything else.

He said, "I gotta talk to you."

He was a strong guy gone fat, with thick black hair that he combed straight back, and a big nose that came straight down from the bridge with no curvature at all. He had on a double-breasted black suit and a gray shirt with a bolero string tie knotted up tight. The sullen woman was much younger than Ventura. She had big hair and a lot of eye makeup, and a pouty lower lip that she was aware of and emphasized by moistening it often. She was wearing one of those silly-looking single-piece top and shorts outfits where the shorts look kind of like a skirt. The outfit was red. With it she wore red heels.

I waved Ventura toward a client chair. Ever the optimist, I had five of them in the office. Ventura sat on one and took a big breath as if the effort had been telling. The young woman sat beside him. She was wearing a wedding ring and a huge diamond solitaire. I put my checkbook away in the left-hand drawer of my desk, and leaned back in my chair and smiled in a friendly way.

"How much you charge?" Ventura said.

He sat with his feet flat on the ground, his knees apart, his stomach resting on his thighs.

"Depends on what I'm doing," I said. "And who I'm doing it for."

"You got an hourly rate?"

"Sure," I said.

I smiled at the young woman. She didn't smile back. She was busy with her lower lip.

"Well, what is it?" Ventura said.

4

I told him.

"That for an eight-hour day?" Ventura said.

"That's for every hour I work," I said. "Might be more than eight. I don't charge you for sleeping."

The young woman had sucked in her lower lip a little and caught it gently in her upper front teeth.

"Who keeps track of your hours?" Ventura said.

"I do."

"Well, that's a pretty soft deal for you now, ain't it."

"Pretty soft," I said.

We were quiet. The late September air moved gently through the window and fluttered some papers on my desk. The young woman pursed her lower lip for a moment as if she were going to whistle "Evelina." But she didn't, she just let it purse there for a moment and then went back to holding it in her upper teeth. It was sort of interesting.

"I heard about you," Ventura said.

I nodded modestly.

"Talked to some people about you."

"Un huh."

"Like your man Hawk, for instance."

"Hawk is some people," I said.

"Says you're a big pain in the ass."

"He's jealous," I said. "'Cause girls like me better."

"Fact is I asked him to take this thing on for me."

"Oh," I said. "That kind of work."

"Maybe," Ventura said. "Hawk says he'll do it, if you do it."

"When I can," I said, "I like to be legal."

"Nothing illegal about this job," Ventura said.

"Un huh."

"You want it? Pay your fee, no argument; expenses, no problem; cash if you want; maybe two, maybe three weeks' work."

"So how come Hawk won't do it unless I do it too?"

Ventura shrugged. "He didn't say."

"He often doesn't," I said. "Whaddya got?"

Ventura glanced at the blonde beside him.

"My daughter's husband took off on her," he said.

"Daddy," the blonde said. "You don't know that. Something coulda maybe happened."

"This your daughter?" I said.

"Yeah."

I stood and leaned over the desk and put out a hand.

"How do you do," I said.

"Yeah," she said. "How you doing."

She took my hand and shook it.

"You know my name," I said.

"Sure."

She licked her lower lip again, quite fast back and forth.

"Her name's Shirley," Ventura said.

"Lovely name," I said.

The lower lip went under the teeth again. I let go of her hand and sat back down.

"So you want me to find your son-in-law?"

"Don't call him that," Ventura said. "My daughter married him. I got nothing to do with it."

"How long's he been missing?" I said.

"Three days."

"That's all, and you're coming to me?"

"My daughter misses him."

"You said he took off on her. She says maybe not. Anyone want to amplify that?"

Shirley looked at her father. Her father shrugged.

"He's a bum," Ventura said. "I give him odd jobs here and there, keep him off welfare. But he's a bum. I figure he took off with some bimbo will work him for what he's got and leave him when he's empty."

"That's not true, Daddy. Anthony loves me."

Ventura didn't say anything.

"No problems in the marriage?" I said.

"Oh, no. He woulda stood on his head for me."

"So what might have happened?" I said.

She looked at me blankly. She showed her top teeth. They were shiny and even, like they'd been bonded. The tip of her tongue poked out under her teeth and moved along her lower lip. Her eyes looked a little random.

"I don't know. Maybe there was an accident, you know. Hit and run, or something."

I nodded.

"Cops?" I said.

Ventura grunted.

"No cops," he said.

"Simple missing person? Why not?"

"You know better," he said.

"You got people," I said. "Why on family business, a

7

wandering husband, only three days gone, would you go to Hawk?"

"We're talking about my kid here, you know? I want the best."

"For a missing hubby? Hawk? And he won't do it without me?"

"You want the job or not. Most people be happy to get it."

I stood up and turned my back on them and looked out my window, down at Berkeley Street where it crosses Boylston. I like the view. You could see up Boylston a good way, and down Berkeley, toward the river. Lot of attractive women worked in the Back Bay, many of them walking about this very corner, and I was trying to stay abreast of this year's fall fashions. I didn't like Ventura. His daughter appeared to be a nitwit. I didn't believe either one of them. I didn't need the money. There was no reason to take the job . . . except that it was the kind of work I did. And there was no one waiting in the hall for the next appointment.

"You got a picture of him?" I said, still looking down at the street life below me.

"Yes," Shirley said.

I turned around and sat back down at my desk. Shirley took a wedding photo out of her purse. There she was in the white gown and veil and elaborate tiara. There he was in his pearl gray tux with the black satin shawl collar. He had a sharp narrow face, with a sharp nose and narrow eyes. His black hair was longish and smooth and thick with mousse, brushed back on the sides, and falling in a darling curl on his forehead.

"Adorable," I said. "When did you see him last?"

"Monday morning when he left the house," Shirley said.

"Same time as usual?" I said.

"Yes. Anthony was very responsible about his work. He felt the responsibility of being Daddy's son-in-law."

I looked at Ventura. He didn't say anything.

"And you didn't have a fight before he left?"

"Oh, no."

"What's the address?" I said.

"Address?" Shirley looked at her father.

"Why you need to know where she lives?" he said.

"Just thought it might be a nice place to start."

"I don't like people knowing any of our addresses."

"Sure," I said. "I understand. No need to tell me anything. I'll just stick my head out the window and yell 'Hey, Anthony.' That'll probably work."

"I'm in a sensitive business," Ventura said. "I don't like people poking around in it."

I held the picture out to Shirley.

"Then take back your picture, and take a walk. You hire me to look for Anthony I'm going to be poking around in your business."

Shirley didn't take the picture.

"I'm going to look through his belongings. I'm going to ask around the neighborhood. I'm going to talk to people who knew him."

"The hell you will," Ventura said.

"We have a condo," Shirley said. "In Point of Pines."

She gave me the address. Ventura stood up and took the picture that I was still holding out toward Shirley.

"Come on, Shirley. Deal's off," he said. "This is family business."

Shirley's face got red and squeezed up and tears began to roll down her cheeks. She clasped both hands together in her lap and lowered her head as if she were studying the grip and began to sob. I sat back in my chair and watched.

"Come on," Ventura said again.

Shirley kept right on sobbing at her lap.

"Goddamn it, Shirley . . ."

Shirley sobbed resolutely. I sat, with my chair tilted back, and waited.

"Oh, fuck!" Ventura said and tossed the picture back on my desk and sat down.

I got a box of Kleenex out of my bottom drawer and placed them on the desk where Shirley could reach them. She plucked one out and dabbed at her eyes with it.

"We're in business?" I said to Ventura.

"Yeah."

Shirley looked up and smiled, and said, "Thank you, Daddy."

Ventura nodded without looking at her. He was looking at me. A hard look. So I'd know how dangerous he was. He was wasting his time. I already knew how dangerous he was.

"You know my occupation, right?" Ventura said.

"Yeah."

Ventura looked an even harder look at me. I managed to keep my poise.

"You learn anything, might be, ah, some kind of problem, you know, you keep it to your fucking self, right?"

"Anyone ever actually faint when you were giving them the hard stare?" I said.

Ventura didn't answer. He kept looking at me.

"You know, sort of gasp with terror," I said, "and slide down in the chair and let their head fall sideways with their tongue hanging out? Like this?"

I demonstrated what I meant. Shirley giggled into the Kleenex she was still using.

"Shut up, Shirley, he ain't funny," Ventura said, without easing up on his hard look.

"You know that, Spenser?" he said. "You ain't funny. You think you are. You think you're a fucking riot, you know? Well, you ain't. My kid wants you to find her husband. Okay, you find him, and I pay you, and you go your way. No problem. But you dick around with me at all, and something will happen that won't be so fucking funny."

Still playing dead, slumped in my chair with my head tilted, and my tongue out, I opened one eye and looked at Shirley. She giggled again. Then I slurped my tongue in and sat up.

"Okay," I said. "Now it's my turn. There's a lot about this deal that doesn't make any sense, because there's a lot

11

you're not telling me. That's all right, I'm used to it. I'll take the case. But when I find out what you're not telling me, I reserve the right, if I don't like it, to quit."

Ventura didn't have a big repertoire. He was back to his hard look again.

"What did Anthony do for you?" I said to Ventura.

"He worked for me."

"Doing what?"

"Doing what I told him."

I looked at Shirley. Her eyes were dry now, though she still held the Kleenex in both fists, clenched in her lap, just in case.

"Anthony was in the financial part," she said as helpfully as she could.

I looked at Ventura. He stared back at me.

I said, "Un huh."

"He chase women?" I said.

"Oh no," Shirley said. "Never. He wasn't like that at all."

"Gamble?"

Shirley's eyes flicked almost invisibly toward her father and then back at me. It was so quick I wasn't entirely sure it happened.

"No," she said firmly. "I mean he'd play cards for pennies with the guys and drink a few beers, and stuff once in like a blue moon, but gamble, no way."

"Any vices at all?" I said. "Booze, coke, too much coffee?"

"Oh no. You have the wrong picture of him. Anthony was very nice, and he was crazy about me."

It went like that for maybe forty minutes more. Me asking questions. Shirley answering, and Ventura sitting like a mean toad giving me the stone stare. At the end of the forty minutes it was clear that Anthony had no reason to take off, and every reason to stay home and drink champagne from Shirley's slipper. Except that Anthony was gone.

Being a trained investigator, I smelled a rat.

CHAPTER

2

SUSAN AND I WERE RUNNING UP AND DOWN THE STEPS AT THE Harvard Stadium late on a Sunday afternoon. At the top of section 7, we paused for a moment to breathe. We were the only ones in the stadium. On the circular track out back of the stadium a few people were jogging. At the far end of the athletic complex, where, across the road, the Charles River curved in one of its big rolling bends, there was a pickup soccer game in progress. Susan wore glistening black spandex tights and a luminescent green top. Her thick dark hair was held off her forehead by a green sweatband, and there were green highlights on her state-of-the-art sneakers. Her thigh muscles moved smoothly under the spandex, there was clear muscle definition in the backs of her arms, and sweat glistened on her face. If I hadn't already done so in a guidance office in Smithfield twenty years ago, I would have fallen in love with her right there.

"I don't get why you agreed to look for whatsisname," Susan said.

"Anthony Meeker," I said. "Julius Ventura's son-in-law."

"Yes," Susan said, "him. How come?"

We started down the stairs again. It was late September, still pleasant. Along the river the leaves had begun to turn but not very many of them and not very much. The white-lined turf on the football field below us was as green as if it were May.

"It's my profession," I said.

"A job that Hawk turned down? Where the employer tells you you'll get in trouble if you investigate?"

We reached the bottom step and turned and started up section 6.

"Hawk didn't turn it down," I said. "He said he'd do it if I would."

"His reasoning being?"

"I don't know. I haven't talked to him."

"But you know him. What would you hypothesize?"

"That it wasn't his kind of work, but if he could get me to do the boring investigation stuff, he'd hang around, maybe hit somebody, and pick up half a fee."

"But don't you think that Mr. Ventura is lying to you?"

"Oh sure," I said.

"And is he not dangerous?"

"He employs dangerous people," I said.

"Do you think the investigation stuff is boring?"

15

"No."

We were at the top of section 4. East of us I could see the two big towers in Back Bay, not very far from my office. My quadriceps were beginning to feel shaky, but Susan showed no signs of slowing down, and of course I couldn't stop before she did—death before dishonor. We turned and headed back down.

"That's part of it, isn't it?" Susan said.

"That I don't find the investigation stuff boring?"

"Yes. You're simply curious. There's a hidden truth in the case. You want to find it out."

I shrugged, which is more awkward than you might think, if you're running down your 1000th stadium step.

"The other part is you can't bear to be told what to do. When Mr. Ventura warned you that you couldn't do A, B, or C, he sealed the deal."

I shrugged again. I was getting the hang of it.

"I'm in the business of selling brains and balls," I said. "And most people value the latter."

"Lucky for you," Susan murmured.

I ignored her.

"And it is not good for the business if people perceive me as someone who can be scared off of something."

We turned and started back up. My quads were beginning to feel as if they were made of lemon Jell-O. Perspiration was soaking through the back of Susan's top. She was the most elegant person I had ever known, and she sweated like a horse.

"It wouldn't matter," she said. I heard no sound of

16

exhaustion in her voice. Her breath was still even. "Even if it were good for business you couldn't let someone chase you off."

Shrugging was even harder going up the stairs. I was concentrating on getting one foot then the other up each step now. I was starting to tie up. I could never understand how the quads could turn to jelly and then knot. At the top of the stairs Susan stopped and rested her forearms on the retaining wall and looked out at the traffic below us on Western Ave.

"I've had it," she said. "Time to stop."

"So soon?" I said. "Ah, frailty, thy name is woman."

She didn't say anything, but she looked at me the way she does, out of the corner of her eyes, and I knew she knew the truth. We walked together around the top level of the stadium, as the light began to fade.

"When will you talk to Hawk?" Susan said.

"Henry says he's out of town."

"So, what's your first move?" Susan said.

"I was thinking of patting you on the backside, and whispering 'Hey, cutie, how about it?' "

"That's effective," Susan said. "I mean the business with the missing husband. What are you going to do first?"

"Deposit Ventura's check," I said. "See if it clears."

"And if it does?"

"Then I'll have to come up with a plan," I said.

"Besides patting me on the backside."

"Besides that."

"But not instead of," she said.

"No. Never instead of."

We stood quietly at the top of the old stadium, our fore-arms resting on the chest-high wall, our shoulders touching lightly, looking out at the declining autumn sun.

"You like that, don't you," Susan said. "Walking into something and not knowing what you'll find."

"I like to see what develops," I said. "See what's in there."

We had been together for twenty years, except for a brief midterm hiatus. The excitement of being with her had never waned. The twenty years simply deepened the resonance.

"And whatever develops, you assume you'll be able to manage it."

"So far so good," I said.

She put her hand on top of mine for a minute.

"Yes," she said. "So far, very good."

CHAPTER
3

Two days later I found Hawk at the Harbor Health Club, in the boxing room, working on the heavy bag. He had on Reebok high tops, black sweats, and a black tee-shirt with the sleeves cut off. In white script, across the front of the tee-shirt, was written, *Yes, it's a black thing.*

"Wow," I said, "militant."

"Dating a B.U. professor," Hawk said. "Impresses the hell out of her."

He dug a left hook into the bag.

"Where you been?" I said.

"San Antonio. Hold the bag."

I leaned into the bag and held it still, which was not relaxing. Hawk had a punch like a jackhammer, and the bag wanted to jump around and say beep beep.

"What were you doing in San Antonio?"

"Looking at the Alamo," Hawk said.

"Of course you were."

"Riverwalk's kind of nice there too," Hawk said. He was driving the left hook repetitively into the bag.

"Yeah. You want to talk to me about Anthony Meeker."

"Who?"

"Julius Ventura's son-in-law."

Hawk grinned and began to alternate three hooks, with one overhand right. The punches were so fast that the sound of them nearly ran together.

"And the cerebral daughter?"

"Shirley," I said.

"Imagine running off from Shirley," Hawk said.

I moved the bag a half step back from Hawk as he started the next combination, and he shuffled a half step forward and maintained the pattern. The reaction had been visceral. He may not have been conscious that I'd moved the bag.

"You got a plan?" he said.

"What makes you think I'm going to do it?"

Hawk smiled and switched to an overhand lead, and a left cross pattern.

"How long I know you?" he said.

"Story smells like an old flounder," I said.

"Sure do," Hawk said.

"You in?" I said.

"Un huh."

"But only if I do it," I said.

"Un huh."

Hawk did three left hooks so fast that it felt almost like one big one as I leaned on the bag. He followed with a right cross, and stepped back.

"You the dee-tective," Hawk said. "I is just a fun-loving adventurer."

"So you want to watch?"

"Gig in San Antonio is finished. Got nothing going right now," Hawk said. He wiped the sweat off his face and naked scalp with one of the little white hand towels that Henry handed out as a perk. "You sure to make Ventura mad. And it'll give me something to do."

"You put us together to see what would happen," I said.

Hawk looked pleased.

"All work and no play," Hawk said.

While I waited for Hawk to shower and change, I honed my observational skills by studying the tightness of the various leotards on the young professional women who made up most of Henry's clientele. It did not escape my attention that there was scant room for anything underneath. When he was through, Hawk went to Henry's office to retrieve his gun from a locked drawer in Henry's desk.

Henry weighed about 134 pounds, and 133 of it was muscle. He had gone twice with Willie Pep in his youth and done as well with Willie as I had with Joe Walcott. It showed on his face.

"That's the biggest fucking weapon I ever seen," Henry said.

21

"Got a lot of stopping power," Hawk said.

He shrugged into the shoulder rig, and slipped on a gray and black crinkle-finish warm-up jacket with bell sleeves and a stand-up collar. He checked his reflection in the window to see how the jacket hid the gun.

"Whyn't you get one of them new nines," Henry said. "Fit nice under your coat, fire fifteen, sixteen rounds a clip."

Hawk made a minute adjustment to the drape of the jacket.

"Don't need fifteen rounds," Hawk said.

"What you carrying?" Henry said to me.

I opened my coat and showed him the short-barreled Smith & Wesson on my belt.

"That's all?"

"It's enough," I said. "Most of the shooting I've ever had to do is from about five feet away and was over in one or two shots. A nine with fifteen rounds in the clip is heavy to carry. I got one, and I bring it if I think I'll need it. Got a three fifty-seven too, and a twelve-gauge shotgun and a forty-four-caliber rifle. But for walking around, the thirty-eight is fine."

"Well," Henry said. "I got a nine, and I like it."

"You safe without no gun, Henry," Hawk said. "You so teeny anybody shoot at you, going to miss anyway."

"Just keep it in mind," Henry said, "I ever come after you."

Hawk and I went out, adequately armed, at least by our standards, and walked along the waterfront through a raw

22

wind blowing off the harbor. When we got to the Boston Harbor Hotel we went in and sat in the lounge looking out at the harbor past the big cupola where the airport ferry docked. We ordered coffee.

Hawk said, "You doing decaf again?"

"Sure. It's good for me . . . I like it."

"'Course you do."

Hawk put his feet up on the low table in front of the couch we sat on. Outside, the airport ferry slid around the end of Rowe's Wharf and edged in to the cupola to unload passengers. The waitress warmed our cups. Hawk asked if she had a bakery basket. She said she did and would be pleased to bring one.

The waitress returned with the bakery basket. There were scones and little corn muffins and some croissants, that were still warm. I had one.

"Goes great with decaf," I said.

Hawk was watching the people file off the ferry with their garment bags and briefcases. He shook his head, and picked up one of the small corn muffins, and popped it in his mouth. I drank some coffee. The ferry picked up a scattering of passengers and backed away from the dock, turning slowly when it was far enough out, sliding on the dark slick harbor water like a hurling stone.

"You think Anthony fooling around?" Hawk said.

"Shirley's a good argument for it," I said.

"I married to Shirley I wouldn't be fooling around with other women," Hawk said. "I be serious about it. You think Julius wants him found so Shirley be happy?"

"Maybe," I said.

"Loving father," Hawk said.

"It's possible," I said. "Hitler liked dogs."

The waitress was looking at Hawk from across the room. Hawk smiled at her. She smiled back at him.

"You figure Anthony took some of Julius's money?" Hawk said.

"Shirley said Anthony was in the financial end of the business."

"That both ends," Hawk said, "for Julius."

I nodded. Outside the window wall a seagull landed on one of the ornamental mooring posts, and tucked his wings up and turned his head in profile checking for the remnants of a bite-sized donut hole that someone might have dropped, or a stray French fry. Gulls were actually pretty good-looking birds. The problem was that there were so many of them, and they were so raucous and eager, that no one ever bothered to notice that they had nice proportions.

"I asked Shirley if Anthony gambled and she had an odd look, just a flicker, before she said no."

"Ordinary man woulda missed it," Hawk said.

"True," I said. "And maybe he'd be right. It wasn't much."

"Think he might be a gambler?"

"If he was it would be a place to start," I said.

Hawk finished his coffee and looked up. The waitress was there, more alert than a seagull, and filled his cup.

Hawk let his voice drop an octave or so and said, "Thank you." The waitress hovered for a moment, managed not to wiggle all over, and went away.

"And if he not a gambler?" Hawk said.

"Got no place to start."

"So he a gambler," Hawk said, "until we find something better."

"Maybe a gambler that fooled around on his wife."

"And took Julius Ventura's money," Hawk said. "To do both."

"So not a smart gambler," I said.

"Maybe not even a live one," Hawk said.

"Except Julius's daughter wants him back."

"Maybe Julius had him chilled and then hired you and me to make it look good for the daughter."

"Not a bad thought," I said. "But why hire you and me?"

"'Cause we too good?"

"Yeah. There's lots of reputable private licenses around that could spend his money, look good, and find zip."

Hawk nodded. "Yeah, he already killed Anthony he don't want us looking into it. 'Cause we going to find out he did it. And you being a Boy Scout, going to tell."

"So he must want him found," I said. "But why us? Why not his own people?"

Hawk smiled.

"Impress the daughter," he said.

"Maybe. Maybe more than that."

"Like maybe the son-in-law done something Julius don't want his own people to find out?" Hawk said.

"You're pretty smart," I said, "for an aging Negro man."

"Sho'nuff," Hawk said.

CHAPTER
4

L~ENNIE SELTZER WAS IN HIS USUAL BOOTH AT THE TENNES-~
see Tavern on Mass Avenue. He was talking on a portable
phone and sipping beer. A laptop computer sat on the table in front of him, the lid up, the screen blank. On the
seat across from him in the booth a briefcase stood open.
As I sat down Lennie nodded at me and made a small
gesture with his free hand at the bartender. I waited while
Lennie listened to the phone. He didn't say anything.
The bartender brought over a shot of Irish whisky and a
draft beer. Lennie always bought me a shot of Irish whisky
and a beer when he saw me. I always drank the beer and
left the whisky, but it didn't discourage Lennie at all. Lennie kept listening to the phone. As he listened he turned
on the computer. I drank some beer. Finally Lennie said,

"Copacetic," and hung up. He typed on the computer for a moment, looked at what he'd written; nodded to himself, hit a couple more keys on the computer, turned it off, and shut the lid. Then he picked up his beer bottle, poured a little into his glass, and drank some. He took a handkerchief from his breast pocket, patted his lips, refolded the handkerchief, and put it back.

"Question?" he said.

"How come you always buy me a shot of Irish whisky and a draught beer, even though you drink bottle beer, and I never drink the whisky?"

"'Cause you're Irish, aren't you?"

"Oh, yeah."

"What else you want?" Lennie said. He had on a brown suit with a tan chalk stripe, a lavender shirt, with a white collar and a wide chocolate-colored silk tie tied in a big Windsor knot. His black hair was parted in the middle and slicked back evenly on both sides of the part.

"Know a guy named Anthony Meeker?"

"Un huh."

"He a gambler?"

"Gambler implies that sometimes you win. I win more than I lose, for instance. It's how I make my living. Anthony don't gamble. Anthony loses."

"Stupid?"

"Yeah, but that ain't it. Stupid you lose more than you win, but even stupid, you win sometimes. Anthony needs it too much."

"The money?"

"Probably not the money. Probably the rush. I don't know. For me it's better than regular work. But it don't make me crazy. For Anthony? I seen him once keep betting in five-card stud when he was beat on the table. You know? Guy had three eights showing with four cards out. Anthony had nothing. Best he could do with a fifth card was a pair. But he kept kicking into the pot."

Lennie drank some beer, poured out the rest of the bottle, and stared at the foam as it settled.

"Compulsive," I said.

"Sure," Lennie said.

"He been losing a lot lately?"

"Don't know. He married Julius Ventura's daughter I wouldn't let him bet with me anymore."

"Julius say anything?"

"No, but I been doing fine these years without pissing Julius Ventura off. I didn't see no reason to start."

"So you don't know firsthand, you hear anything?"

"People don't talk about Julius Ventura's son-in-law, Spenser. He's in hock to them they stay low about it, you know."

The bartender brought Lennie a new bottle of Budweiser.

"How many beers you drink a day?" I said.

"Maybe sixteen," Lennie said. "Why you asking about Anthony."

"He's missing."

Lennie nodded.

"Julius hired me to find him," I said.

29

"You're shitting me."

"Nope."

I drank some beer.

"He fool around with women?" I said.

"Julius Ventura hired you to find his son-in-law?"

"Me and Hawk," I said. "What kind of beer is this?"

Lenny shrugged and called to the bartender over his shoulder.

"Jackie, what kinda draught beer you serving us?"

"New Amsterdam Black and Tan," Jackie said.

"New Amsterdam Black and Tan," Lennie said.

"Thanks," I said. "His answer was much too hard for me."

"Why the fuck is Julius hiring you and Hawk, for crissake?"

"Julius's a first-class guy," I said.

"You know he ain't," Lennie said. He lowered his voice when he said it. "What's going on?"

I shrugged.

"Anthony fool around with women?" I said.

"I don't know," Lennie said.

"Can you find out?"

"No."

"I like a man knows his limitations," I said.

"I know gambling," Lennie said. "I don't know shit about fooling around."

"Your wife will be pleased to hear that."

"She's the reason I don't know."

I finished my New Amsterdam Black & Tan. I wanted

another one, but I was used to that. I always wanted another one. Lennie picked up his portable phone and dialed a number.

"It's Lennie," he said into the phone. "Gimme what you
got."

I got up from the booth, shot Lennie once by dropping
my thumb on my forefinger, and left the bar, and headed
down Newbury Street.

CHAPTER

5

It was a Grand Wednesday afternoon on Newbury Street. The sky was blue, the temperature was in the low seventies, and people trying to look like Eurotrash were sitting outside having various kinds of fancy coffee and looking at each other. A college-aged woman in tight jeans, high boots, and a red St. Lawrence Hockey jacket walked by with a black Lab on a leash. The Lab wore a red bandana around his neck. Most black Labs you saw in the Back Bay had red bandanas around their neck, but not every one was color-coordinated with its owner. I walked down from Mass Ave. toward my office, past boutiques, designer shops, handmade-jewelry stores, sidewalk cafes, tiny chic restaurants, pet stores that sold iguanas, places that sold frozen yogurt, Hermès scarfs, hand-hammered silver, decorative furniture, muffins, scones, wine, cheese, pâté. Behind me across the street in front of a sign that advertised boysenberry sorbet was a big guy in a watch cap who had as much business on Newbury Street as I did. I had seen him outside my office earlier this morning, and he had been behind me when I went to talk with Lennie. Now he was looking in the window of the ice cream store, his hands deep in his jacket pockets while he studied the options to boysenberry sorbet, paying no attention to me. And being blatant about it.

I walked on to Dartmouth Street and turned right toward Copley Square. Across from the public library, I turned right onto Boylston Street and went past H. H. Richardson's other church back toward Mass Ave. By the time I reached Exeter Street, the guy in the Patriots football jacket was turning up Boylston. I stopped outside Morton's Steak House and leaned on the doorway. He walked on past me and crossed Exeter Street and leaned idly against the streetlight post, musing on the new addition to the library. Probably agreed with me that the new addition was ugly. I walked across Exeter Street, and stood beside him on the corner, looking at the new part of the library.

"Looks like corporate headquarters for an oil refinery," I said. "Don't you think?"

"You talking to me?" he said.

"Doesn't it just leave a sour taste in your mouth when an architectural treasure is esthetically debased?" I said.

"Sure, pal. I'll be talking to you."

"That why you're following me around?" I said. " 'Cause you want to talk to me?"

"Following you? What the fuck are you talking about?"

He started to walk away. I walked along beside him. At Fairfield, he turned right and I turned right with him. He stopped. I stopped.

"Buzz off," he said.

I smiled at him. He walked again, across Newbury down to Commonwealth. I walked with him. He stopped.

"Keep it up, pal," he said, "and I'm going to knock you on your ass."

"Probably not," I said.

"I warned you," he said.

We crossed the inbound side of Commonwealth and turned right on the mall toward The Public Gardens. He was stepping out smartly.

"Don't you think this is a great stretch of city?" I said.

He kept walking.

"I don't know if I've seen another stretch of urban space like it," I said. "The brick and brownstone townhouses, the wide pedestrian mall in the center, all the statues, the trees, the flowering shrubs. You know any other places like it?"

Apparently he didn't.

"And you can see the full length of it, from Charles Street to Kenmore Square, because it's dead flat, you know?"

Apparently he knew.

At Clarendon Street he stopped under the arching trees, near a bench. I stopped too. A gray-haired woman in a black and white checked pant suit passed us walking a honey-colored spaniel on a red leash.

When she had passed the big guy said, "You don't know who you're fucking with, pal. Now you either get lost or I knock you on your ass."

"Who am I fucking with?" I said.

The big guy led with his right, which is effective only with amateurs. I pulled my head out of the way and smiled. He followed up with a meandering left hook which I avoided also.

"You loop your punches," I said.

He lunged at me and I stepped sideways and played him past me with my hands.

"You're going to hurt yourself," I said.

He stood staring at me, breathing hard. Then he lowered his head and charged at me. I slipped the charge again and drove my right fist into his left kidney as he went by. He grunted and fell face forward. I stepped away from him.

"See," I said. "Short punches. The one I hit you with didn't travel a foot, but I turned into it when I threw it and got a lot behind it."

He got to his hands and knees, and then to his feet. He stood crookedly, as if his left kidney were hurting, which it surely was, and stared at me.

"We going to walk some more?" I said.

He unzipped his jacket with his right hand and reached inside. By the time he got his hand on his gun, mine was out and pointing at him.

"Silly to walk around with your gun zipped up inside," I said. "I know you didn't expect you'd need it, but once I got annoying, you should have at least unzipped just in case."

He didn't know what to do. He stood staring at my gun, holding his gun half out from under his coat.

"Did the folks who told you to follow me also tell you it would be okay to shoot me in the middle of Comm Ave. at ten-thirty in the morning?"

He let the gun slide back into its place and took his hand away from his coat.

"No."

"Good," I said. "Why don't you zip the coat up good, and I'll just sort of keep my piece handy here in my pocket."

"Why don't you kiss my ass," he said. And turned and started walking toward The Public Gardens again. I walked with him. My gun was the short-barreled Smith & Wesson .38 and I could easily hold it inside the pocket of my green windbreaker. We reached Arlington Street in silence and crossed and went into The Public Gardens which was still bright with flowers in the early fall. Near the big statue of George Washington on horseback he stopped again.

"You going to follow me home?" he said.

"Sure," I said.

"You're making me look bad, you know? You're gonna get me in trouble, following me like this."

"Un huh."

Ahead of us the swan boats were still in the water, full of people, trailed by a convoy of hungry ducks to whom the tourists gave peanuts.

"Whyn't you gimme a fucking break, pal?"

"Naw."

He stood some more. He looked at Washington above him. He looked back at the Swan Boat Lagoon, and the boats full of people being slowly pedaled about by college kids with quads of steel. He looked back at me.

"Okay," he said. "I'm fucked. What do you want?"

"I want to know why you are following me."

"Guy asked me to."

"Who?"

"You gotta promise me, you don't say I told you, you know. It don't make me look real good."

"Don't feel bad," I said. "You just weren't ready for what you got. You're used to collecting overdue vig from some guy fixes timing chains for a living. Doesn't matter you loop your punches, you still hit him. You don't need to have your gun where you can get at it quick."

"You gotta promise," he said.

"Sure."

"They find out I let you roust me, it won't do me no good."

I waited. Behind him one of the swan boats drifted under the little bridge. The ducks glided behind it.

"Marty told me to see who you talked to," the Big Guy said.

"Marty who?"

"Marty Anaheim," he said. There was surprise in his voice that there could be another Marty.

"Works for Gino Fish," I said.

Again the guy looked startled.

"He don't work for him, man. Marty's his number-one guy," he said.

"Awesome," I said. "You know why he wanted me followed?"

"Naw. I'm just a fucking laborer, you know. Grunt work. They don't tell me shit."

"When did Marty tell you to start following me?"

"Sent me out this morning."

"How long were you supposed to stay on me?"

"Till he told me to stop."

"Okay, here's what you do. Tell him I made you, and you decided the wisest course was to bail out on the tail. You got that?"

"The wisest course . . . ?"

"Ad-lib if you want to."

"Yeah, but Marty'll put somebody else on you."

"Tell him not to," I said.

"I can't tell Marty Anaheim what to do."

"Anyone else follows me around I'm going to speak to Marty direct."

"Jesus, you can't do that, he'll know I told you."

I shrugged and turned and walked away from him. I

crossed Arlington Street at the light. Down at the corner of Newbury Street people were going into the Ritz, probably having lunch in the cafe. The bar would be open. I wondered if they served New Amsterdam Black & Tan these days. I looked back at the Big Guy. He was still standing there beside Washington. Next to the monumental sculpture he looked small.

CHAPTER
6

I WAS SITTING AT MY DESK WITH MY FEET UP, READING THE *Globe*, when Hawk came into my office with a bag of donuts and two large cups of coffee. My windows were open behind me and the sound and scent of morning traffic drifted up, along with the smell of bacon cooking somewhere, and beneath it, the smell from the river five blocks away. Even though it was September, it still smelled like summer.

"Got you some delicious decaffeinated," Hawk said.

"You drinking real coffee?" I said.

"Guatemalan dark roast," he said.

"Keep drinking that stuff you'll be bouncing around like one of the Nicholas Brothers."

Hawk set out the coffee for each of us and put the bag of donuts between us. He hooked one of my client chairs over near the desk where he could reach the donuts and sat down. He was wearing a dark blue suede jacket made to look like denim, over a white silk tee-shirt. His jeans were pressed and his black cowboy boots were hand tooled from the skin of some reptile I didn't recognize.

"Just up tempo my natural rhythm," he said. "What we going to do about Marty Anaheim?"

"Sort of a problem," I said. "I told the slugger I wouldn't spill the beans."

"That you made him, and he told you who sent him?"

"Yeah."

Hawk stared at me for a time. Then he shook his head.

". . . obedient, cheerful, thrifty," he muttered, more to himself than to me, "brave, clean, and reverent."

"I'm not too obedient," I said.

"You ain't too fucking reverent either," Hawk said, "but you still a goddamned Eagle Scout."

"I told him I wouldn't," I said. "You know what Marty's like."

"I remember once Marty beat a guy to death with a pool cue," Hawk said. "They playing pool, and the guy kidding Marty. Saying how Patriots folded against the Bears in the eighty-five Super Bowl. Marty likes those Patriots. So he starts hitting the guy with the butt end of the pool cue."

"Guy overestimated Marty's sense of humor," I said.

Hawk nodded.

"Your slugger probably be in some trouble, you tell Marty he screwed up the tail job."

"He's a dope," I said. "He couldn't tail a bull through a china shop. No need to get him killed."

"Everybody know Marty's a psycho. You work with him, you gotta be prepared to deal with that."

"I sort of promised."

"Okay," Hawk said. "I know what you like. How we going to do it?"

I ate a plain donut and drank some decaf. Hawk sipped his Guatemalan dark roast.

"Well, the best guess is that Marty, or more likely Gino Fish, knew that Julius hired me. And they wanted to see who I talked to and what I found."

"Julius hired *us*," Hawk said.

"You're so sensitive," I said.

"Nobody follow me."

"For crissake," I said. "You haven't been doing anything."

"I waiting for my kind of work," Hawk said. "I don't do gum-shoe work, rattle fucking doorknobs."

Hawk stood and went to my window and looked down at the corner of Berkeley and Boylston. It was a fine bright morning. There was a lot of foot traffic at ten of nine, people going to work at the big insurance companies that littered the Back Bay. The young women were still in their summer dresses. The young men wore no topcoats.

"'Cross Boylston," Hawk said. "Corner near Louis'."

I stood beside him and looked.

"Sort of tall with square shoulders," Hawk said. "Fishing hat, tan raincoat, looking uninterested."

"I see him," I said. "Newspaper under his arm."

"So he can lean on a lamppost and read it," Hawk said.

"He's doing everything but," I said.

"Your guy?"

"No," I said. "They wouldn't send the same tail two days in a row."

"They haven't been too smart so far," Hawk said. "You made the first guy as quick as we made this one."

"Not the same thing," I said. "We were looking for this one."

"Sure," Hawk said. "Why don't we just go see Marty, see what he wants?"

"You know where to find him?"

"Sure," Hawk said.

"'Course it's possible," I said, "we brace Marty Anaheim, we get ourselves in trouble."

"Or him," Hawk said.

CHAPTER
7

THE GUY IN THE RAINCOAT FOLLOWED HAWK AND ME TO A bar on Canal Street, near the old Boston Garden.

"Marty here about every morning," Hawk said.

The bar was called Poochie's, and through the big plate glass window in front we could see that Marty was there with a couple of other guys in suits drinking draught beer, and watching a motorcycle race on the big color television over the bar.

"Why don't you wait out here and confuse the tail," I said.

Hawk smiled and leaned against the entrance wall. The guy in the raincoat was across the street, near the MBTA entrance, pretending to count his change.

"He'll doodle around out here for a while," Hawk said. "Trying to figure out if Marty'll be mad, and then he'll come in."

"That's about right," I said.

I walked in and sat on a bar stool next to one of Marty's companions and ordered a beer. Marty glanced at me and away, then he let his glance drift back to me out of the corner of his left eye. The guy in the raincoat was decisive. After a minute or so, he came in and spoke to Marty, standing on the other side of Marty, whispering so I couldn't hear. Marty listened without taking his eyes off the motorcycle races.

"Okay, Dukes, beat it," Marty said when the guy in the raincoat finished whispering. "I'll talk to you later."

Marty glanced casually past me at the street through the big window, then let his glance drift disinterestedly over me. I gave him a big friendly smile. He didn't smile back. Marty was a bodybuilder, and a successful one, if you judged by the way his suit didn't fit. He was clean shaven with shoulder-length blond hair and a dark tan. He had a small scar at the left corner of his mouth. And his right eye seemed to wander off center. There was a gold earring in his left earlobe, and a very big emerald ring on his right pinky. The two guys with him were weight-room types. The one next to me had a medallion of some kind on a gold chain around his neck. On the television another motorcycle race was under way. I didn't watch. Marty and his pals did, with Marty occasionally glancing

ROBERT B. PARKER

at me. I waited. Finally it was more than Marty could stand. He leaned forward and looked at me from the other side of his buddy with the medallion.

"How you doing," he said.

He had a surprisingly high voice.

"Fine," I said.

The beer was growing slowly flat in front of me, but ten in the morning seemed a little early. Marty kept leaning forward. His two friends were looking at me too.

"I know you?" Marty said.

"Sure you do," I said. "I'm your hero. You want to be just like me."

"That a wise remark?" Marty said.

"Yeah. I'm just practicing on you, in case I meet somebody smarter."

Marty's tan darkened, and a small nerve in his right cheek began to twitch, below the walleye. He slid off the bar stool and stepped around his associate to stand beside me.

"You come in here looking for trouble?"

"No, but your guy Dukes was tailing me. Thought I'd ask you about it."

"My guy?"

"Guy in the raincoat. I wanted to see who sent him. And sonovagun, Marty, it was you."

"I don't know no Dukes."

"Sure," I said, "and you don't know no Spenser either, and you didn't have a guy on my tail."

Marty took a half step back and folded his thick arms.

His two friends were both turned on the bar stools toward me. I noticed the friend without the medallion sported some crude prison tattoos on his forearms. The bartender had moved as far down the bar away from us as he could and was busy slicing lemons. Marty kept his pose as he stared at me. His coat sleeves pulled tight around his upper arms. His Rolex watch gleamed at me from his left wrist.

"Chills," I said, "run up and down my spine."

"Whaddya doing for Julius Ventura?" Marty said.

"Why do you want to know?" I said.

"'Cause I'm softhearted," Marty said. "Give you a chance to tell me what's going on, and maybe walk out of here with your balls still swinging."

I had a couple of killer responses to that all ready, but I didn't get to use them because Hawk came in. He stepped inside the bar and took off his sunglasses and tucked them into the side pocket of his suede-denim jacket. Then he unbuttoned the jacket and walked down the bar past where we were sitting, and leaned on the wall behind Marty and his pals. It was nice theater and also made it harder for all of them to concentrate on giving me the hard eye. Which had been getting pretty boring anyway.

"So," I said. "Why do you want to know what I'm doing with Julius Ventura?"

Marty was still looking at me, but his two pals had swung farther around in their seats and were looking at Hawk.

"The colored guy don't make no difference," Marty said.

"The hell he doesn't," I said.

"Still three to two," Marty said.

"Yeah, but one of the two is me," I said. "And the other one's him."

Marty wasn't scared of me, or of Hawk. Marty was much too predatory to be scared. But he was confused. He'd put a simple tail on a guy and ended up having the guy, so to speak, on his tail. He was used to scaring people to death. He wasn't used to smart talk. His natural response to it would be violence. He was almost certainly doing what Gino Fish had told him to do, so he couldn't just kill me. He was supposed to find something out.

"You doing anything for Ventura got to do with Anthony Meeker?" Marty said.

The nerve near his eye was twitching faster.

"Who wants to know?" I said.

"Who the fuck you think? Who's asking you? Geraldo fucking Rivera?"

"Gino interested in this?"

Marty shrugged.

"Sure he is," I said. "And when he found out Ventura hired me, he wanted to know what I knew."

"So?"

"So he told you to have me followed, and you did."

"So?"

"So, why's he want to know?"

"None of your fucking business," Marty said. It was starting to occur to him that I was finding out more than he was.

"And how'd he know so quick that Ventura hired us?" I said.

"That's it," Marty said. "Meeting's over."

"He's got somebody in Julius's organization."

"Get lost," Marty said.

Marty put his thick hand on my chest and shoved. I was supposed to stagger backwards. But I didn't. I rolled a little away from the shove and Marty's hand slid off my chest and Marty actually staggered a half step forward. He caught himself on the bar and tried to look like he hadn't staggered.

"You okay?" I said solicitously.

The tic in his cheek was vibrating like high C. His hand started toward his coat.

Hawk said, "Marty."

Hawk never talked especially loud. But you could always hear him. He seemed to be in the same position leaning on the wall that he had assumed when he came in. Except the big-barreled .44 Mag that he always carried was now out and aiming at Marty Anaheim.

Everything stopped.

The bartender ducked down out of sight behind the bar.

The motorcycles kept zooming around the track.

Hawk nodded toward the door.

Nobody said anything for a moment. Then Marty jerked his head at the two gym rats and the three of them headed out. At the door Marty turned back, his cheek in full tic.

"Another day," he said, his high voice shaking, "you're both dead meat."

Hawk grinned at him.

"Gotta watch them steroids, Marty. You be talking soprano pretty quick."

Marty looked at Hawk with a look that would have scared us both if we weren't so fearless. Then he turned and went out the door followed by the gym rats. Hawk put the big Magnum away, and leaned over the bar.

"You got any Krug?" he said to the bartender, who was still crouched on the floor behind the bar. "Maybe an eighty-six?"

The bartender didn't know what Krug was.

CHAPTER
8

I HAD LUNCH WITH SHIRLEY VENTURA AT A NEW JOINT ON Huntington Ave. called Ambrosia. You could eat well, and have quite a nice time examining the spectrum of Boston chic which regularly gathered there. Shirley studied the menu for a long time. She was wearing a low-cut electric blue slip dress that was designed to enhance long legs and a narrow waist. Shirley was short and chunky. The effect was different. A number of the women lunching that day appeared to notice the difference.

"You got any, ah, like maybe a roast beef sandwich?" Shirley said to the waitress.

"We have a wonderful sandwich of grilled portabellas with Asiago on country bread dressed with extra virgin oil and served with julienne of jicama and blood orange," the waitress said encouragingly.

"What's a portabella?" Shirley said to me.

"A big mushroom," I said.

She looked at the waitress and frowned.

"A mushroom sandwich?"

The waitress smiled enthusiastically.

"Why don't we each have the paillard of chicken, and a green salad and some bread."

"Of course, sir. Anything to drink with that?"

"Wine," Shirley said.

"Anything special?" the waitress said.

"Some white wine," Shirley said. She'd lost interest in ordering and was looking around the room at the other diners.

The waitress looked at me. She didn't have to be a weatherman to know which way the wind was blowing.

"Bottle of Sterling Sauvignon Blanc," I said.

The waitress smiled as they always do to tell me how much she admired my choice of wines, and hurried away to tell the wine steward.

"What's that pallard thing you ordered?" Shirley asked.

"Breast of chicken flattened with a mallet and quickly sautéed."

"Sounds terrible," she said.

"Drink enough wine," I said, "you'll think you like it."

Shirley picked up a roll from the bread basket and bit into it the way you eat an apple. She looked around the room some more until the waitress returned with the wine.

"You care to try it?" I said to Shirley.

"Sure," she said.

The waitress opened the bottle and poured a splash in Shirley's glass. Shirley looked at it.

"Come on, lady, pour me some wine," Shirley said.

I nodded to the waitress.

"Pour it out," I said. "I'm sure it's fine."

The waitress smiled happily and poured us both a glass of wine, and put the bottle in the ice bucket. Shirley picked up her glass and drank half of it. She smiled at me.

"Hits the spot," she said.

"You bet," I said.

She glanced out toward Huntington Ave. where her father's big Lincoln sat near the curb. The driver was behind the wheel, reading the *Globe*.

"See if Jackie's watching," she said with a big confidential smile. "They don't like it, I drink wine at lunch."

"Your secret's safe with me," I said and made a slight toasting gesture with my glass. Shirley drank the rest of her wine and reached behind her to get the bottle from the wine bucket. She poured another glassful. The waitress brought our salads. The salad chef was long on presentation. There were various colored greens arranged into a somewhat precarious-looking vegetable spray. Shirley studied it for some time, sipping her wine without a word. I ordered a second bottle of wine from the waitress.

"So what can you tell me about Anthony?" Shirley said.

She stuffed a forkful of greens into her mouth.

"Haven't found him yet," I said.

"So why we having lunch. So you can tell me you haven't found him?"

"Tell me a little more about what he did for your dad," I said.

"Money stuff," Shirley said.

She washed the greens down with more wine.

"What kind?" I said.

"What kind of what?"

"What kind of money stuff," I said.

I took my first sip of wine. If I drank a lot at lunch, I needed a nap. Shirley didn't seem worried about that.

"He used to pick up money from people," she said. "Bring it places, and give it to other people."

"Bookies?"

"I don't know. I'm a girl. They don't talk about business with girls."

"Of course not," I said. "He carry a lot of money around?"

"Sure. Daddy trusted him like he was his own son."

"Sure," I said.

The waitress arrived with our chicken paillard. Shirley poked at it with her fork for a moment, and put the fork down and drank some wine.

"Daddy never had sons of his own, just me."

"Only child, huh?"

"Yeah, my mom said it was too hard."

"I'm an only child too," I said.

Shirley nodded. It didn't seem to make us closer. I drank another small swallow of wine.

"You and Anthony ever have any, ah, little spats?"

"Never, I told you before, he'd stand on his head for me."

I nodded. She drank the rest of the wine in her glass and reached around to the ice bucket and poured out the remainder of the first bottle.

"Well sure, I know a woman who'd stand on her head for me, unless she was wearing a skirt. But now and then we might disagree about something."

Shirley laughed loudly. Her face was flushed.

"I bet she wouldn't," Shirley said between guffaws, "if she was wearing a dress. I bet she wouldn't."

She laughed very loudly again.

"Well, luckily, Anthony doesn't wear a skirt," she said. "So he can stand on his head whenever he wants."

"When he stands on his head, do you forgive him?"

She was still giggling.

"Depends how long he stands." She had trouble saying it because she was giggling so hard.

I laughed along with her. She tried to get it under control by having some more wine, but it only made her more giggly.

"What's the longest you ever made him stand on his head?" I said. Jovial.

"Well, of course he never really stood on his head. But there was the time when I found out about him and the cocktail waitress at The Starlight," she said.

Her face was bright red now, and she spilled a little of her wine as she drank.

"He paid big for that one," she said. "He paid for that big time."

"I'll bet he did," I said, bursting with mirth. "I'll bet he never tried that again."

"You kidding?" she said, leaning forward toward me over the table. "Little fink would fuck a snake, you hold it for him."

"Really?" I said.

"I'm telling you," she said.

"How you feel about that?"

"I won't hold one for him," she said. And leaned back in her chair and laughed hard. I had a bite of chicken and glanced around the room. The chic lunch crowd was grimly ignoring her.

"You ever catch him with anyone else?" I said.

"Naw. That time I caught him I laid down the god-damned law. He's too scared to try and step out on me," she said.

"Your father know about this?"

"Gawd no," she said. "That's what I told Anthony. 'I tell Daddy about this,' I told him, 'and he'll have them cut off your balls.'"

I nodded.

"That would be discouraging," I said.

She giggled again.

"'Course I wouldn't really want them to snip off his

balls, you know. Wouldn't be in my best interest, you know what I mean. Little bastard is something in bed, I'll tell you."

"I'm glad to hear it," I said.

Shirley stood up quite suddenly.

"'Scuse me," she said. "I gotta go to the little girls' room."

I stood, ever gallant, and watched her as she wove among the tables, showing too much of her chunky legs, looking sadly vulnerable with the little dress draped badly over her big butt. People stared at her as she wobbled among the tables. *Not our kind.*

I sat down and looked at nothing much. Shirley had eaten half her salad and none of her chicken. But the second bottle of wine was nearly empty. I caught a couple of people peeking over at me, wondering who would be lunching with *her!* I'd have to come here with Susan and try to recoup. The long dining room was impressive. Along the front, picture windows looked out onto Huntington Ave., and across at the Prudential Center. The bar was across the far end of the room, and the ceiling was two stories high. The kitchen was, apparently, at the top of a flight of stairs to the right of the hostess station, which must have been an added benefit for the wait staff. Earn a living while developing the quadriceps of a long jumper.

The maître d' came to my table. His brass name tag said *Jose.*

"Excuse me," Jose said. He spoke with the silken hint of an accent. "I'm afraid your companion has had a small accident in the ladies' room."

"She pass out?" I said.

"I'm afraid she has, sir," Jose said. "But unfortunately not before she was sick."

"Okay, Jose," I said. "Keep the other ladies out of there for a couple minutes and we'll get her out."

"Jose," the maître d' said. "I'm Brazilian. In Portuguese you pronounce the J."

"Jes," I said, and went to the front door of the restaurant and gestured at her driver. Jackie was more alert than I had thought. He came rolling out of the car very quickly, with his hand inside his coat. He was a tall rangy kid, with a lot of black hair cut short on the sides, left long on the top.

"She passed out in the ladies' room," I said.

He took his hand out of his coat.

"You give her something to drink?"

"Some wine," I said.

Jackie nodded. "Probably two bottles, right?"

I nodded.

"Which way?" Jackie said.

We went into the ladies' room and found Shirley asleep on the floor in one of the stalls, her cheek resting on the toilet seat, her white thighs exposed by the skirt that had hiked up above her hips. She looked like a clumsy little girl who'd eaten too much Halloween candy. I wanted to put my coat over her, or something.

"Goddamn it," I said.

Jackie pushed past me. He straddled her, got his arms around her waist, and hoisted her up.

She mumbled something that sounded like "hey."

Jackie turned her toward the sink.

"Clean her off," he said to me.

I wet one of the hand towels and did the best I could. She wasn't cooperative but she was too zonked to put up much resistance. I used a second towel to finish the cleanup and a third to dry her off.

"Okay," I said. "Want me to take an arm?"

Jackie shook his head.

"Easier I just do her around the waist like this. You can go ahead and open doors."

"Done this before, I gather."

Jackie didn't say anything but he let his eyes roll upwards in their sockets for a moment. We got her through the restaurant, out the door, and into her father's car. She slumped over when Jackie put her in the backseat. He went around to the front, got in behind the wheel, nodded at me, power-locked the doors, and drove her away.

I went back in to pay the check.

"I hope the lady is all right, sir," Jose said.

I gave him my American Express card.

"I don't think she'll ever be all right," I said. "But she'll be no worse for this experience."

Jose went away with my card.

No wonder they didn't like her to drink wine at lunch.

CHAPTER
9

"I FEEL LIKE CHESTER THE MOLESTER," I SAID TO SUSAN.

We were walking Pearl the Wonder Dog along the Charles River, on the Esplanade, near the Hatch Shell.

"Getting a young woman drunk and pumping her for information?"

"Yeah," I said.

"Are you familiar with the term 'Consenting Adult'?" Susan said.

I nodded. Susan was wearing black high top sneakers, black sweats, a black baseball cap with the words "Community Servings" printed in white over the visor, and a yellow all-weather jacket which said "DKNY Athletic" in black letters on the back.

"Did you find out things that will help you?"

"I found out that her husband handles a lot of money. I found out that he has cheated on her and seems inclined to again, except he's afraid that her father will have someone cut off his testicles."

"Well, it would render the question of adultery moot," Susan said.

"Conventionally defined."

"Good point," Susan said.

"I also found out from Lennie Seltzer that Anthony, that's Shirley's husband, gambles a lot and loses."

"And," Susan said, "you found out that Anthony is married to a stupid, coarse, spoiled, self-indulgent, childish drunk."

"You shrinks have a real knack for saying things so they don't sound bad."

A platoon of people in elbow pads, helmets, and spandex pants Rollerbladed by with various degrees of grace. Pearl gazed after them with what might have been scorn, or even derision. I wasn't sure. Dogs are hard to read.

"I'd love to do that," Susan said. "I think I'll take some lessons."

I made no comment. Pearl returned to straining against her leash, sniffing the grass along the edge of the sidewalk, alert for a wayward Zagnut wrapper.

"So what you have is a picture of perhaps a compulsive gambler with a wandering eye, married to an undesirable wife, with access to a great deal of money," Susan went on. "That you had to find some of this out by sitting quietly while Shirley Ventura got drunk and made an ass of herself seems a fair exchange for a man in your business."

"You ought to try Rollerblading, at that," I said. "And if you don't like it you can always eat the skates."

"Oh come on," Susan said. "You complain that I'm hard. You're the hardest person I've ever known. And I'm in a fairly tough profession, myself."

"Including Hawk?"

"Okay, one of the two hardest people I've ever known," Susan said. "And most of the time you accept it. In fact most of the time you enjoy it, except when you have one of these little sentimental spasms."

"Thanks," I said. "I needed that."

We walked quietly for a bit. Pearl spotted a couple of sparrows and went into her bird dog stalk, head extended, body tense, each step infinitely deliberate as she seemed to steadily elongate toward the birds until they flew away. As they rose in the air Pearl looked back at me expectantly.

"Bang," I said.

Pearl returned to the Zagnut hunt.

"Of course," Susan said, "I love you for having the little spasms of sentimentality."

"I know," I said. "That's why I have them."

Pearl paused to roll vigorously on an earthworm which had gotten squashed on the sidewalk, probably the victim of a reckless Rollerblader.

"Ick," Susan said as Pearl rolled. "Why do they do that?"

"I don't know," I said.

"Dogs are sometimes mysterious," Susan said.

The small sailboats that people rented from the public boat club bobbed not very gracefully around the basin where the river widened behind the dam. They had small sails and flat bottoms and the people in them were mostly amateurs, but the scatter of white sails on the blue-gray river looked nice anyway. On the other side MIT stretched along Memorial Drive, its gray stone buildings and its domes looking technical and serious.

"I also have a connection between Gino Fish and Julius Ventura," I said.

Pearl got through with the worm and got up and shook herself and proceeded. We went with her.

"Who's Gino Fish," Susan said.

"Sort of filled the number-one slot," I said, "when Joe Broz got old."

"Broz retired?"

"Not really, but his kid's a bust, and Vinnie left him, and he's about seventy, and his heart's not in it anymore."

"And where does Shirley's father rank in all of this?"

"If it weren't for Gino, he'd have Broz's slot," I said. "He might get it anyway. He's ambitious."

"So what's the connection?"

"Gino's guy Marty Anaheim had some people following me."

"And you're sure it's about Whatsisname, Shirley's father?"

"Better than that," I said. "Hawk and I braced Marty

and he asked if Julius hired us to do anything with Anthony Meeker."

"Why are they interested?"

"Don't know."

"What would you speculate?"

"Money."

Susan smiled.

"That would always be a reasonable guess, wouldn't it," she said.

"Yes."

"And the other guess would probably be sex," Susan said.

"So young," I said, "so beautiful, and yet so cynical."

CHAPTER
10

THERE WERE MAYBE A DOZEN PLACES IN THE PHONE BOOK with the word Starlight in their name. I eliminated places which wouldn't employ waitresses, like Starlight Video, or the Starlight Laundry, and narrowed it down to The Starlight Lounge in Lynn, and a roadhouse called Starlight Memories on the beach in Salisbury. I took the wedding picture of Anthony and Shirley with me and went to check out the waitresses.

The Starlight Lounge was closest, out at a traffic circle near Lynn Beach where the causeway to Nahant branched off. It had been built after the war and was called the Redwood: a lot of glass windows, a lot of exposed pine stained red, the kind of restaurant that sold fried clams and hamburgers and frappés before the fast food franchises were invented and put them out of business. After that for a while it had been a bait and tackle place, and then it was a place that sold ceramic lawn statues, and then a pizza joint, and then, for a long time, an abandoned building except for a month in the winter when Christmas trees were sold out of the parking lot. In 1989 somebody painted it all over a dark blue, windows included, put in a bar and a bunch of cheap tables and chairs, installed a spinning strobe light in the high center of the room, hired a bunch of waitresses to work topless, and The Starlight Lounge was born.

It was still bright daylight when I parked there at 5:20 in the afternoon. There were a couple of motorcycles parked outside and a truck full of cement sidings was nosed in at an angle taking a space and a half, as if the crew hadn't been able to wait a moment longer when quitting time came.

The inside of the place was painted the same dark blue as the outside. I took off my sunglasses and waited for my pupils to dilate. The strobe reflector in the ceiling turned slowly, scattering the light like confetti. There was heavy rock music playing. I didn't recognize it, but I didn't expect to. All rock music sounded to me like glass being ground.

To my right there was a long, nearly empty bar, where once maybe there had been a soda fountain. I went over and leaned on the end of it. One of the bartenders came down to get my order. He was wide faced and curly haired with the sleeves of his white dress shirt rolled up over his thick freckled arms. He put a paper napkin down on the bar in front of me and said, "What'll it be?"

"Got any draft beer?" I said.

"Nope. Bottle only."

"Got any New Amsterdam Black & Tan?"

The bartender grinned at me.

"You got to be shitting," he said.

"What have you got?" I said.

"Bud, Bud Light, Heineken."

"Bud," I said.

The bartender got me a long neck, popped the cap, put a glass beside it, and went away. I looked around the room. The guys from the forms truck were at a big table down the bar drinking beer and making small talk with the waitresses. There were two guys in motorcycle jackets at another table, and there were four waitresses. All of them bare chests and short shorts and a lot of hair. Leaning on the far end of the bar opposite me was a guy with a round head and sloping shoulders. He too was wearing a white dress shirt with the sleeves rolled. The music banged away through a couple of speakers up high somewhere in the dark blue top of the dim room. I drank my beer. The bartender returned.

"You want another one?" he said.

"Not yet," I said. "Who's in charge of this joint at the moment?"

"In charge?"

"Yeah. There a manager or anyone?"

"Me and Vic, I guess," the bartender said.

"Vic the guy at the other end of the bar?"

"Yeah. Mostly he's the bouncer. It get real busy he comes back here with me. But usually one man can handle it. It's a beer crowd, not a lotta mixed drinks, you know."

"How about if the bouncer end gets real busy."

"Oh, sure, I'll come around, give him a hand. But Vic don't usually need much help. Whaddya need?"

"I'm a private cop, looking for a guy's missing," I said. "I want to show his picture around to the waitresses, see if any of them know him."

"Yeah?"

"I don't want trouble from Vic, or you," I said.

The bartender shrugged.

"I don't see no harm to it," he said. He turned and jerked his head at Vic, and turned back to me.

"You got some sort of license or something you want to show me?" he said.

I took out my wallet and showed him. Vic moved down the bar toward us, casual, just strolling down to see what's up. Nothing he wouldn't be able to handle. Up close he was shorter than I was, but thick, and long armed. His short crew cut was flecked with gray. There was some buildup of scar tissue around his eyes, and his nose was thick and flat.

"Guy's a private eye," the bartender said. "Wants to ask around after a missing person. I said I didn't have no problem with that. You?"

"He show you something?" Vic said. His voice was a soft rasp.

"Yeah. He's legit."

"You make the piece?" Vic said to the bartender. The bartender grinned.

"Right side, back on his hip," the bartender said.

Vic nodded approvingly. He was studying my face.

"You used to fight," he said.

"Yeah."

"Tough way to make a living."

"Had its moments," I said.

"Yeah," Vic said in his soft rasp. "It did. Who you looking for?"

I took out my picture.

"Name's Anthony Meeker. Been gone about a week. He may have dated one of your waitresses."

Vic and the bartender both looked at the picture. Then they looked at each other.

"Yeah," Vic said. "That's Anthony."

"Tony the Phony," the bartender said.

"Tell me about him," I said.

"You know who his father-in-law is?" Vic said.

The waitress who was serving the forms guys yelled, "Vic."

Vic turned easily, rolling against the bar so he was looking at her.

"This jerk was grabbing my tits," the waitress said, nodding at a long-haired kid in cement-stained white overalls. He and his four friends were laughing, secure in their numbers.

Vic walked slowly over from the bar toward the boy.

"That's like the only rule in this joint," the bartender said. "You can't touch the waitresses. You start letting them touch the waitresses and they'll be fucking them on the floor in a half hour. Place would turn into a zoo, wasn't for Vic."

"Think he'll need some backup?"

"Vic? Naw. Watch."

Vic stopped about three feet from the table, and spoke in his soft rasp.

"Look all you want, don't touch. Capeesh?"

"Hey, Vic," the kid said, playing to his friends, "she's flapping them hooters in my face, you know? Hard not to take a bite."

Vic nodded.

"You kids are new here. You didn't know. Now you do. You touch one of the waitresses again, you gotta leave."

"What if we don't want to leave?" the kid said.

Vic said something too softly to be heard. The kid leaned forward in his chair.

"What was that?" he said.

Vic hit him a nice left uppercut that looked like it didn't travel more than six inches. It knocked the kid out of his chair and sprawling backwards on the floor. Vic stepped maybe a step back, and stood balanced easily, hands hanging loose near his hip. The kid lay on the floor a moment, dazed. The other three were frozen in their seats. They were probably tough enough kids in their neighborhood. But this wasn't how fights started in their world. First there would be some smart remarks and then some threats and then one guy would push another guy and some other guys would usually break it up, and maybe one time in ten a few punches were thrown, and then someone broke it up.

"You think I can't take all four of you?" Vic said in his soft rasp.

I couldn't see his face. But the forms guys could and it told them something. None of them said anything. The long-haired kid on the floor was sitting up now, his forearms on his knees, still listening to the bells ringing. Vic turned and walked back to the bar.

"He's the one hired me," I said.

"Phony Tony's father-in-law?"

"Yep."

"Julius Ventura?"

"Yep."

"Why's a guy like him hire a guy like you?"

"Hero worship," I said.

The long-haired kid got his legs under him finally and wavered over toward Vic.

"You sucka-punched me, you sonovabitch," he said.

Vic looked at him without interest.

"You wanna try that when I'm standing up facing you?"

Vic looked at me without expression for a moment and back at the kid. The other three guys at the table had stood and were looking half ready to come to Long Hair's aid.

"Look at something," I said to the kid. "Look at how

you're standing. Then look at how he's standing. You see? All you need is a bull's-eye painted on your face. Look at him. See how he's balanced? He looks like he's still leaning on the bar, but see where his hands are? It's the difference between amateurs and professionals. And if you're going to be a tough guy it's a difference you better learn."

The kid looked at me hard for a minute as if he were trying to focus. He'd been half gassed even before Vic hit him. And, probably, on his best days, he wasn't a thinker.

"You a tough guy?" he said finally. But there was no bite to it. He was just talking to talk.

"But oh so gentle," I said. "Go sit down."

"Either you guys want to arm wrestle me?" the kid said.

The bartender snorted. Vic's expression didn't change.

"Guy with arms like you? I wouldn't have a chance," he said.

"Goddamned better believe it," the kid said. "Any one of you want to try me, I'll put your arm flat fucking down."

"I believe you would," I said.

"Appreciate it if you'd go over and calm your buddies down," Vic said. "Keep them in line for me, if you would."

"Yeah, sure," the kid said and began to move away from the bar. "You change your mind on the arm wrestling, anytime. You unnerstand. Anytime you wanna try me . . . flat fucking on the bar . . ."

His voice trailed off into some sort of mumble and

then silence as he went back to his table, and told his buddies how he'd outfaced Vic over arm wrestling.

"Arm wrestling," Vic said softly. "Arm fucking wrestling."

"So tell me about Phony Tony," I said.

The bartender moved down the bar to open four Bud long necks for one of the waitresses.

"Always flashed a lotta dough," Vic said. "Always come on to the waitresses. Flirt with them, tip them big. But no touching, which was good. I didn't want to have to throw Julius Ventura's son-in-law out on his keister."

"But you would," I said.

Vic shrugged. "Have to, he touches the girls."

"But he didn't," I said.

"No. He was pretty much no trouble. Always acted like he was dangerous, let everybody know who his father-in-law was. But he never caused no trouble."

"Was he dangerous?"

Vic smiled softly.

"The arm wrestler would clean his clock," Vic said. "Used to bet on stuff. Be a basketball game on the tube, say. He'd bet who'd score the next basket. What the score would be in one minute, whether a guy would make both free throws, who'd commit the next foul. Crazy! Bet with anyone, guy next to him at the bar, the waitress." Vic pointed with his chin at the bartender. "He'd bet Keno whether the next beer order would be Bud or Heineken."

The room had filled some as people got off work. And the waitresses were hustling beer and bowls of Spanish peanuts to the tables. Four or five guys were at the bar. Most of the customers were men, but there was one table with three women at it. All three were smoking.

"He date any of the waitresses?"

"Yeah, Dixie. She's the one with the red hair, down here, just picking up."

"Mind if I talk with her?"

"No. I'd just soon you talked in the back room though. People won't think she's standing around gabbing while they're waiting for their drink."

He gestured around the corner of the bar toward a black door with an opaque frosted glass window in it. There was a hole in the door frame where a doorknob used to be. I pushed it open and was in a storeroom piled high with cases of beer and cases of empties. There was an old school teachery-looking desk shoved into an open space on one wall under a small window set high. And a light bulb hanging on a cord from the ceiling fixture. I leaned my hips on the desk and waited. In maybe a minute the door pushed open and Dixie came through.

She said, "Hi. I'm Dixie Walker."

"Your father a Brooklyn Dodger fan?"

She smiled.

"I guess so. My real name's Frances, but he always called me Dixie."

I said, "My name's Spenser. I'm a detective. I'm looking for Anthony Meeker. You used to date him?"

"Yeah, sort of, I guess. You can look at my tits, you want to, I'm used to it. I don't mind."

CHANCE

I glanced down at her chest. Her breasts were quite small, with long nipples.

"I'm trying to keep my mind on Anthony Meeker," I said gallantly. In fact, I thought women walking around topless looked kind of . . . not silly, exactly, more like sad.

Dixie smiled.

"Sure," she said. "I just didn't want you feeling uncomfortable."

"Thank you. Tell me about Anthony."

"Well, you know who his father-in-law is?"

"Yeah."

"He made a lot of that," Dixie said.

"So you knew he was married."

"Oh sure—you got that kind of hang-up?"

"Just the facts, ma'am," I said.

"He's a grown-up guy. He wants to fool around, ain't my business to straighten him out, you know?"

"Was he fun?" I said.

Dixie shrugged.

"That's the thing. You think he's going to be. You know, kind of a wild guy likes to spend money, always got a smart remark. Promises a lot."

"But?"

"But he's not fun. He'd pick me up after work and we'd go to a place he's got down the road and drink a little Southern Comfort, maybe a joint, and do the deed. He doesn't really spend money. He just gambles. And when he's not losing his dough on whatever he can find to lose it on, he's talking about his plan, how he's got a system, and how he's going to go to Vegas and bust the town with it. He's pretty boring."

"That's why Vegas is there," I said. "Guys like Anthony to bust it."

Dixie smiled.

"Yeah. I used to tell him, 'Anthony, they ain't in business for you to win, out there.' But he had his system, he said. And as soon as he got a kitty together, he was going out and come back rich."

"He say where he was going to get the kitty?"

"No."

"He say what his system was?"

"Yeah, he talked about it all the time, but I got no idea what he was talking about. I never paid no attention."

"Atlantic City's closer," I said. "Hell, there's a place in Connecticut the Indians run. Be a two-hour drive."

She shook her head.

"It was like his dream," Dixie said. "Go to Vegas and bust the town. It was like his whatchamacallit, the thing people say when they meditate."

"Mantra," I said.

"Yeah, it was like that."

"When'd you see him last?"

"Oh, not for a while. Last year sometime. His wife found him out, and that was it."

"You think he's faithful to her since."

Dixie looked at me as if I had asked her about pigs whistling.

"He told me it was his wife, but he was ready to dump me anyway, something better came along."

"So you figure he's got a girlfriend now?"

"Anthony's always going to have a girlfriend. It ain't just sex. He needs somebody to brag to."

"Would he leave his wife, you think?"

"Wife's his ticket to ride," Dixie said. "Anthony needs a lot of money and he don't know how to earn it."

"Anthony sounds like kind of a lizard," I said.

Dixie smiled a little.

"Phony Tony."

"How come you went out with him?"

Dixie shrugged. Her small naked breasts looked vulnerable in the unshaded light from the bare bulb above her.

"I ain't got that much else going right now," she said.

CHAPTER
11

"WHY IS SOMEONE A COMPULSIVE GAMBLER?" I SAID TO Susan.

We were having dinner at her place in Cambridge, sitting at her counter eating Chinese takeout. Susan gave Pearl the Wonder Dog a Peking ravioli with her chopsticks. I was eating with a fork.

"I don't know," Susan said.

"But you're a goddamned shrink," I said. "You're supposed to know stuff."

"I know a lot of stuff, and one bit of stuff that I know is that it is unwise to generalize about the causes of compulsive behavior."

I ate some chicken with cashews.

"Can compulsive gamblers be helped?"

"Sure," Susan said. "Same old conditions. If they want help. If they are able to do the work."

"Is it the hope?" I said. "The chance for the big hit?"

"Often it's losing," Susan said.

"The thrill of defeat?" I said.

Susan shrugged. "Something like that, maybe. Sorry I'm not more helpful."

"Only idle curiosity," I said. "I don't need to know why he's compulsive to find him."

"I doubt that your curiosity is ever idle," Susan said.

There were a few grains of rice on the countertop near Susan's elbow, spilled when Susan had served it from the carton. Pearl got up with her forepaws on the counter and lapped it off.

"She likes a balanced diet," Susan said.

Susan's office was downstairs and she had come from work to dinner, still dressed in the conservative gray pants suit and understated jewelry that was part of her Dr. Silverman look. Her thick black hair was shiny. Her eyes were very large, and full of thought. She had a wide mouth, faultlessly made up. Her perfume smelled like rain.

"Hawk and I are going to Las Vegas Monday," I said. "We'd like you to join us."

"What about my appointments?"

"Can you reschedule for a few days?"

"Will Henry take Pearl?"

"Yes."

"Will we see Wayne Newton?"

"I can't promise anything," I said.

79

"Can I sleep with you?" she said.

"I can't promise anything," I said.

"The hell you can't," Susan said. "I'll reschedule next week."

"Ever been to Vegas," I said.

"Years ago, with my first husband."

"Suze," I said. "He's your only husband."

"Well, technically. Since you refuse to marry me."

"I thought you refused to marry me," I said.

"Hard to keep track, isn't it," Susan said.

"I think Anthony's in Vegas," I said.

Susan was drinking a glass of Merlot. She always chose red wine, regardless of what she was eating, because it didn't need to be chilled.

"With some of his father-in-law's money?"

"Yes. I figure he was carrying money between Ventura and Gino Fish. I don't know why—but it would explain Marty Anaheim's interest. And I figure he either skimmed some, or simply took off one day with a bag of it."

"And Mr. Ventura doesn't want either his own people or Mr. . . . . what's his name?"

"Fish," I said. "Gino Fish."

"Or Mr. Fish to find out. So he hires you to look for Anthony."

"Yeah. But Fish finds out about me. And very quickly."

"Which means that Mr. Fish has some source of information in Mr. Ventura's organization," Susan said. "In fact, if he's trying to keep the whole thing secret it's probably someone very close to Mr. Ventura."

"Likely," I said.

"And Mr. Fish sends his man . . ."

"Marty Anaheim," I said.

"And Marty Anaheim sends some people to follow you to find Anthony."

"Which means what?" I said.

"Which means Mr. Fish either knows he's been robbed, or is suspicious."

"You therapists are a smart bunch," I said.

She shook her head.

"It's not because I'm a therapist," Susan said. "It's because I'm Jewish. Jews are very smart."

"I've heard that," I said. "I've also heard that their women are desperately oversexed."

"Some of them are, it's true."

"How about yourself?"

"Desperately," she said. And smiled her postlapsarian smile.

"I like that in a woman."

CHAPTER
12

I WAS IN MY OFFICE ON THE PHONE BOOKING OUR LAS VEGAS trip when Vinnie Morris came in with a tall, angular, gray-haired specimen whom I knew to be Gino Fish.

Fish sat in one of the client chairs, directly in front of my desk, firmly upright, elbows on the chair arms, hands folded in his lap. He glanced slowly around the room and then looked at me as if he were interested. Vinnie leaned on the wall to the right of the door. I nodded at him.

"Do you know who I am?" Fish said.

His voice was dry and faintly hoarse, like wind whispering over sandpaper. His diction was precise.

"I do."

"Vinnie says you can be trusted."

"Under the right circumstances," I said.

"Vinnie says if you give your word, you will keep it."

"Generally," I said.

"Vinnie is not given to praise," Fish said. "So his regard for you is impressive."

"Impresses the hell out of me," I said.

"Vinnie also said you are inclined to be flippant."

"Vinnie thinks flippant is the name of a dolphin," I said.

Fish smiled as dryly as it was possible to smile and not be frowning. His teeth were remarkably white. I wondered if he had them bonded.

"I did in fact rephrase Vinnie's remark," Fish said.

"I thought Marty Anaheim walked around with you," I said.

Fish shook his head very slightly.

"Marty is my business associate," Fish said. "Vinnie has kindly agreed to be my bodyguard."

"You and Broz never patched it up," I said to Vinnie.

"Kid's in the way," Vinnie said.

"Kid wasn't the best thing that ever happened to Joe," I said.

"He knows that," Vinnie said. "But what's he gonna do."

Fish seemed in no hurry. He sat perfectly still with his hands folded and waited for us to finish. He was wearing a gray three-piece suit with a gentle glen plaid pattern. His shirt was blue with a white tab collar, and his tie was a gray and blue geometric. While he waited he examined the sink in the corner, the big green file cabinet to the right of the window with the head shot of Paul Giacomin on top of it, the picture of Susan with Pearl on my desk.

"I have a problem," he said.

I tilted back in my chair and waited. Behind me the September air, with only the smallest edge of fall inside the still summery softness, drifted in through the half-open window that overlooked the Boylston-Berkeley intersection.

"May I assume that this discussion is entirely confidential?" Fish said.

"No," I said.

Fish looked mildly surprised and glanced at Vinnie.

"He's just being a hard-on, Mr. Fish," Vinnie said. "He does that. Means he'll decide whether it's confidential after he hears it. Go ahead and tell him."

"I have been in business a long time," Fish said, "and I have learned prudence. I have learned that if you have associates you have to trust them."

He spoke slowly, with pauses between words that required no pauses, so you never quite knew when he was through talking. I waited.

"But I have also learned never to trust them beyond the limits of their venality."

"You go to Yale?" I said.

Again the driest of possible smiles.

"I have very little formal education," he said. "But I have always valued language and during a long period of incarceration when I was very much younger, I took it upon myself to master language."

"Are you sure you're a bad guy?" I said.

"Yes," Fish said. "I am."

I waited. Fish seemed to be thinking about something. Somewhere below me on Boylston Street I heard the *boop beep* of someone's car alarm remote.

"So, I have instituted a system of, ah, checks and balances in my organization. No single person is solely responsible for the management of money. Sometimes there are two, sometimes more than two, people who control a particular source of income and are responsible for its accounting. These people are generally not known to each other, or, two people are known to each other, but there may be a third or even a fourth who is unknown to the others, indeed, whose very existence is unknown to the others."

"Labyrinthian," I said.

"I value precision and control," Fish said.

"And you caught somebody stealing," I said.

"I told you at the beginning that I had a problem," Fish said, and his velvet fog voice was suddenly metallic. "If I had *caught* someone stealing, I would not have a problem."

I let that pass.

"You have, I believe, recently had dealings with Marty Anaheim."

"Marty had a tail on me," I said. "I backtracked the tail to Marty and expressed my dismay."

Leaning on the wall, Vinnie almost smiled.

"You are intrepid," Fish said. "Marty is extremely dangerous."

"But does he value precision and control," I said.

"Did Marty tell you why he had a tail on you?"

"No, but he seemed very interested in whatever I might be doing for Julius Ventura," I said. "And he seemed quite interested in Julius's son-in-law."

Fish pursed his lips for a moment and blew short silent whistles through them.

"What are you doing for Julius," Fish said.

I shook my head. Fish nodded sadly.

"If I need to know," he said, "I will make you tell me. For the moment the point can remain moot."

"Maybe you can tell me something," I said. "Was Marty acting for you when he put a tail on me?"

Again Fish whistled silently for a moment.

"Marty is ambitious," Fish said.

"And charming," I said. "I understand that Julius's son-in-law used to courier cash between you and Julius."

"He has done some work for me. Julius and I have areas of common interest in which we are cooperative."

"It's what life's all about, isn't it?"

Fish ignored me. We both sat quietly for a time.

"Do you know why Marty was interested in Anthony Meeker?" Fish said.

The name was up in the front of his brain. Did that mean Gino knew Anthony because he'd done some work for him, because he was Julius's son-in-law, or because he had recently become interested in him?

"If Marty was working for you, I'd say Anthony was skimming. If Marty's on his own in this, I don't know."

Fish nodded.

"Maybe Marty is skimming," I said.

"Why would that cause him to be interested in Meeker?"

"It would explain why you were interested in Marty," I said. "Maybe they were both skimming."

"Many people, ah, skim," Fish said. "It is human. But it doesn't seem an answer sufficient to my questions."

"Don't you hate it when that happens," I said.

Fish didn't answer. He sat still and looked thoughtfully at me, his long hands folded quietly in his lap.

"Well," Fish said, finally. "Neither of us has learned as much from the other as he would have wished."

"True," I said, "but I enjoyed listening to you talk."

Fish did his imitation smile.

"Perhaps we'll talk again," he said.

He stood and walked toward the door. Vinnie opened it, Fish walked through. Vinnie, his face expressionless, shot me once with his forefinger and walked out after him.

CHAPTER
13

JULIUS VENTURA DIDN'T LIKE IT MUCH THAT I WAS GOING to Vegas to look for Anthony. He wanted me to find Anthony in East Boston, or maybe Scituate at the outmost.

"You sure you ain't holding me up for a trip to Vegas?" he said.

We were in his office, in the back of a bar room called Cutter's on Atlantic Ave., near Quincy Market. Shirley was there too, sober, in a flowered dress with puffy sleeves and a very narrow skirt with a flared hem.

"Sure," I said. "Me and Hawk. The dream of a lifetime. Vegas! Who could blame us?"

"I ain't paying for you two clowns to go on no joy ride," Ventura said.

"But, Daddy, if Mr. Spenser thinks he's there . . ."

"Mr. Spenser thinks there's a good time there," Ventura said.

He was going to okay the trip and we all knew it. This was just foreplay to Julius, who felt like being a hard-nosed guy. I didn't mind. Julius needed to feel like a hard-nosed guy, and I had plenty of time.

"I could have said he was in Paris."

"He wouldn't go to Paris," Shirley said. "Did he go to Las Vegas with anyone?"

"Don't know," I said. "Got anyone in mind?"

"No. Not at all, I was just wondering."

"You and Hawk both got to go?" Ventura said.

"We'll find him quicker," I said. "With two of us looking."

"Just why is it you think he's there?"

"I'm told he's always dreamed of it. That he's got a system and as soon as he could get the dough together he was going to go out and bust Vegas."

"And where you think he got the dough?"

"From you," I said, "or Gino Fish, or both."

"You think we give it to him?" Ventura asked.

"No, I think he took it."

Shirley stood up as if there was a spring in her chair.

"That is absolutely not so," she said. She had her fists resting on her hips. "Anthony made a very good salary and he was as honest as the day is long."

"That honest?" I said.

"And besides, if he was going anywhere because he had

a dream he'd take me with him. He wouldn't go anywhere without me unless he was forced to."

"So you think he's been kidnapped and taken to Vegas?" I said.

"I don't know where he is. You said he was in Las Vegas, mister smart-ass detective."

She almost stamped her foot. It was as if she'd learned how to be mad by watching old Doris Day movies.

Ventura said, "Shut up, Shirley. What makes you think he lifted money from me or Gino?"

"He's got a gambling problem. He collected money for you. Now he's gone and you're looking for him, but you don't want people to know and Gino seems to be trying to find out what I find out."

I shrugged and spread my hands.

"He doesn't have a gambling problem," Shirley said. She was sitting again, her knees tight together, her fists clamped together in her lap. Her top teeth were on her lower lip again.

"Shirley, I tole you shut up," Ventura said. "This is business, you unnerstan? I'm trying to think about business here."

Shirley looked down at her folded hands. She spoke very softly, as if to herself.

"He wouldn't go without me."

Ventura stared at me hard for a while. I waited.

"Gino's been trying to find out what you're doing?"

"Marty Anaheim," I said.

"Same thing," Ventura said.

"They put a tail on me as soon as I started looking for Anthony. They knew about me the day I started."

Ventura's eyes were on me but they weren't seeing me. The tip of his tongue rested for a moment on his lower lip. He sat that way for a while.

Finally he said, "I do some business with Gino."

"Cash," I said.

"Yeah, a course." Ventura looked at me as if I questioned the law of gravity.

"And Anthony bagged the money back and forth."

"Some," Ventura said. "Sometimes, for good faith, because he was, you know, family, he'd do some pickup for Gino."

I waited.

"You sure about this Las Vegas shit?"

"I talked to some people. I'm sure he gambles bad and loses worse. I'm told he had a plan for winning big in Vegas."

"How come I don't know anything about it?" Shirley said. She was still looking at her fists in her lap. Her voice was still very small. "If he was like that I'd know. We were closer than anything."

Ventura ignored her.

"You don't say nothing about this. Especially you don't say nothing to Gino or Marty Anaheim."

"Normally," I said, "I stay in business by being a blabber-mouth, but since you asked so nice . . ."

"I don't want no talk about this anywhere," Ventura said.

"That your son-in-law stole your partner's money?"

"You don't know what he did," Ventura said. "All you know is he's missing and you better find him."

"He wouldn't steal anything," Shirley murmured.

"So we're off to Vegas," I said.

"Yeah, and right now. And don't stay in no fucking Caesars Palace, you unnerstan?"

"Probably just sleep in the airport," I said.

CHAPTER
14

I ALWAYS SUSPECTED THAT LAS VEGAS AIRPORT WAS BIGGER than Las Vegas, but I'd never seen any hard stats on it. Hawk and I were carrying one shoulder bag each for our clothing and two suitcases each for Susan's clothing. Slot machines lined the concourse.

"You planning on changing clothes every hour?" Hawk said.

"You never know when I may meet Wayne Newton," Susan said. "I have to be ready."

"Long as you don't have to carry it," Hawk said.

"Jewish American princesses do not carry luggage," Susan said. "That's why there are goys."

"I wonder if we could pick up a couple of little red caps," I said.

Hawk shook his head.

"Don't issue them to white guys," he said.

At the limousine pickup area there was only one other party, a man and a woman. Susan studied them for a moment and then made a covert head gesture to Hawk and me.

"Wayne?" Hawk said.

"Shh. No. That's Robert Goulet," Susan whispered.

Hawk put down the suitcases.

"You need to change?" he said.

"No," Susan said. "What I'm wearing is fine for Robert Goulet."

A slender light-skinned black man in a white suit came into the waiting area. He had short reddish hair. Inside the door, he took off his aviator sunglasses while his eyes adjusted.

Hawk said, "Lester."

"Hawk, my man," Lester said.

Hawk introduced us. We stayed with the air-conditioning while Lester hustled the luggage out to the car.

"Lester runs a specialty limo service," Hawk said. "Hotels bring in some high rollers. Lester picks them up, drives them around, gets them dinner reservations, girls, or boys, or both, if they want. Makes sure they go to the casino that sponsored their trip."

"And he owes you a favor," I said.

Hawk shrugged.

"He got some time free," Hawk said. "For *pro bono* work."

Lester came back in.

"Okay, folks, car's waiting."

We left Robert Goulet and his companion, and went through the brief band of desert heat outside the terminal and into an air-conditioned white Lincoln.

"You folks want a little tour of Vegas on the way in?" Lester said.

"Lester," Hawk said. "We ain't tourists."

"Sure. There's booze in the bar, you want."

"How do you know Hawk, Lester?" Susan said.

I smiled. I knew she wasn't making conversation. Susan actually wanted to know.

"Knew Hawk in Cuba," Lester said.

Susan looked at Hawk.

"Cuba?" she said.

Hawk shrugged. Behind us a maroon Buick Regal pulled away from a pickup zone and fell in behind us.

"What were you doing in Cuba, Lester?"

"Little of this, little of that," Lester said.

"Oh."

Susan turned to look at Hawk. The maroon Buick passed us on an open stretch. Usually when that happens the car keeps going and leaves you behind. The Regal pulled in two cars ahead of us and stayed there.

"And you?"

"Same thing," Hawk said.

We left the airport and headed north on Paradise Road. The Buick pulled off into the drive-up at the Best Western. When we passed, it came out of the Best Western and fell in three cars behind us. There was no doubt that the Regal was following us. Nothing is so conspicuous as the attempt to be inconspicuous.

The Regal stayed where it was the rest of the way. We drove down Las Vegas Boulevard, passing people in pink shorts and plastic hats walking past pirate coves and fake volcanos. A flaunting show of waterfalls and fountains danced in the middle of the desert as if they had not only defeated nature but wished to rub it in.

Lester turned in at The Mirage porte cochère and popped the trunk. The bell staff pounced on our luggage before we were out of the car. The Regal stayed on the strip, moving slowly with the traffic. Susan looked anxiously after the luggage as it disappeared through the bell door. I reached for my wallet as Lester opened the door for us, but Hawk shook his head.

"You got my beeper number," Lester said to Hawk. "I be around."

Hawk nodded. Lester got back in the Lincoln and drove away.

The lobby of The Mirage was positively sylvan. There were jungle plants and waterfalls, and a small bridge over a stream.

Hawk said, "Wait here."

He went into the guest services office and in maybe two minutes he was back with three keys. We walked across the bridge and through the casino jiving with the implacable music of the slots, to a bank of elevators next to the in-house shopping mall. In front of our rooms on the fourth floor, Hawk handed Susan and me each a key.

"Case you get bored," Hawk said. "Volcano erupts every fifteen minutes, until midnight. You can see it from your windows."

"The fun never lets up," I said.

"Round the clock," Hawk said. "Got the room next door, you do something romantic try to keep the noise down."

"I don't know if I can promise that," Susan said.

Hawk laughed, which he does, as far as I can remember, only at Susan.

I unlocked the door and Susan went in.

"You make the Buick," Hawk said to me.

"Yeah."

"You got a thought who that might be?"

"I'm losing track," I said.

"You do that easy," Hawk said and unlocked the door to his room.

I followed Susan into mine. It was a one-bedroom suite. The ceilings were high. The walls were banked with windows, the decor was multicolored southwestern mixed with Catskills. The woodwork was dark. The living room was bigger than my apartment in Boston, with a bar, a huge walnut armoire concealing a television, two red couches, four blue armchairs, a large round dining room table finished in black, and six black dining room chairs. There was pottery and there were paintings and there was beige wall-to-wall carpeting. I went across the room and opened the curtains. The volcano was there as promised. Not, at the moment, erupting. But if I were patient . . . the doorbell rang, and Susan let the bellhop in with the luggage. He put the bags in the bedroom. I tipped him. He left.

Susan picked up a printed card off the bar.

"'Dear VIP Guest,'" she read. "'Welcome to our VIP Level. Please call the VIP office with any requests you may have. We are at your service twenty-four hours a day.'"

"That's us," I said. "VIP guests."

"On the VIP Level," Susan said. "Is it because you are a famous detective?"

"No. Hawk knows somebody here that owes him something."

"Are we paying for this?"

"I don't think so."

Susan went into the bedroom. In a moment I heard her say, "Oh, oh."

I looked in. The bags were open on a black king-sized bed big enough for pony races, and the ceiling was mirrored.

"Oh? Oh?" I said.

"The mirrored ceiling," Susan said.

"I'll shut my eyes," I said.

"You'll pretend to," Susan said.

"You can watch too," I said.

"I'd rather go dancing with Howard Stern," Susan said.

"Oh come on," I said. "It's not that bad to see."

"And I am desperately oversexed," Susan said.

"Yes you are."

"And it's probably better than watching the volcano," Susan said.

"Yes it is."

"So." Susan shrugged, her eyes gleaming.

"So?"

"So peekaboo," she said.

CHAPTER
15

Vegas is not a big town, but if you want to gamble there, they have lots of places to do it. All we had for a plan was to cruise the casinos until Anthony appeared.

"And if he doesn't appear?" Susan said.

I shrugged. "Then we assume he's not here, and we look for him someplace else."

"Maybe he's in New York," Susan said, "hiding out at Bergdorf's."

We were at breakfast, sitting in a grotto of tropical vegetation, some of which was real, at the rim of the casino, soothed by the permanent harmonics of the slot machines which, when you're in Vegas, becomes like the music of the spheres.

"Susan and I will go north on the Strip," I said to Hawk. "You go south."

"What about all the joints off the Strip?" Hawk said.

"If he's the guy I think he is, he'll be in one of the big casinos. Here, Caesars, MGM Grand, that kind of place. What I gather, he's got something to prove."

"You gonna break the bank, you don't want to do it in some Motel Six in Laughlin," Hawk said.

I nodded.

"So first we hit the biggest and gaudiest. He's got a system. So we start with the blackjack tables. Could be something else, but most guys with systems play black-jack."

"Can a system win?" Susan said.

"Over a long time," I said. "Like most things it depends some on the guy using the system. In some places, for instance, you can surrender early—dealer shows a ten card and you don't like your first two you can turn them back to the dealer and forfeit half your bet. Gives you a quarter of a percent edge on the house."

"My God, that's not very much return on your investment."

"About a quarter for every hundred you play. But it's sort of illustrative. There are things that will give the player a positive edge. Most systems have to do with card counting; they can work if you play enough."

"How long is enough?" She was eating half a papaya with some lime squeezed on it. She had cut a small wedge off one end and picked it up and took a small bite. Even when she ate with her fingers, she seemed entirely delicate and proper. After I ate, I always looked like I'd been in a food fight.

"Two, three hundred hours," Hawk said.

Susan looked at him with horror.

"Two or three hundred?"

"Gambling ain't for lazy people," Hawk said. "You going to make a living at it."

"Wouldn't it be easier to work?" Susan said.

Hawk smiled.

"Or do what we do," he said.

"The thing is most people don't gamble hundreds of hours," I said. "Most people come to Vegas, say, for a weekend. Most of them don't have a system. They just play because that's what you do here."

"And they lose," Susan said.

"Absolutely," I said. "If they didn't enjoy the experience they might as well mail in a check."

"I'd love to try it," Susan said.

"Blackjack?"

"Anything. It sounds like fun."

"You got a system?"

"Of course I do. You and Hawk tell me what to do."

Hawk looked at me without expression.

"Be a first," Hawk said.

"She won't do what we tell her," I said.

Susan smiled.

"I will if I want to," she said.

In the lobby bar a young woman with a tight red dress and a blond ponytail was belting "Hey Look Me Over" to three guys at the bar and one woman sitting near the lounge feeding coins into a nickel slot. I looked at my watch. It was 7:45 A.M.

Susan and I stood for a moment outside The Mirage watching Hawk move away down toward the Strip. He was wearing a white straw planter's hat, a dark blue linen shirt, white slacks, and blue suede loafers. People studiously avoided looking at him until he was past them. Then they stared at him over their shoulders.

"People notice him," Susan said.

"Yeah."

"He frightens them."

"Yeah."

"Have you ever figured out why?"

"They know," I said.

"Yes," Susan said. "They do."

We stood for another minute watching Hawk's progress. Then the tram from Treasure Island arrived and we were swarmed with heavy people in colorful shirts. We fought our way through them and went first for a look at the white tigers in their climate-controlled habitat. Then we backtracked, and looked at the people lounging by the pool.

"It's amazing that no matter how small women's bathing suits get, they still manage to cover all they're supposed to," I said.

"Do I hear disappointment in your voice?" Susan said.

"Yes."

The desert air lived up to its clichés. It was hot, but the dryness made it seem less hot. We moved north along Las Vegas Boulevard, casino by casino. The hotels were garish, but the north side was less so than the south. It was Hawk who got to go into Caesars Palace, which looked like ancient Rome, and the Luxor, which looked like a pyramid, and Excalibur that looked like a fortress, and MGM Grand, which looked like Oz. We had only Treasure Island, which looked like a Caribbean seaport, though we did get the live pirate show where one ship sinks another in the Treasure Island Lagoon, while the mist machines on the perimeter cooled us down. The rest of the hotels on our part of the strip looked like big ugly hotels, a fifth-grader's dream of luxury, and nighttime excess, shopworn in the unblinking Nevada sunlight.

The street crowd was mostly the same kinds of people who dream those kinds of dreams, people who'd decided this year to come to Vegas instead of Disneyland, people who looked like they'd just come from a square dance, people who looked like they'd just arrived on a freight car, pink shorts, small plastic mesh baseball hats, small children, Instamatic cameras, white boots, large bellies, plaid shirts, high top sneakers, camcorders, just married, street peddlers—mostly black and Hispanic, private security people wearing black shorts and yellow shirts, riding bicycles, and carrying Colt Python revolvers, people in pointed shoes and checked sports coats with dark glasses and their shirts unbuttoned, a little guy with a big nose, wearing a flowered short-sleeved shirt and a Panama hat, and a perfectly dressed sophisticate from Boston with his stunning companion.

Inside the hotels, the casinos seemed interchangeable: air-conditioned, windowless, artificial light, no clocks, the pinball colors of the slots dominating the room, the carnival chatter of the slots overpowering all other sounds. We stopped at a blackjack table, watched some games, moved on to the next table, watched some games. The little guy in the Panama hat was better on foot than he was in a Buick. He wasn't obvious, but, if you're looking for a tail, there's not much the tail can do to avoid being seen. He was in the casinos when we were in them, lingering near the exit. He was on the other side of the street, down a ways, when we were strolling between casinos.

"Would he play poker?" Susan said.

"Might. But in poker you play against the other players, not against the house. I have a sense that Anthony wants to bust the MGM Grand or somebody."

"Not only money, but notoriety," Susan said.

We checked the poker tables. Only two were in use this early. The blank-faced dealers expertly distributed the cards, presiding over a game in which they had no stake. We strolled past the blackjack tables again on our way out.

"No one seems to smile here," Susan said.

"It's about money," I said.

"Of course," Susan said. "No wonder they're so serious."

"Want to play?" I said.

"Certainly," Susan said. "If you'll stay beside me and tell me what to do."

"Of course," I said.

Susan bet five dollars. She got a seven and a nine. The dealer had a ten showing.

"Stay," I murmured.

"Hit me," Susan said.

The dealer gave her a jack.

"I lost," she said.

"Un huh."

We played for another fifteen minutes in which Susan lost a hundred dollars. She paid no attention to what I told her to do. On the fourth hand I said nothing. She glared at me.

"What should I do?"

She had a three and a five.

"Hit," I said.

She got a ten.

"Stay," I said.

"Hit," Susan said.

She drew a five.

"I hate losing," she said.

"Well, I don't mean to be critical," I said. "But why are you taking a hit with eighteen?"

"I don't want to just stand there," Susan said.

"Of course you don't," I said.

We didn't find Anthony that day, or the next one. But

Susan did locate something called the fashion mall, down past Treasure Island.

"Maybe they have a Victoria's Secret in there. You could buy one of those seductive floral nighties."

"You know I don't wear nighties," Susan said. "We've known each other a long time now. It's okay, I think, for you to see me naked."

"Oh good," I said.

"But not right here," Susan said.

"Give with one hand, take with the other," I said.

CHAPTER
16

I CAME TRUDGING BACK IN THE LATE AFTERNOON OF DAY three. Susan had taken the afternoon to explore the shops in Caesars Palace next door, and I had cruised the casinos alone, swinging off the Strip this time just to vary the monotony. The little guy in the Panama hat stayed with me. I wasn't expecting to find a Vegas Buster at the Debbie Reynolds Hotel. And I didn't. The little guy had trouble at the Debbie Reynolds Hotel. The lobby casino was too small to be unnoticed. He did his best, feeding quarters into one of the slots aimlessly, while I was not finding Anthony.

"Debbie'll sign her book for you," the clerk said. "Comes right out every night after her show and talks with people." He gestured toward the coffee shop. "Right outside there. I can sell you tickets. Show starts at eight."

I thought about getting two tickets, one for me, and one for the little guy, but decided that I wasted too much time being self-amusing.

When I came into the lobby of The Mirage, I was thinking about beer. At the casino entrance on the rude bridge that arched the artificial flood, Hawk was leaning on the rail, looking at the water.

"Anthony's here," Hawk said. He nodded toward the casino.

"Blackjack?"

"Un huh. He a guest here."

We started toward the blackjack tables.

"You know that for a fact?"

Hawk looked at me.

"Of course you do," I said. "It pays to have contacts."

"You know you got a tail," Hawk said.

"Little guy, big beezer, Panama hat," I said.

"Un huh. You don't want to brace him?"

"No. Let's let it play out," I said. "See what happens when he sees us with Anthony."

"You figure he's from Gino?" Hawk said.

"Or Julius, or Marty Anaheim, or all three, or Wayne Newton, for all I know. But I figure it's Anthony he's trying to find."

In person Anthony was better-looking than his wedding picture. He was taller, more graceful. His nose was less pronounced. His eyes looked less beady. He was nicely dressed in a collarless white shirt buttoned to the neck, and a tropical-weight tan blazer that fit him well. He was standing at a $100 blackjack table, his face blank, watching the cards come out. Hawk and I separated as we approached and stood to either side, a little out of the game, spectators. There was nothing unusual about Anthony's play. He was as serious as any other hundred-dollar player. As I watched I counted cards for a while. Plus one for the low cards, minus one for the high ones, zero for the rest. After maybe half an hour I had a very low count, which meant that a lot of high cards had come out. That left a lot of low cards, which favored the dealer. Anthony looked at his watch, handed in his cards, picked up his chips, and left the table. Hawk and I followed him to the bar. He ordered a scotch and soda, and idly fed a dollar coin into one of the poker machines set into the bar. He won three dollars. He played it again and lost. Hawk sat down on one side of him, and I sat down on the other. He looked sideways at me, then at Hawk, and fed another coin into the machine.

Hawk ordered a couple of beers.

I said, "How you doing, Anthony?"

"Do I know you?"

"Not yet," I said. "My name's Spenser. The gentleman on the other side of you is Hawk. We need to talk a little."

"Nothing wrong with right here," Anthony said. He drew one mechanical card on the poker machine, and failed to fill a flush. "Whatcha want to talk about?"

"You, Shirley, Julius, money, stuff like that."

To his credit he didn't waste time pretending.

"You from Julius?"

"Julius and Shirley. They're worried about you."

"You with the outfit?"

"Nope, I'm a private detective."

"A private dick? No shit. Him too?"

Hawk smiled to himself.

"He's more like a soldier of fortune," I said.

"So you found me. Now what are you supposed to do."

"I guess we're supposed to bring you back."

"You got any paper, something like that, says you can make me come with you?"

"Nope."

"Then I don't have to go," Anthony said.

"He didn't say that," Hawk murmured. "He just said he didn't have no paper."

"You talking about kidnapping?"

"We're just talking, Anthony, trying to see how it is," I said.

The bartender set the beers down in front of Hawk and me. Without being asked, he put another scotch and soda in front of Anthony.

"You talking kidnapping, I'm talking cops, you dig?"

"How come you took off?" I said. "You scoop some money?"

"If I did, nobody I scooped it from is in a position to go to the cops."

Anthony sounded confident but occasionally he would look at Hawk for a flickering moment out of the corner of his eye.

"You think Julius Ventura spends much time calling the cops?" I said. "They usually take care of things like this themselves."

"Yeah, so how come he sent you?"

"I've been wondering that myself. Any thoughts?"

"I figure he isn't going to rough up his own son-in-law."

"You got a better opinion of Julius than I do," I said.

Anthony dipped into his second scotch. He took a mouthful, raised his head, and tipped it back so that the drink could trickle down his throat. When he'd swallowed he looked at me and winked.

"Shirley wouldn't let him touch me," he said.

"She's got that much influence with Julius?" I said.

"Shirley gets her way," he said. He saluted Shirley with his glass and took another drink.

"How much influence she got with Gino Fish?" I said.

Anthony finished his drink, and got an ice cube in his mouth. He chewed on the ice cube and shrugged.

"I don't know. I don't think she knows Mr. Fish."

"You know him?"

"Sure, I met him."

"You ever carry any of his money?"

"Sure. It's what I been doing, working for Julius. So sometimes I bring money from Julius to Mr. Fish and sometimes I take money from Mr. Fish to Julius."

Hawk was leaning his back against the bar, his feet outstretched, looking at the casino. He appeared to have no interest in what Anthony and I were talking about.

"You know what the money's for?"

Anthony shrugged elaborately.

"What are you, from the IRS? You got a wire maybe? You think I'll say anything you can use, good luck to you, pal."

Anthony gestured the bartender for another scotch. I shook my head no to another beer.

"You know Marty Anaheim?" I said.

Anthony stared at me for a moment before he caught himself.

"Yeah," he said.

"Got any idea why he might be interested in you?"

"Marty?"

"Yeah."

"Interested how?"

"Like he might want to know if I found you?"

Anthony looked at the mirror behind the bar, and I realized he was scanning the room behind him. If he saw the little guy halfway across the casino, watching roulette, he didn't react.

"I don't want nothing to do with Marty Anaheim."

"But he might want something to do with you," I said.

"Does he know I'm here?"

"Not from me," I said. "You take some of Gino's money?"

"No. I swear on my mother, I never took no money from Gino. Has Marty been asking you about me?"

Still watching the room without any apparent interest, Hawk spoke to Anthony.

"How about we give Marty a call, tell him you here?"

"Jesus, don't do that."

"Why not," I said.

"You know him?"

I nodded.

"Then you know he's a fucking animal. I mean he likes to kill people, for crissake."

I nodded again. The bartender brought Anthony a fresh scotch and soda. Anthony took a long pull on it.

"So why would he want to kill you?" I said.

"Who knows," Anthony said, "an animal like that."

Hawk and I were quiet. Anthony drank a little more of his scotch, though not as if he was in desperate need. He stared at the half-empty glass for a moment while he swallowed.

"Listen," Anthony said. "I'm on to something here. It's going to pay off for me, big time, you unnerstand? But I need a little breathing room. You guys want to be in on it, give me some of that breathing room, in a manner of speaking, and I can cut you in on a very nice chunk of change."

"You got a system?" I said.

Anthony shook his head.

"I can't tell you, you're going to have to trust me. But

you stick with me on this, and I can make it worth your while. In capital letters, worth . . . your . . . while."

Hawk said, "Un huh."

"Two days, three at the most and I'll have all the money there is. I give some to you. I pay back Julius; and Shirley and I buy a nice house in Lincoln. Gimme two, three days."

"What if Marty Anaheim shows up?" Hawk said.

"You guys keep him off me."

"Lemme see your room key," I said.

"How come?"

"Want to see where you'll be if I need you."

"Why not just ask me?" Anthony said.

"Anthony," I said, "you told me the time, I'd want a second opinion. Gimme the key."

He produced it. It was a Mirage key. Room 1011. I gave it back to him.

"You here alone?"

"Yeah."

I spoke to Hawk.

"You want to give him time to break the bank?"

"Sure."

"Think we can keep Marty Anaheim off his back? If he shows up?"

Hawk turned his head slowly and looked at me from the other side of Anthony. He smiled.

"We could do that," he said.

CHAPTER
17

ANTHONY TOOK HIS SYSTEM BACK TO THE BLACKJACK TA-
bles. We sat at the bar and watched him. Hawk was sipping Krug, from a fluted glass. The bottle was in an ice
bucket on the bar. I had a beer.

"You think he's got a system?" Hawk said.

"Don't know," I said. "He doesn't seem to be counting."

"Maybe one of those progressive betting systems,"
Hawk said. "Casinos love them."

"Anthony was born to lose," I said. "He'll play till he
does."

Hawk nodded more in agreement with himself than
with me.

"So how come we didn't just grab him and call Julius?"
Hawk said.

"And then what?"

"Then it's up to Julius," Hawk said.

"I don't want to leave it up to Julius," I said.

"Or Shirley," Hawk said.

"Her even more," I said.

"So who we leaving it up to?"

"There's something wrong here," I said.

"Anthony did seem to be thinking 'bout Marty Anaheim a lot."

"He reacted different to that name than the others," I said. "When I first brought up Gino's name, you notice, Anthony didn't have any reaction. He didn't react to Gino until after we mentioned Marty."

"You believe him he didn't take no money from Gino?"

"He swore on his mother," I said.

Hawk smiled.

"That did it for me," he said.

"You got a friend at the hotel," I said.

"You are an ace detective," Hawk said, "figure that out."

"We didn't have to register and everything's free," I said.

Hawk grinned.

"You don't miss nothing, do you, Bawse."

"Nothing," I said. "So maybe you could ask her if Anthony is registered here with anybody."

"How you know my contact is a her?" Hawk said.

"Ace detective."

We were quiet. Hawk took the bottle from the ice

bucket, poured a little more Krug, and put the bottle back in the ice bucket.

"You think there's something between Anthony and Marty?" Hawk said.

"We been looking at Marty Anaheim and seeing Gino Fish," I said. "What if Gino's got nothing to do with it. What if it's Marty? Gino didn't seem too sure about Marty when he came to see me."

"So what's that got to do with Julius?" Hawk asked.

"Maybe nothing. Maybe there's two sets of things going on. Julius you can figure. Anthony stole some money from him and it makes him look bad. Julius wants the money—and Anthony—back without anyone knowing about it."

"And Marty?"

"I don't know. If he's not working for Gino on this . . . be kind of hard to drag Anthony back to Boston, he doesn't want to go," I said.

"Sure," Hawk said. "That be really hard for just the two of us, him being such a bad ass and all."

A woman wearing a designer baseball cap and carrying a coin cup slid into the bar beside Hawk. She ordered a bourbon old-fashioned, looking covertly at Hawk while the bartender mixed it. When it came, she put it down in three swallows and headed back to the slots.

"Okay," I said, "so we can drag him back to Shirley if we wanted to. Let's wait and see first if we want to."

"During which time we hang around and protect him from Marty Anaheim. If Marty were to show up. For whatever reason, which we don't know, that Marty might have. If Anthony needs protection from Marty."

"Which he thinks he does," I said.

"Or which he lets us think he thinks he does," Hawk said.

"Unless we misinterpret."

"Unless that," Hawk said.

Hawk was looking at the casino floor as he talked. His face was expressionless. His eyes always seemed to see nothing and everything simultaneously. After a minute he looked back at me and grinned.

"You know what you're doing?" Hawk said.

"No."

"But you trying to do the right thing, soon as you know what it is," Hawk said.

"Yes."

"And meantime we going to fuck around with Anthony until we find out who to save."

"That's my plan."

"So we going to cover him twenty-four hours a day, you and me?"

"I don't think he'll run," I said.

"Why not?"

"He's not going anywhere," I said, "until he loses all the dough. We'll sort of cover him while he's playing."

"So Marty Anaheim won't come and scare him to death," Hawk said.

"Marty's pretty scary," I said.

"What you going to do about Julius," Hawk said.

"I told Anthony I wouldn't blow the whistle on him yet."

"Yeah but Julius paying us," Hawk said.

"I'll let him know we've located Anthony, see what he has to say."

"And if he say bring him right back?"

"I'll tell him, soon."

"And if he say now?"

"I'll tell him, soon."

"You got to do it your way," Hawk said, "don't you."

"I don't do kidnappings."

"The hell you don't," Hawk said. "I seen you do more than kidnappings, you think it's what you should do."

I shrugged and took a sip of beer. I had nursed it so long that what was left was warm. I pushed the bottle away.

"For something important, maybe," I said. "Not for Julius Ventura's money. Not to send Anthony back to Shirley."

"You decide," Hawk said.

"Who else," I said.

Hawk grinned. "Don't ask me. I don't worry 'bout things like that. I just do what I feel like."

"So why you asking?"

Hawk smiled his still smile.

"You ever think about running for Pope?" he said.

"Some," I said.

CHAPTER
18

IT WAS SUPPERTIME. HAWK HAD THE FIRST WATCH ON AN-
thony and I was in my hotel room waiting for the volcano
when Ventura called me.

"What the fuck's going on?" he said.

"Just fine thanks, and yourself?"

"Never mind the wiseass shit, what'd you call me for?"

"Let you know that your son-in-law is in Vegas."

"My daughter with him?"

"Your daughter?"

"Yeah, asshole, my daughter, you know? Shirley? She
out there?"

"I haven't seen her," I said.

"Well, she's not here," Ventura said.

"How long's she been gone?" I said.

"She had Jackie drive her to the airport an hour ago."

"If she's on her way here, it'd be a little soon to expect her," I said.

"What are you, a fucking travel agent? My wife's driving me up a fucking tree about it."

"Why would she come here?"

"Her asshole husband's there ain't he?"

"How would she know that?" I said. "I only found him about three hours ago."

"You said you thought he was there," Ventura said. "Maybe he fucking called her. I didn't hire you to ask me a bunch of fucking stupid questions."

"You hired me to find Anthony Meeker," I said. "I found him. He's here, with money, gambling."

"Well, stay with him, see if my daughter shows up. She does, you grab her and hang onto her and call me."

"And then what?" I said.

"I'll send some people to bring them back."

"And?"

"And you take your fucking fee and buzz off."

"Can I use you as a reference on my next job?" I said.

"You find her you call me, any fucking time, twenty-four hours, you understand? It's fucking three in the morning, you call me. Somebody'll answer."

"I'll be in touch," I said.

I sat after I hung up and thought about this, and the more I thought the more I didn't know what the hell was going on.

I heard the key in the door and then a lot of fumbling,

which I knew would be Susan. She always had trouble with keys and locks, and was always a little annoyed about it if I opened the door to save her the struggle. After a stiff resistance, the door succumbed, finally, and Susan came in carrying a lot of expensive-looking bags.

"So many shops," she said. "So little time."

"You can do it," I said.

"I think maybe I did," she said.

She gave me a friendly kiss on the mouth and began to take things out of the bags.

"Any luck today?" she said.

"Yeah, we found Anthony."

"Oh," Susan said. "Excellent. What now?"

"We talked," I said. "And we decided to await developments."

"How about Anthony's wife?"

"She seems to have disappeared. Last seen at Logan Airport an hour ago. Ventura thinks she's on her way here."

"Looking for Anthony?"

"That's what Ventura thinks."

"Why did she decide to come now?" Susan said.

"Yeah, I wondered about that," I said. "Maybe she just got restless."

"Maybe she wanted to share in Anthony's dream," Susan said.

"Imagine having Vegas dreams," I said. "But why now? It's almost like she knew we found him."

"How would she know?"

"There's been a guy following us."

"Here?"

"Yeah, little guy, big nose, Panama hat," I said.

"I haven't noticed him."

"You haven't been looking," I said.

"Why is he following us?"

"Don't know," I said.

"Who do you think sent him?"

"Don't know," I said.

"Do you think he told Shirley?"

"Maybe," I said.

"Right on top of this, aren't you," Susan said.

"Well, the tail's good news in some sense, so is Shirley, if she comes out here. Means things are stirring."

"The hardest part, in therapy, is when nothing's happening," Susan said.

"That's the idea," I said. "Ventura wants us to sit tight and grab her if she shows up."

"You want to sit tight anyway, don't you?"

"Yeah."

"Perfect."

Susan held up a yellow linen jacket. When I first knew her I would say things like *Don't you already have a jacket like that?* But I have learned much since those early days.

"Looks great," I said.

"You like the color?"

"Yellow," I said.

"Jonquil," Susan said with some scorn. "You like it?"

"Love it," I said.

She took it to the mirror and put it on and turned around and checked the rear view and made nine or ten minute adjustments in the way it hung. She also took advantage of the moment to fluff at her hair a little. Finally she nodded as if somewhat satisfied and hung it in the closet.

"I have to go home tomorrow," she said. "I have patients."

"I know," I said. "You see Shirley Ventura hanging out in a terminal at DFW or someplace, grab her, and give her some psychotherapy."

"Or call here and give you some," Susan said.

"Either one is nice," I said.

Susan held a black silk blouse against herself and studied it in the mirror.

"Aren't you supposed to do that before you buy it?" I said.

"And after," Susan said. "And every time you pick it up for the rest of your life. Does it look cute?"

"Cute," I said, "is far too small a word."

Susan looked at it some more, turning to see it from all angles, smoothing it down as she did so.

"I hate to go home without you," she said.

"Sexual deprivation?"

"And luggage."

"At least it's both," I said.

The phone rang and I answered.

"Anthony's registered as Ralph Davis," Hawk said. "There's a Mrs. Davis with him."

"He still playing?" I said.

"See him from here," Hawk said. "Hundred-dollar table. He's winning."

"Think your contact could get one of us into his room when it's empty?"

"Un huh."

"Ventura called," I said. "Says Shirley's missing, thinks she might be out here."

Susan was taking a pair of hand-painted cowboy boots out of a bag that had a polo pony imprinted on it.

"Maybe it's Mrs. Davis," Hawk said. "He got instructions for us?"

"Stay put, watch Meeker. Look for Shirley."

"Better do what he say."

"Certainly," I said. "Susan and I are reviewing her shopping. I'll talk to you later."

We hung up. Susan was holding up the colorful cowboy boots.

"What do you think?" she said.

"You know," I said, "what would be a great look?"

Susan put her finger to her lips.

"I'll try them on," she said.

She took the cowboy boots and went into the bedroom. Outside the volcano began to rumble. I got up and went to the window. It would be embarrassing to go home and say I'd never seen it. I stared down at the plastic volcano as flame and smoke erupted from the top and fire ran down the sides mixing with the water which flowed from the fountain. This went on for several minutes and then stopped. And the mountain turned back into a waterfall. I stared at it for a while. Maybe it would be embarrassing to go home and say I had seen it. I turned back toward the room. Susan came into the living room with her cowboy boots on and no other clothes.

"Howdy," I said.

I'd seen her naked often. But in all the time I'd known her, I never saw her naked without a sense that if I weren't so manly I'd feel giddy. In fact I never saw her at all, dressed or undressed, without that feeling.

"Every time I buy boots you have the same suggestion as to how I should wear them," Susan said.

"Well," I said, "you can't say it's not a good suggestion."

"No," Susan said. "I can't."

"The gold necklace is a nice touch," I said.

"Thank you."

"You're welcome."

Susan's eyes narrowed slightly, and she looked at me sort of sideways as if squinting into the sun.

"You want to canter on into the bedroom," she said. "Buckaroo?"

"You sure you want to do that now?" I said. "The volcano's due to go off again in fifteen minutes."

She smiled the smile at me, the one that could launch a thousand ships and burn the topless towers of Ilium. She walked slowly toward me.

"So are you," she said.

CHAPTER
19

T HE NEXT MORNING HAWK JOINED US FOR BREAKFAST.

"Where's Anthony?" Susan said.

"Never comes down till noon," Hawk said. "He play till four-fifteen this morning."

"Poor thing," Susan said. "It's only seven-thirty. You must be exhausted."

"We don't get tired, Missy," Hawk said. "Just sing some songs, and keep on picking cotton. Little guy in the hat getting kinda frazzled though."

Bob, the waiter, brought Susan one pancake with honey. Hawk and I had steak and eggs. I had some decaf.

"Why do they just keep watching him," Susan said. "Why doesn't somebody act?"

"My guess is it's because he's winning," I said. "If the little guy is watching him for Julius, or Gino, or Marty, or any combination thereof, they want their money back. Figure they'll wait until he wins as much as he can."

"And he'll start to lose eventually, won't he?" Susan said.

"Don't know his system, but Lennie Seltzer tells me he's a loser. And everything I know about him supports it."

I was finished with my breakfast. Hawk was eating his last piece of toast. Susan poured another gram of honey onto her pancake and took a second bite.

"You got a view on losers?" Hawk said to Susan.

"You mean once you've eliminated stupidity and bad luck?"

"Which is eliminating big," Hawk said.

He sipped some of his coffee. It reeked of caffeine.

"With many people for whom gambling is an obsession, there's a lot of guilt," Susan said. "They know it's obsessive, and destructive. They see it as a vice. And they are angry with themselves for doing it."

"Like alcoholics," Hawk said.

Susan nodded.

"Yes, and as is sometimes the case with alcoholics, the vice becomes its own punishment."

"So they gamble 'cause they have to, and lose to punish themselves," Hawk said.

"Something like that," Susan said. "Sometimes."

"If you right, and Lennie Seltzer right, and we right, Anthony bound to lose and when he start to lose they may just whack him."

"Who?" I said.

"Find out when he starts to lose," Hawk said.

"I was hoping for prior to," I said. "You seen any sign of the woman he's registered with?"

"Nope. Stays in the room as far as I can tell. Eats off the room service menu. She goes out she does it when I'm watching Anthony."

"Seems kind of odd," I said.

"It do," Hawk said.

"No trips to the blackjack tables to cheer on her man? No expeditions to the Fashion Mall?"

"Unthinkable," Susan said. She had already finished half her pancake.

"I guess she didn't want to be seen," I said.

"By whom?" Hawk said. "We the only ones watching, until Panama Hattie showed up."

"Maybe after we go to the airport I'll take a look into that a little."

"Toward that eventuality," Hawk said, lengthening the initial *e*, "ah has acquired us a key."

He handed it to me and I put it in my shirt pocket.

Bob appeared with the check.

"You want to chahge it to your room?" he said. "Or put it on a credit cahd."

All three of us looked at him simultaneously. A song of home.

"You from Boston?" I said.

"Yeah, Dawchestah. How'd you know?"

"A wild guess," I said.

When I signed the check, I overtipped Bob because he talked right.

Hawk and I drank the rest of our coffee, caffeinated and decaffeinated. Susan finished all but two bites of her pancake, and it was time for the airport.

Lester was waiting out front. Susan was wearing her jonquil jacket, and carrying her makeup bag as we got into the Lincoln. The little guy with the Panama hat was nowhere in sight. No Buick Regals followed us to the airport.

"What happened to all the luggage you brought out?" I said. "Plus the stuff you bought?"

"The hotel is shipping it for me," Susan said. The hint of a triumphant smirk played at the corners of her mouth.

"Boy," I said, "now if they could just do that with sexual gratification."

"Yes," Susan said.

On the backseat of the Lincoln was a newsprint magazine titled *Boobs-Are-Us.* I picked it up. The cover featured a woman with a chest appropriate to the title. She had blond hair and a lot of dark eye makeup and she had her tongue sort of half stuck out. Two pink telephones concealed her nipples.

"Tasteful," Susan said.

There was a phone number to call and a picture of a Visa card and a MasterCard, presumably so you could call the blonde right up on the phone and charge it. I looked through the magazine. It consisted of a series of pictures of seminude women, many with the perennially popular little hearts pasted in crucial spots. Each picture had a brief sales pitch, like "shy but sweet" or "nude and naughty." With each there was a telephone number.

"I like the ad for hot sexy feet," I said.

"I figured you for that," Lester said.

"All these years," Susan said, "I've been wasting time on nudity."

"What happens if you call these folks," I said to Lester.

"Besides the chilling effect on our relationship," Susan said.

"Prostitution is legal in Nevada," Lester said. "But it's on a county by county basis. It's not legal in Clark County, where Vegas is, so you pay a hundred bucks for a girl to come to your room, get naked, and give you a massage. You want more you make a private deal with the girl. If she wants to. Or I can take you about an hour down the road, next county, and you get it legal in a whorehouse. That's why I have the magazines. People ask about the girls and I can steer them to the brothels."

"Maybe later," I said.

Susan made a sound that in someone less elegant would have been a grunt.

"Well, keep it in mind," Lester said. "I get a nice commission on that."

He pulled the car up in front of the airport.

"I'll be here," he said.

I walked with Susan through the brief wedge of dry heat into the air-conditioned terminal. We went along the concourse past the people on their way home desperately trying to recoup with one last dollar in one last slot until we got to the security gate.

"Did anyone follow us out here?" she said.

"No. Once they located Anthony they jilted me," I said.

"That would suggest that it was Anthony they were looking for."

"Yes."

"Do you think he's in danger?"

"Hawk's with him," I said.

"I wish you knew if there were danger, where the danger was coming from," Susan said.

"Where's the fun in that?" I said.

We stood silently for a moment. Then Susan put her arms around me.

"I love you." she said.

"There's a certainty," I said.

"Maybe the only one."

"Maybe the only one necessary," I said.

She nodded as if I'd said a smart thing and smiled up at me.

"Take care of yourself," she said.

"I'll call you."

"Often," she said.

We put our arms around each other and kissed each

other gently. This kiss was loving but not big and smoochy. Susan never did big smoochy kisses while wearing lipstick.

"You got your ticket," I said.

She held up the ticket which she had in her left hand. Then she put her right hand on my face for a moment and turned and went through the gate. Watching her I felt the little knot in my stomach that I always felt when I left her. She walked a ways down the concourse, and looked back and waved and then turned a corner and was out of sight. I still stood for a moment, looking at the last place I had seen her, being careful not to be routine, while I became the other guy again, the one I was without her. It took a couple of minutes. And then I was him. He wasn't a bad guy; in fact sometimes I thought he had strengths that the other guy didn't have. Certainly he wasn't worse. But he was no one I wanted to be all the time. I turned back and headed for Lester and the Lincoln.

CHAPTER
20

When I got back to The Mirage there were a couple of Las Vegas detectives waiting for me with a hotel security guy in the corridor outside my room. When I put the key in my door, one of them showed me his badge.

"Your name Spenser?"

I confessed to it, and unlocked the door.

"May we come in?"

"Sure," I said.

They looked for a moment at the security guy.

"Let me know if there's anything you need," he said.

Both of the cops looked at him without speaking. The one who'd showed me his badge nodded slightly. The security guy went off down the corridor and we went into my room.

"Nice," one of the cops said.

The one who'd showed the badge was leathery and tall and gray haired with a thick gray moustache. His partner was much younger with stylish blond hair, wearing good clothes.

"This is Detective Cooper," the gray-haired one said. "I'm Detective Sergeant Romero, Las Vegas Police Department."

"You know I'm a famous detective, and you came here looking for crimestopper tips," I said.

"Never heard of you," Romero said, "until we found your card at a crime scene."

"Pays to advertise," I said.

"Oh good," Cooper said, "a funny one."

"Yeah," Romero said. "Makes it so much nicer when they're funny."

"Just think of me as lighthearted," I said. "Tell me about the crime."

"Woman's been killed," Romero said. "Couple Mex cleaning workers found her body in a vacant lot this morning when they got off work."

"You know who she is?" I said.

"No, we thought we'd bring you over, see if you knew."

"Sure," I said, "let's go."

The vacant lot was a half mile down the Strip behind an out-of-business restaurant. There were half a dozen cop cars parked there, a fire department rescue truck, a vehicle from the coroner's office, and a couple of civilian vehicles. They took me to the body.

"This is how we found her," Romero said.

She was naked, lying on her back with the desert sun baking down on her. There were a couple of bruises on her face, and one eye had swollen half shut. There was bruising on her throat. And the tip of her tongue protruded slightly between her swollen lips. But the damage didn't disguise her. It was Shirley Ventura Meeker, her white body dimpled and pudgy in the comfortless sunlight.

"Know her?" Cooper said.

"Name's Shirley Ventura. She's married to a guy named Anthony Meeker. I don't know which name she used."

"Coop," Romero said. "Start checking the hotels. Try the MGM Grand first."

Cooper had a small notebook.

"Meeker with two *e*'s?" Cooper said.

"Yes."

Cooper scribbled in his notebook for a moment.

"Got a next of kin?" he said.

I told him and he wrote it down and headed for the car.

"How you know her?" Romero said.

"Her father hired me to find her missing husband."

"You find him?"

"Not yet."

"And you think he's out here?"

"Yeah."

"So you came out looking for him."

"Yeah."

"She come out here with you?"

"No."

"So what's she doing here?"

"Maybe she came out to look on her own."

"You know where she was staying?"

"No."

"Think she found her husband and he killed her?"

"I doubt it," I said. "He doesn't seem like that type, what I hear. And I'm pretty sure she was too dumb to find him anyway."

"You know the husband?"

"No."

"Got a picture?"

"Yeah."

"Might want to borrow it."

"Sure."

"Got any thoughts on this?"

I shrugged.

"Maybe if you told me what you know so far."

A police photographer appeared. Romero took my arm and steered me carefully away from the crime scene, so the photographer could take pictures. We leaned against the back wall of the defunct restaurant. It was late morning and the dry heat lay hard and flat over everything.

"Couple Mex night workers, got off work at six this morning, say they were just cutting through the lot on their way home. Except home isn't in that direction. I figure they scooped a six-pack from the hotel kitchen and came out in the lot to drink it."

"Going to notify robbery?"

Romero smiled.

"Probably not," he said. "Anyway they found her and one of them called us and here we are. You see the way she was when we found her. No clothes. No purse. Mexican could have taken it, but I don't think so. If they had, they wouldn't have called us."

I nodded.

"M.E. will want to look at her more closely but it looks like the cause of death was manual strangulation."

"She been raped?"

"Almost certainly."

"And somebody beat her up."

"Yeah. Happens a lot with rapes."

"I know," I said. "Where'd you find my card."

"On the ground near the body. I figure it was in her clothes, maybe tucked in her bra or someplace, and it fell out when the guy made her disrobe."

"How'd you know I was at The Mirage?"

"There were two phone numbers written on the back. We called them both. One was the MGM Grand. They never heard of you. The other was The Mirage. Bingo!"

"What happened to her clothes?"

Romero shrugged. "Maybe it happened someplace else, maybe he brought her here."

"Why would he do that?"

Romero shrugged again.

"If she disrobed someplace else, what did my card fall out of?"

Romero shrugged again.

"You trying to make this harder than it is?" he said.

"What happened to the purse?" I said.

Romero shrugged.

"She was traveling," he said. "She probably had cash."

"Why take the purse, which is incriminating? Why not take just the cash, which isn't?"

"Guy was in a hurry," Romero said. "Took the purse and beat it. Emptied it out later. We'll probably find it empty someplace. Or he emptied it where he undressed her. Left it there. Give me a little time, pal. I just got on the case."

"Didn't take her rings," I said. "Or the necklace."

"Didn't want to get caught trying to turn them over," Romero said.

"Maybe he took the purse because he didn't want us to know who she was."

Romero shrugged again.

"Maybe he took the clothes for the same reason. You hadn't found my card you wouldn't have, excuse the expression, a clue."

"Maybe," Romero said. "We find out where she's registered, might help. I figure the thing happened sometime between dark last night, say nine o'clock, and six A.M. this morning. You account for yourself during that time?"

"I was with my sweetheart," I said.

"Can we talk to her?"

"She went back to Boston this morning. She won't get there until six tonight."

"We can call her," Romero said.

Cooper came back across the lot from his car.

"Anything?" Romero said.

"She's not at the Grand," Cooper said. "Still checking around."

"Get a list of the guests?"

"They're running it off for us," Cooper said. "I sent a car over to get it."

Romero turned to me.

"Give you a copy of the list, you check it for names?"

"Sure."

"How about Boston?" Romero said to Cooper.

"Talked to the Homicide commander," Cooper said. "Guy named Quirk. Says the hawkshaw is legit."

"Just legit?" I said.

Cooper continued speaking to Romero as if I hadn't spoken, but there was a trace of humor at the corners of his mouth.

"Says he'll lie to you, he thinks it's a good idea. But he wouldn't rape and murder anyone."

"Good to know," Romero said.

"He say anything about brilliant?" I said. "Or dauntless?"

"No."

"I'll send a copy of the list over to your hotel," Romero said to me. "You need a ride back?"

"No," I said. "Just as soon walk."

Romero nodded.

"You know why the husband disappeared?" Romero said.

"I don't think he was happy in his marriage," I said.

"Well, that won't be a problem for him now," Romero said.

CHAPTER
21

HAWK AND I WENT OVER THE LIST OF GUESTS AT THE MGM Grand that Romero had sent over. We recognized no one.

"Why don't I go stand by the elevators in the MGM Grand," Hawk said, "watch who gets on and off, see if I recognize anybody, might not be using their right name."

"Don't get sidetracked by the *Wizard of Oz* display," I said.

"Be hard," Hawk said. "But ah does have a will of iron."

"And a head to match," I said.

Hawk almost smiled as he left.

I went down and sat at the bar in the casino with Anthony Meeker. He didn't like being at the bar. He wanted to be at the tables.

"I got a hot table," Anthony said. "I need to get back to it before it cools off."

"Okay, I won't waste time," I said. "Your wife was found murdered today in a vacant lot about a half mile from here."

"My wife?"

"Shirley," I said.

"Here?"

"Un huh."

Anthony glanced back at the blackjack table he'd left.

"She's dead?" he said.

"Yes."

"The cops know?"

"Yes."

"They know about me?"

"They know you exist. They think you're in Vegas. They don't know you're here," I said.

"You think they can find me?"

"Yes," I said. "They have your picture. They'll circulate it. It's only a matter of time."

"They know about you and me?"

"They know I'm looking for you."

Anthony glanced at the hot table again.

"But you didn't tell them you'd found me."

"No."

Anthony put up his hand to high-five me.

"All right, Spenser, my man," he said.

I didn't high-five back, so he put his hand down.

"I'm up big," he said. "Couple more days is all I need."

"I need to know who you're here with," I said.

"Me? Nobody. I'm here alone. Just me and Lady Luck."

"You registered as Mr. and Mrs. Ralph Davis. Who's Mrs. Davis?"

"Aw, I just did that in case I met somebody, you know?"

"Sure," I said. "I know how prudish they are out here about a woman in your room."

"Yeah, I guess it does sound crazy, but it's just a habit. I always do that when I travel."

"So there's nobody in there living off room service, staying out of sight."

"No."

"Then you won't mind giving me your room key so I can stroll up and see for myself."

Anthony looked at me, and looked back at his table, and looked at me again.

"I don't want you to go in my room," he said finally.

"I don't care," I said, and put my hand out for the key.

"Spenser, c'mon, I got a right to some privacy for cris-sake."

"And I got a right to go home and let Marty Anaheim find you when he finds you."

"Marty? Is he here?"

I did a big shrug.

"Where's Hawk?" Anthony said.

He was looking at the casino floor again in the bar mirror.

"I go, Hawk goes," I said.

Anthony looked over his shoulder again at his table.

He scanned the rest of the room. He looked at me, and at the table again.

"Okay, I got a girl with me."

"Who?"

"Just a girl I know, name's Bibi."

"Why does she stay in the room all the time?" I said.

"She's kind of shy."

"Shy?"

"Yeah. She's sort of, ah, intimidated by the casino scene and all. She stays in the room, reads, watches TV."

"And eats three meals a day off the room service menu? And never goes to a show? Or shops? Or swims?"

Anthony was quiet.

"I think we need to talk with her, Anthony."

"Okay, but not right now, you know? I'm missing quality time at the table."

"Anthony," I said. "Your wife's been killed. You are a suspect. When the cops questioned me, I lied about several things, including you. I got to know what's what before they find you so I can save my ass, and maybe yours as needed."

"Me? I didn't kill her. I been playing blackjack since I got here."

"She was killed sometime prior to six A.M. this morning. Hawk left you at four-fifteen this morning. That's an hour and forty-five minutes when you could have done it."

"For crissake. I was in my room, Bibi can tell you."

"My point exactly," I said. "Let's go and ask her."

146

Anthony sat for a moment without moving. Then he got up from the bar, glanced regretfully at the hot blackjack table, and we headed for the elevators.

At his room, Anthony unlocked the door with his room key, opened it just enough to stick his head through.

"Beebs, you decent?" he yelled.

I could hear a television laugh track giggling and guffawing inside the room. I heard a woman's voice, and then Anthony opened the door wider and we went in.

Mr. & Mrs. Davis had a one-bedroom suite. They were not neat. The room service wagon was still in the living room, bearing the disorganized remnants of cereal and toast, orange juice and coffee. There were shirts and panty hose, socks and blouses all over the room. The luggage was open on the floor, half unpacked. A hair drier lay on the coffee table. An uncapped toothpaste tube lay on the bar with some toothpaste drooling out. Through the open door to the bedroom I could see that the bed hadn't been made up yet. Sitting on it, fully dressed and made up, was a red-haired woman with pale skin and a faint scatter of freckles. She had a parenthesis-shaped scar a little to the right of, and below, her right eye. Her hair was long and thick. She wore a green dress with some sort of white print in it, and white sling-back heels. She stood and came out of the bedroom.

"Beeb, this is Spenser," Anthony said. "Spenser, Bibi."

"Bibi what?" I said.

"Anderson," Anthony said. Unfortunately, Bibi said, "Davis," at the same time.

There was a white leather woman's handbag on the dresser, a big one, the kind you hang off your shoulder. I picked it up and looked in.

"Hey," Anthony said. "What the hell are you doing."

"You can't even agree on what her name is, I thought I'd look for a clue."

There was a dark red compact, some loose tissues, a pair of radiant blue Oakley sunglasses, some bills and coins, a bottle of Advil, some keys, a fat-free granola bar, some lipstick in a dark red tube, two tampons, and a wallet. Anthony looked like he wanted to take the purse away from me, and knew he couldn't so he settled for standing around wishing he could. Bibi said nothing and showed no evidence that she cared one way or another if I rummaged in her purse.

"You got no right to look in there," Anthony said.

I took out the wallet. It had credit cards in it and a Massachusetts driver's license. The picture on the license was Bibi. There was a Medford address, and the name on the license was Beatrice Anaheim.

"Marty's wife?" I said.

"Yes," she said.

"Leapin' lizards," I said.

CHAPTER
22

"OKAY," ANTHONY SAID, "NOW YOU KNOW."

"Now I know."

"It's not what you think. We love each other."

"That's what I thought," I said.

"I finish here, we're going someplace, get married."

"How's Marty feel about this?" I said.

Bibi had her arms folded across her stomach as if she were sick, or cold. She squeezed herself a little tighter when I asked the question.

"Marty don't matter," Anthony said. "We clean out this place and we're gone."

"How do you feel about it?" I said to Bibi.

She shook her head.

"She feels great about it," Anthony said.

"Either of you worried that Marty Anaheim might be jealous and try to find you and, ah, attempt to correct your behavior?"

Bibi seemed to be getting colder; she hugged herself tighter.

"That's what I got you and Hawk for," Anthony said.

I passed that by without comment.

"Anthony with you last night?" I said to Bibi.

She nodded.

"All night?"

She nodded.

"From midnight to four-fifteen?" I said.

She nodded.

"No," Anthony said. "Bibi, you remember I was playing blackjack until four-fifteen. Hawk saw me. I was with you from four-fifteen on."

Bibi nodded.

"Sure," she said. "That's right."

"Isn't that swell," I said.

"You through now, man. I gotta get back to the table before it goes cold."

"Sure," I said. "Hawk's not there. So stay in full view."

"You think Marty's here?"

"Better to act like he might be," I said.

"Aren't you going to come with me?"

"I'll stay and talk for a while with Mrs. Anaheim," I said.

"Don't call me that," Bibi said.

"Man, you're supposed to be guarding me."

"I was supposed to be bringing you back to your wife," I said.

"Well, that's over," Anthony said.

I stood. Bibi sat. Anthony looked at me and at the door and at his watch. He shifted from one foot to the other.

"You coming?" he said.

"Nope."

"Man, the table's getting cold on me while we stand here."

I waited. Anthony looked at Bibi.

"I got to get to the table," he said.

She nodded. Anthony looked back at me.

"Yeah, sure. Okay. I'll be right there at the tables. Nobody's gonna try something right there, in the middle of the casino."

I smiled encouragingly. Anthony shifted again and then headed for the door.

"I'll be playing," he said.

The door closed behind him and the ornate room was quiet. Bibi sat on the couch looking at me. I glanced around the room. There was nowhere to sit without moving a pile of clothing. Bibi didn't seem to care if I stood or sat.

"Want some coffee or something?" she said. "I can call down."

"No," I said. "Why don't we go downstairs and have lunch."

"What if somebody sees me?"

"Bibi," I said, "somebody killed Shirley Ventura Meeker in a vacant lot a half mile down the Strip."

"Who did it?"

"I don't know, but it makes everything different. A lot of people are going to see you before this thing gets straightened out."

"This thing?"

"This thing," I said. "Whatever it is. Let's eat."

I put my hand out to help her up. She ignored it and stood and hesitated and then went out the door ahead of me. She never said a word down in the elevator, across the casino, and into the restaurant, where, only this morning, Susan and I had eaten breakfast together. I looked at my watch. She'd be landing in about an hour. She'd stop at Henry's, get Pearl, and go home. She'd feed Pearl, unpack and hang everything up carefully, iron things that had wrinkled, take a bath, put on the pajamas she usually wore when she slept without me, get in bed with Pearl, have a half cup of frozen chocolate yogurt sweetened with aspartame, and watch a movie. Pearl would burrow under the covers and then Susan would fall asleep with the television still on.

"Hey, Boston," the waiter said, "how ya doin?"

It was Bob from Dorchester. Bibi ordered a glass of white wine. I had decaf. Bibi asked for a cheeseburger and fries. I ordered something called a Roman salad. I didn't know what it was, but Vegas was very taken with ancient Rome, and I wanted to be with it.

"What do you want to talk about?" Bibi said when Bob went away.

"You."

"Oh God," Bibi said. "You know how many times I've heard that line?"

"Tell me about yourself."

"Yeah. You know what it means?"

"Sometimes it means tell me about yourself," I said.

"Mostly it means, 'Let's fuck.'"

"Tell me about you and Marty and Anthony," I said.

Bob brought the decaf and white wine. I looked at Bibi. She was a handsome woman with very big greenish eyes, and a wide mouth. There was very little life in the eyes. Besides the scar under her right eye, there was some thickening to her nose, not much, but a little the way fighters sometimes get it. A little like mine. Her teeth were white and even and might have been capped. There was about her the quality, almost the aroma, of sexuality. Susan always would ask how I knew. I could never tell her exactly, except that when I'd seen it before and put it to the test, I'd nearly always been right.

"What's to tell," she said. "I was with Marty, now I'm with Anthony."

"How was it with Marty?"

She shrugged.

"Marty's a pretty dangerous guy," I said.

"He's a pig," she said.

"Yes, he is. That why you left him?"

"Yes."

"Why'd you marry him?"

Bob returned with the Roman salad and the cheese-burger. The Roman salad looked very much like a tossed salad except that it had green olives and wedges of arti-choke heart in with the cherry tomatoes and shredded car-rots and red leaf lettuce. Bibi took a small bite of her cheeseburger.

"Was he a pig when you married him?" I said.

Bibi chewed carefully and swallowed. She picked up a French fry and ate it.

"He's always been a pig," she said. "But I didn't always know it."

"He treat you right?" I said.

"He beat the shit out of me," she said.

Everything she said was flat and offhanded as if noth-ing mattered more than anything else, and she was kind of bored to have to tell me.

"At least he's consistent," I said.

"I think he liked to do it," she said. "I think it gave him a thrill."

"He do it often?"

"Yeah."

"And you didn't leave."

"No."

I nodded and took a bite of my Roman salad. Bibi had stopped eating and sat staring past me as if she were look-ing at her own past, just beyond my left ear.

"I didn't have any money," she said. "He kept it all. I

didn't even have a credit card. He'd give me money for food shopping once a week, two hundred dollars, and he'd check the register receipt when I came home and make me give him the change."

I didn't say anything. You do it long enough and you get a sense when somebody is at the start of a long talk. The best thing is to give them space and wait for them to fill it.

"I didn't have a credit card. I didn't have anyplace to go, even if I had one. He wouldn't let me work. You know I never had a job? I married Marty right after high school."

Bibi shook her head. Her face was blank but there was painful self-mockery in her voice.

"Fairhaven High School, nineteen seventy-seven, most congenial. Met him down the Cape, bar in Falmouth we used to go to 'cause they didn't card you. He picked me up. He was dangerous. Everybody was scared of him, but me. I thought he was exciting, you know? A real man."

Bibi stared down silently at her cheeseburger for a time.

"You got married right away?"

"Three months."

"Kids?"

She made a sound that had it been less bitter might have been a laugh.

"Marty didn't want kids. Didn't want my figure get ruined, he said. I think he didn't want to share me with a kid, you know?"

"Well," I said. "Your figure didn't get ruined."

She gave me a little automatic smile to acknowledge the compliment.

"Let me join a health club, aerobics, body shaping, that stuff; Marty said he liked me looking good."

Bob came by and poured a little more decaf in my cup. I looked at it gloomily. It was better than nothing. It was not, on the other hand, better than an Absolut martini on the rocks with a twist. And the more Bibi Anaheim talked about her marriage, the more I wanted the martini.

"He used to like to punch me around," she said. "And then have sex. Called it making up."

I nodded.

"He had a lot of trouble," Bibi said, "getting it up, you know? I'm not sure he could get it up, he didn't rough me up first."

"Probably wasn't pleased that you knew that."

"No, he wasn't. Said it was my fault. Said he had no trouble with the whores."

"Probably because they were whores," I said.

She shook her head impatiently.

"I don't know anything about that," she said. "He used to go to the whores a lot. Good. Keep him away from me. Bastard gave me the clap once."

I was quiet. She sat thinking back, looking past me at the lush artifice of the Las Vegas restaurant and probably not seeing it.

"And then Anthony came along," I said after a while.

"Funny thing," she said. "Marty introduced us. He

never did that, you know, but he introduced me to Anthony. Figured Anthony was safe, I guess. He's not a tough guy like Marty. And he was married to Julius Ventura's daughter. I guess Marty never thought Anthony would be the one."

"He was a friend of Marty's?"

"Marty had a lot of guys hang around him. I don't think he had any friends. Everybody was scared of him."

"So what was his relationship with Anthony?"

She sat staring past me as if she hadn't heard me and then her eyes came slowly onto my face.

"You scared of Marty?"

"No."

She kept her eyes on me for a while. Then she nodded her head slowly.

"No, maybe you're not," she said, still looking at me. "But you should be."

I waited.

"Marty and Anthony had some deal going," she said, finally.

"Do you know what it was?"

"No."

"Was Gino involved?" I said.

"I don't think so."

"I assume the deal is now off," I said.

She nodded.

"Marty finds out you're here, what happens?" I said.

"He'll kill Anthony. Probably with his hands. Marty likes that. And he'll take me home and beat the shit out of me and it'll be like it was. Except this time he'll probably hurt me worse."

"We'll have to see to it that he doesn't do that," I said. "Can Anthony stand up to him?"

"Oh, God no," Bibi said. "Nobody can."

"Somebody can," I said. "You love Anthony?"

She made the bitter laugh sound again.

"Better than Marty."

"And he was a way out," I said.

"He was. Now it's all shot to hell," Bibi said. "He's gotta break the bank or whatever he thinks he's going to do, and we sit here and wait until he does it, and now the stupid wife shows up and gets killed and Marty will hear about it and know I'm out here and find us and . . ."

She shrugged.

"Or not," I said.

She shook her head.

"There's no *or not*," she said. "You can't stop him. He'll find me and do what he's going to do and no one will stop him. Nobody can."

"I might stop him," I said.

She shook her head, and kept shaking it, slowly back and forth. Tears formed in her eyes and came down her cheeks. She lowered her head, and I could no longer see the tears but I could see her shoulders shake. I put a hand out on top of hers. She didn't move except for her head swaying back and forth and her shoulders shaking. I guess she didn't believe me.

CHAPTER
23

I WAS SITTING AT THE BAR DRINKING CLUB SODA, WATCHING the gamblers, and thinking of the Kipling poem ... something about piling all you own on a single bet and losing and smiling and walking away. *Yours is the Earth and everything that's in it, and—which is more—you'll be a Man, my son.* Kipling had never been to Vegas. I was drinking club soda because in recent years beer in the middle of the day made me sleepy.

I didn't want to be sitting at the bar in the middle of the day, wide awake, drinking club soda and thinking of poetry. But I didn't know what else to do, and at least this way I could keep an eye on Anthony Meeker while he mourned his wife at the blackjack tables. I knew Julius would show up to take his daughter home. I figured sooner or later Marty Anaheim would show up to straighten out his marital circumstances. The Vegas cops might or might not catch whoever murdered Shirley. Hawk would or would not spot someone at the MGM Grand which would explain why Shirley had the number written down.

I wondered if I was still employed. The question of returning Anthony to his wife was no longer pressing. Murder spilt a lot of milk. And if Julius really had wanted me to find Anthony before word got out that he skimmed some money, it was too late, that probably being some of the milk that was spilt. I wondered if the stolen money was part of Anthony's deal with Marty Anaheim. Gino's visit to my office made me think that something was wrong between Gino and Marty.

I fed a dollar coin into the poker machine at the bar and won ten dollars. I fed the money back into the machine mindlessly until I lost it. It wasn't that I liked to gamble. Gambling mostly bored me. I just had nothing else to do and I didn't want all those dollar coins clanking around in my pocket. Eventually I managed to get rid of about thirty dollars. The bartender asked if I wanted another roll.

"No thanks," I said. "I've got to let my pulse rate settle."

The bartender put a fresh club soda on the bar in front of me.

"On the house," he said. "I'm supposed to cozy up to the high rollers."

"You've got a real instinct for the job," I said, as Hawk slid onto the bar stool next to me.

The bartender looked at him. Hawk shook his head.

"Marty Anaheim," Hawk said.

"At the Grand?"

"Yeah. Little guy's been tailing Anthony is with him."

"Okay, that answers one question," I said.

"Cops find where Shirley staying?" Hawk said.

"No," I said. "I called Romero this morning. As far as they can tell she wasn't registered anywhere."

"So where's her luggage?"

"Romero says maybe she didn't have any."

"Romero ever travel with a woman?" Hawk said.

"I asked him that. He admitted that mostly they bring luggage."

"So where is it?"

"They don't know. They figure the murderer stole it."

"A woman's luggage?" Hawk said. "You knew Shirley, would she have luggage?"

"She'd have luggage like Susan has luggage."

"So our guy rapes this woman," Hawk said. "And strangles her, and then runs off carrying her handbag and three, four pieces of luggage?" Hawk said.

"Or," I said. "He rapes her and kills her someplace else and carries her nude body to a vacant lot and drops it."

"And your card, 'less she still clutching it in her lifeless hand and he don't notice."

I sipped some club soda. The slot machines chanted

their endless song in the background. There was very little night and day in Vegas. There were no windows in the casinos, no clocks, no closing time, no last call. Only if you went outside, for which there was very little reason, or waited at your window for the volcano to erupt, did day or night matter.

"He wanted to prevent her identification," I said.

"Un huh."

"And went to a lot of trouble to do it," I said.

"Un huh."

"Which means he can be tied to her. Otherwise why bother?"

"Which mean the finger of suspicion point to Anthony," Hawk said.

"Or Marty Anaheim."

"Marty ain't tied to her."

"So why'd she have the number for me and The Mirage and the MGM Grand written on the back of my card?" I said.

"Got any tighter fix on time of death?" Hawk said.

"Cops say no. Anytime that night before she was found."

"I got Anthony until four-fifteen," Hawk said.

"And his girlfriend says he was with her the rest of the night."

"'Course she might lie."

"She might. She's Marty Anaheim's wife."

Hawk stared at me for a moment, which was as much surprise as he ever showed.

"Anthony got a death wish," Hawk said.

"Marty and Anthony had some kind of deal going."

"Did it include Mrs. Anaheim?"

"No, he ran off with her after, as far as I can tell, double-crossing Marty."

"Be quicker for Anthony," Hawk said, "he just stepped in front of a train."

"And more pleasant," I said.

"How's he doing?"

"Don't know," I said. "Right now I think he's counting, and betting progressively."

"If he loses doubling the last bet?" Hawk said.

"Something like that," I said. "I don't study his technique."

"He'll find a way to lose," Hawk said. "Anybody double-cross Marty Anaheim and run off with his wife knows how to lose."

I sipped a little more club soda. Refreshing. Hawk gazed absently at Anthony Meeker across the room at one of the blackjack tables. He was dressed today in a black blazer and a white silk shirt with vertical black stripes like a successful referee.

"Cops still holding out for a random rape and murder?" Hawk said.

"I doubt it. They don't like to complicate things if they don't have to, but Romero doesn't seem stupid to me. Of course they'd have a better chance if I told them all I know."

"Why don't you?"

"I'm trying to protect our client," I said. "And I'm trying to figure out who did what to whom before I sic the cops on them."

"Just who is our client," Hawk said. "And why we still working for him? Shirley's dead and Julius knows where Anthony is."

"Well, we can't let Marty Anaheim run around loose here," I said.

"Why not?"

"His wife took off with Anthony because Marty abused her," I said.

"You're surprised Marty Anaheim would abuse his wife?" Hawk said.

"He'll abuse her more if he finds her here."

"So we working for her now?" Hawk said.

"She hasn't hired us. But I sort of told her we wouldn't let Marty get her."

"Sure you did," Hawk said. "She's probably good looking and sad and you do four or five back flips and say we gonna eat Marty's lunch for him, he comes near her."

"I didn't do that many back flips," I said.

Hawk signaled to the bartender and ordered a glass of champagne.

"Marty Anaheim," he said thoughtfully, "is the meanest man I ever knew. He lost his hands, he'd bite you to death."

I didn't say anything.

"Marty Anaheim," Hawk said again, shaking his head slowly.

I shrugged.

The champagne arrived. Hawk drank half of it, and toasted me with the remainder.

"You often been a headache," he said. "But, babe, you never been a bore."

CHAPTER
24

I WAS IN MY ROOM READING SIMON SCHAMA'S NEW BOOK ABOUT landscapes when Anthony called me.

"Spenser," he said, "get up here."

"You're awful bossy, Anthony, for a guy who's not paying me."

"For God's sake," Anthony said, "Julius is here."

"With you?" I said.

"In the hotel. He called me on the house phone, but I wouldn't tell him where my room was."

"What was his posture?" I said.

"What?"

"How was he acting?"

"He said he was going to kill me."

"Oh," I said. "That posture."

"So get Hawk and get your asses up here," Anthony said.

I indulged a cruel streak.

"Did you know Marty Anaheim was in town too?" I said.

"Marty?"

"Yeah. He's staying down the Strip."

"Oh my God," Anthony said.

His voice was very small. I heard the murmur of another voice in the background and Anthony's voice, muffled, as if his hand were over the mouthpiece, saying Marty's here, and a louder murmur and Anthony's voice saying, "For crissake, Bibi," then his voice on the phone again.

"You and Hawk said you'd protect me," he said. "You gotta come up right now."

"Stay in your room," I said. "We'll be along."

When we got there Anthony was drinking scotch out of a short fat glass. His coat was off, his dark blue linen shirt was unbuttoned nearly to the waist. The cuffs too were unbuttoned. Bibi sat on the couch, hugging her knees, her back wedged into the angle of the arm. Her feet were bare. She had on designer jeans and a white sleeveless top.

"So tell me about Julius," I said.

"Fuck Julius," Anthony said. "Where's Marty Anaheim?"

"MGM Grand," I said.

"How do you know?"

167

"I saw him," Hawk said.

"You know he's staying there?"

"Seems likely," Hawk said. "He coming out of the guest elevators when I spotted him."

"Maybe he was just visiting somebody?"

"Maybe," Hawk said.

"What difference does it make?" I said. "He's staying someplace. He's here in Vegas."

"Yeah, yeah. Of course. Right. What difference does it make. You haven't seen him here, in this place?"

Hawk shook his head.

"Step at a time," I said. "Far as we know, Marty doesn't know where you're staying. Julius does. Tell me about Julius."

"You think Marty's here looking for me, though."

"Center of attention," I said. "Tell me about Julius."

"Oh God," Anthony said.

He finished his scotch, went to the ice bucket on the table, put a handful of ice in his glass, and poured more scotch over it. Bibi continued to watch us, peeking over her clenched knees. Hawk leaned on the wall near the door. I waited, standing in front of Bibi. While I waited I patted her knee. My father used to do that, give me a pat once in a while, without comment. Anthony drank some more scotch.

"Julius blames me for Shirley's death," Anthony said.

I nodded.

"Said if I hadn't run off like I did she'd be alive today."

I nodded.

"Hey, it's too bad somebody killed her, but I ain't going to pretend she was like, you know, Meg Ryan or somebody. I had to get away from her. I had to get a new start."

"You could have killed her," I said.

"I was right here with Bibi, you asked her yourself."

I patted Bibi's knee again.

"She might lie to protect you."

"I was gonna kill her, would I wait till I got out here?"

"You thought you were free and clear," I said. "You were winning, your system was working, and then she showed up. You could have done it."

"For crissake, I thought you and him was gonna protect me."

"Julius threaten you?" I said.

"Yes. He said I was as good as dead."

"Was he alone?" I said.

"I dunno, I just talked to him on the fucking phone," Anthony said.

He drank more scotch.

"Probably he wasn't alone," I said.

"Probably not," Hawk murmured.

"So," I said. "How you want to handle this?"

"Me?"

"Yeah. It is, if you'll pardon the expression, your ass. I figure you might want some input in how to save it."

"How much to eliminate them?"

"Them?"

"Both of them, Julius and Marty."

"How about Gino Fish?" I said. "Don't you have some of his money?"

"I don't know. That was Marty's part."

"Part of what?"

"Of our deal. I'll tell you about it later. Right now we got to get rid of the immediate threat."

"By shooting it," I said.

"Yeah. You guys are good. I've heard about you. Ten thousand each. Cash on the barrel head."

I looked at Hawk.

"On the barrel head," he said.

"It's a nice idea," I said. "But it might turn into a career, we have to kill everybody you annoy."

"No, no. Just these two guys. You want more than ten each. Okay. I can do that. You name it, I'll do what it takes."

"We'll hold that option in reserve," I said, "until we talk with the other principals."

"Talk?"

"Yeah. Hawk and I will go talk with Julius, see what he has in mind. Then maybe we'll find Marty, see what he's thinking, then we'll report back to you."

Anthony drank some scotch as if it were an antidote to madness.

"Talk?" he said. "Fucking talk? You can't talk to them, for God's sake. You try talking to them and they'll kill you, for crissake, and where the fuck does that leave me?"

"Nice to be needed," I said.

Bibi was sitting as she had been, motionless, her eyes seeming to grow larger and more empty as we talked.

"You all right in this?" I said to her.

"No," she said. "All I can do is sit here and wait for the men to do whatever they'll do. How all-right is that?"

"We can get you out of this," I said. "Have you on a plane out of here in an hour."

"To where?" she said.

I didn't answer. I knew the question was rhetorical.

"She stays," Anthony said.

"She does what she wants to," I said.

"I'll stay," Bibi said.

Her voice was small and nearly empty. The words were its only content. I nodded.

"Okay," I said. "Sit tight. No one knows quite where you are. There's two doors. This one and the one in the bedroom. Leave the door in the bedroom chained and bolted. Use the living room door. Check everybody through the peephole. No room services. No messages. No housekeeping services. Nobody but me or Hawk. There's trouble call hotel security."

"You don't even know where his room is," Anthony said. "Maybe he's not even staying here, how you going to find him?"

"He'll find me," I said. "Technically, he's still my client."

"You going to sell me out to Julius," Anthony said. His voice was shrill. "You gonna leave me here and sell me out, like a goddamned sitting duck?"

"You could call the cops," I said.

"You guys are scared," Anthony said. "And you won't admit it. That's the fucking problem, isn't it? You're yellow."

"Maybe we could shoot him," Hawk said, "and go get ten thousand from Julius."

"Hell," I said, "we could double-dip. Get ten from Julius, get ten from Marty."

"Hey," Anthony said. "Don't kid around, you know. This is a fucking life-or-death deal."

"Ain't it always," I said.

I patted Bibi's knee again and headed for the door.

"We'll be in touch," I said.

CHAPTER
25

WHEN HAWK AND I CAME INTO MY ROOM, I THOUGHT THE air-conditioned stillness hinted at the memory of Susan's perfume, but maybe it was nostalgia. The message light was flashing on my phone.

"A Mr. Ventura called, please call him in his room."

Hawk smiled and shot me with his forefinger.

Julius had several rooms in another wing, without a view of the volcano. I wondered if he knew he was not A list. Hard to be sure. There might be people closer to the volcano than I, who thought I wasn't A list. His suite was bigger than mine, though it was smaller than Delaware. A fat guy named Steve, whom I knew slightly, let us into the living room. He was in his shirtsleeves and had a Glock 9mm on his right hip. There were four other men in the living room, all in shirtsleeves, all with guns. One of them was Jackie, Shirley's driver. I nodded at him. He nodded back. A pump shotgun lay across a hassock near the couch. The remnants of lunch littered the coffee table and the bar top, and spilled off the rollaway room service table. A bottle of red wine stood on an end table.

"Julius was looking for us," I said.

Hawk stepped to the side of the doorway and leaned on the wall again. There was nothing specific about the way he leaned but somehow it projected menace.

"He's in with the missus," Steve said. "She's pretty shook up about Shirley."

"Probably is," I said. "Can you let him know we're here?"

Steve went into one of the bedrooms, and stayed a moment. The four men in the room looked at Hawk and at me. No one said anything. Steve came out of the bedroom.

"Julius says come in."

Hawk and I went past him into the room. There was an old woman dressed in black lying on the bed with her shoes on. The shoes were black. Julius sat on the bed beside her. There was a plastic ice bucket full of water on the bedside table. Julius wet a facecloth in the ice bucket and wrung it out and wiped his wife's face with it. Her face, even refreshed with the cold water, was pale, and her eyes were puffy. She had thick eyebrows and a thick prominent nose. Her hands rested on her stomach below her bosom and her thick fingers were moving rosary beads through them, though she gave no outward sign of prayer.

"She don't want me to leave her," Julius said.

"Here is fine," I said.

The woman opened her eyes and looked at Hawk and me, without much focus.

"I don't know you," she said.

Ventura said softly, "They work for me, Iris."

"The colored man, too?"

"Yes."

"Did you know Shirley?" she said.

"Yes," I said.

"She's dead, you know."

"I know," I said. "I'm sorry."

"Did you know her?" she said to Hawk.

"Yes ma'am," Hawk said. "I'm sorry for your loss."

"Yes," she said. "It is a loss."

We were quiet. The old woman closed her eyes again and in a moment tears began to seep from under the lids. Sitting beside her, Julius wiped her face again with the wet facecloth. Then he put the cloth back into the ice water and picked up her hand and held it and patted it with his other hand.

"We come to bring her home," Julius said to me. "You know who did it?"

His voice was a deep slow rumble, like a subway train passing far below the surface.

"No," I said.

"Hawk?"

"No," Hawk said.

"You know where Anthony Meeker is?"

"Yes," I said.

"Tell Stevie," Julius said. "Then go home."

"Can we talk?" I said.

"Nothing to talk about," Julius said.

"Yeah, there is."

"No," Julius said. "I don't know if it was him actually put his hands on her. But he ran off on her. She wouldn't have been out here, he hadn't run off on her. She wouldn't be gone."

He slowly patted his wife's hand as he spoke.

"Did you know he has some kind of game going with Marty Anaheim?"

"He did, he didn't, don't matter. That's business, this is blood. You understand anything?"

"You don't know the game between him and Marty?" I said.

The old woman on the bed opened her eyes. Her voice scraped harshly out between her thin bluish lips.

"Don't talk business, my daughter's in the morgue."

"No, Iris," Julius said. "No business."

"Only business is killing him," she said.

"Yes," Julius said, still holding her hand, still patting it.

I looked at Hawk. He shook his head. I nodded.

"We'll find him anyway," Julius said. "Save us a little time, you tell Stevie."

"Sure," I said.

"I'll pay you through today," Julius said. "Tell Stevie, he'll give you cash."

"Sure."

"No more business, Julius," Iris said. "Kill him."

He reached across and closed her eyes gently with his fingertips.

"Try to sleep," he said.

Hawk and I left the room. In the living room I spoke to Steve. He took $100 bills from a suitcase in the closet and gave some to me. I folded it once and put the money in my pants pocket without counting it, and we left.

CHAPTER
26

On the phone Susan's voice had the same quality of promise that it had in person.

"I talked to a policeman from Las Vegas on the phone. He wanted to know if you were with me the night before I left."

"Yeah. They found Shirley Ventura dead with one of my business cards near her."

"My God! I told them the truth on the assumption that had you wished otherwise, you'd have gotten to me first."

"Honesty is the best policy," I said.

"Usually," Susan said. "When are you coming home?"

"Why is it," I said, "that the simplest question, about

the most ordinary subject, when you ask it comes freighted with the hint of God knows what excitement?"

"Perhaps it has to do with the auditor, more than the utterer."

"Utterer?"

"I have a Ph.D.," Susan said.

"Of course you do," I said. "You think I'm projecting?"

"Yes. All I said was, 'When are you coming home?' "

"And the possibilities I hear implied are me not you."

"Certainly. When are you coming home?"

"Well, as of yesterday I'm on my own. Julius paid me off."

"So now you have no client."

"True."

"But . . . ?"

"Well, Julius blames Anthony for Shirley's death and plans to kill him. And Marty Anaheim's in town, and may want to kill Anthony. Might want to kill Bibi too."

"Bibi?"

"Anaheim's wife; she's here with Anthony."

"Oh my."

"Yeah. And there's something else going on, in the background, that I don't quite get."

"Do you think Anthony killed his wife?"

"Killing was pretty brutal. Raped and strangled by hand, left naked with no ID in a vacant lot."

"And you don't think Anthony's capable of that?"

"Doesn't seem his style."

"Still it sounds like a crime of anger. Rape and manual strangulation."

"Or a crime made to look like that."

"By whom?"

"Anytime there's a brutal crime and Marty Anaheim is around, it's worth thinking he might have done it."

"Why?"

"I don't know."

"But you don't want to come home not knowing?"

"No."

"And you wouldn't want to abandon the charmingly named Bibi to her fate."

"No."

"Of course not," Susan said.

"Is Hawk willing to stay on?"

"I don't know," I said.

"I hope he will. I feel better when he's with you."

"Hell," I said, "so do I."

"But you'll stay whether he stays or not."

"Yes."

"So, when are you coming home?"

"I miss you," I said. "I'll come home as soon as I can."

"Good," Susan said, and there was that sound in her voice again. "Because I intend to boff your brains out when you arrive."

"Sure, I'm projecting," I said.

CHAPTER
27

I LEFT HAWK IN ANTHONY'S ROOM TO WARD OFF JULIUS, AND strolled down the Strip toward the MGM Grand on a bright desert morning. It was about 105 and the perspiration on my forehead evaporated as soon as it formed. Traffic was heavy along the Strip, an equal mix of limousines and pickups. A lot of young women with big hair and thick thighs were on the Strip, and men with big bellies hanging over low jeans were on the Strip. Neon lights were blinking, in the bright sunshine, and ahead of us the MGM Grand rose greenly from the gravelly desert. The emerald palace. I was going to look for Marty Anaheim. When I found him I was going to talk with him. About the current situation. Or whatever. Because I didn't have any idea what was going on and I didn't know what else to do.

I went into the vast lobby chattering with slot machines. It was about forty degrees cooler inside. I walked past the *Wizard of Oz* exhibit in the front of the lobby, past the crap tables, and took up residence in sight of the guest elevators. It was of course possible that Marty wasn't staying here, that he'd been visiting someone else. According to the list the Vegas cops came up with he wasn't registered under his own name so I had no way to find out. Except to stand here and watch until I saw him. Or I didn't. Or hell froze over.

The MGM casino seemed bigger and more crowded than the Mirage, and noisier and more garish. People in short-sleeved shirts and Bermuda shorts and tank tops milled about the slots and crowded around the crap tables and marched reverently past the life-sized statues in the *Wizard of Oz* display, and ate in the restaurants and had drinks and came and went on the elevators. None of them was Marty Anaheim. After a couple of hours I looked at my watch. I'd been there twenty minutes. At the crap table to my far right a small cheer pushed through the routine hubbub. Big winner. I tried standing first on one foot then the other. Make use of the time. Improve my balance. That way, when I did find Marty and he gave me a shot in the mouth I'd be less likely to fall over. The morning went that way. I varied my balancing exercises by doing toe raises. I stretched my lower back by flattening the hollow against the wall. I did isometric exercises, pressing my palms together or against the wall. I stretched my neck. I stretched my shoulders. I laced my fingers, turned my palms out, and stretched the muscles in my forearms. I thought about doing push-ups but concluded that people might notice. I looked at my watch. I began to count the number of women getting off the elevator that I would want to sleep with. They had to be getting on or off the elevator. Women strolling past didn't count. After forty minutes the count was lower than it once would have been. When I was seventeen, the count would have been every.

Just before noon, while I was doing toe taps to guard against shin splints, the little guy in the Panama hat got off the last elevator to the left and walked on past me.

I said, "Hey."

He stopped and turned slowly, looking at me under the snap brim of his hat. His small black eyes were close on either side of his big nose.

"You talking to me?"

"Yeah. Where's Marty."

"Marty who?"

"Marty Anaheim that's been paying you to follow Anthony Meeker around."

"Buzz off," the little guy said.

He turned away. I reached out and got hold of his right arm. He stopped in half stride and turned his head back slowly toward me.

"Keep your hands off me," he said.

"I want to see Marty," I said.

He made no effort to get his arm free. He stood perfectly still, his eyes steady on me.

"He might even want to see me," I said. "Why don't we go to a house phone and you call him. Tell him I've seen his wife."

The little guy kept looking at me. I kept hold of his arm.

"Okay," he said. "I'll call him."

I let go of his right arm. He flashed his right hand in under his coat and came out with a short stainless-steel automatic. He pressed it against my stomach, standing close so that no one would see.

"What kind of gun is that?" I said.

"Next time you put your hands on me," he said softly, "you'll be breathing through your navel."

"Fast little guy aren't you."

"Remember it," he said and put the gun away with a small deft movement.

"So what kind is it?" I said.

"What?"

"The gun, looks like a short Colt."

"It is, nineteen ninety-one A-one Compact."

"Forty-five?" I said.

"Yeah, six rounds."

"Nice gun," I said.

He looked at me with no expression in his slatey little eyes.

"Gun's as good as the guy who holds it," he said.

"Sure," I said. "Call Marty."

Which he did.

There was a pedestrian overpass across the Strip so people on the other side would have no trouble dashing over to the MGM Grand and dropping a bundle. Marty met me in the middle of it. He was wearing a blue silk suit and a blue silk shirt buttoned to the neck.

"Okay, Bernie," he said to the little guy, "take a walk."

"I'll be over here, Marty," the little guy said.

He walked a ways toward the west end of the overpass and leaned on the railing, watching us.

"Tough little guy," I said.

"He can shoot," Marty said. "You seen my wife?"

"Yeah."

"Where is she?"

"Where do you think she is?"

"What is this, some kinda fucking game?"

"Sure," I said. "I'm trying to find out what you know, without letting you know what I know. You know?"

"This is what I know, asshole. I come down here to talk with you. I could throw you off this fucking overpass instead."

"Or not," I said.

"You don't think so?"

"Marty," I said. "You don't scare me, any more than I scare you. One of us is wrong, but do we have to find it out right now?"

"You called me, pal."

I nodded. I was thinking about what to say. Since I didn't know what was going on there wasn't much to think about. I turned to one of Spenser's rules. When in doubt tell the truth. It was a brand-new rule, and it might be worth testing.

"Your wife's with Anthony Meeker," I said.

"Tell me something I don't know."

"You know where?"

"At the Mirage," Marty said.

"You know Julius is there too?"

Marty didn't say anything.

"Julius is going to kill Anthony," I said.

"He better hurry."

"Julius's daughter, Shirley, was killed Sunday," I said. "Cops found her in a vacant lot up the Strip a little."

"Yeah?"

"Julius is upset," I said. "He blames Anthony."

Marty said nothing. Below us on the Strip, cars moved steadily in both directions. Across a short spread of scrub desert, Route 15 was busy with trucks and cars and RVs heading west to California and east to Utah and the north-west corner of Arizona.

"I'm under the impression," I said, "that you and Anthony were in on some scam together."

"Lying little fucker tell you that?"

"I got that impression."

"It's bullshit."

"So why are you here?"

"I'm going to kill him and take my wife back."

"He didn't do anything to you," I said. "She did."

"Don't matter who did what. He dies. She comes back."

"And if she doesn't want to come back?"

"She'll come back."

"Or?"

"No *or*. She'll come back."

"And you'll forgive her," I said.

"Fuck forgiveness. Forgiveness got nothing to do with it," Marty said. "She's with me, you unnerstand? That's how it is."

"Maybe not," I said.

"You going to get in my way?" Marty said.

"You kill Shirley Ventura?"

"Why the hell would I kill Shirley Ventura?"

"What was the deal with Anthony?"

"I got no deal with Anthony, asshole. He collected money for Julius, passed some of it along to Gino."

"Through you?"

"Everything goes to Gino through me," Marty said.

"Makes it easy to skim," I said.

"Any skimming was done by Anthony."

"Bibi says you and Anthony were playing a two-man game," I said.

"You're a fucking liar," Marty said. "Bibi don't know nothing about my business."

"Says you introduced her to Anthony," I said. "Says she ran off with him to get away from you. Says you're a pig."

It was a gamble to get him mad enough to say something wrong. It didn't work. He didn't say anything. He swung at me. He telegraphed it some, and I was able to turn my hips against the railing as it came. The punch landed on my right cheekbone, and rocked me backwards, and sent me staggering along the railing. Marty could hit. If I hadn't half slipped it I would have gone down. I could feel the shock of it through my head. Everything darkened and for a minute I didn't see well. The railing helped keep me up.

"I'm sick of you, Spenser. You got that? I see you again and I'm going to fucking beat you to fucking death."

My head was clearing. I steadied against the railing as my legs resolidified and my knees unbuckled. Fighting with Marty Anaheim wasn't going to help me figure out what was going on.

I said, "Not here, Marty. Not now."

He extended his arm straight out from the shoulder and pointed his finger at me.

"You been warned," he said and turned and stomped back toward the emerald palace.

I glanced down the overpass in the other direction. The little guy with the Panama hat was leaning on the railing looking at me and shaking his head. I felt my cheekbone. It was hot and already puffy. I had learned nothing and gotten popped on the kisser in the process. I was willing to take one on the chops now and then if it furthered my cause. I wasn't sure my cause had been furthered. But Marty would probably be overconfident next time. Which was a good thing. And Hawk would be amused. No cloud without a silver lining.

The little guy strolled down the walkway and tucked a small business card into my shirt pocket.

"Take a pretty good punch," he said.

"Yeah, it's one of my best things, but I try not to do it too often."

"I'm in business out here," he said. "You ever need some work done, gimme a call."

"You figure I need help?" I said.

The little guy shrugged.

"I know I need business," he said, and strolled off toward the MGM Grand.

CHAPTER
28

WHEN I GOT BACK TO THE HOTEL HAWK AND BIBI WERE SITting in my room.

"Anthony's gone," Hawk said.

"Tell me about it," I said.

"Went in the bedroom to lie down," he said. "Turned on the television, left the door ajar. 'Bout twenty minutes ago she went in to use the bathroom. He was gone. Chain off the hall door from the bedroom. I could look for him or I could stay with her."

Bibi sat forward on the front edge of one of the easy chairs near Hawk.

"Well, he didn't hire us to keep him in," I said.

"What I thought."

"He got any money left?" I said to Bibi.

She shook her head.

"He took ours," she said.

"Ours?"

"We had five thousand put aside, win or lose, to take us out of here, and give us a start. I had it in my makeup case. It's gone."

"Anything else?"

Bibi shook her head.

"He was going to be the one," Bibi said. Her voice was quiet. There was no hint of tears behind it this time. "He was going to be the one got me out of it, away from Marty. Find some town on the Oregon coast, start a store or something. Bookstore, maybe. I like books. He was going to bust The Mirage and then we were going to go to Oregon and open a bookstore."

"You have any money left?"

She shook her head again. Her face was still, her eyes were empty. If she felt anything it showed only in the slump of her shoulders as she sat on the edge of the chair.

"I was going to run it, read up all the new books, tell people when they came in what was good. Get a cat maybe, a store cat, let him sleep on the books in the window. You know how they stretch when they wake up and sort of slide around?"

"You got a plan?" I said.

"Even if he lost everything," she said softly, as if I hadn't spoken, "we had the five thousand. That was my idea. I kind of knew what Anthony was, and I wanted some money to be mine so he wouldn't lose it, and we could at least get to Oregon. I could maybe get some waitress work. I know he wouldn't work, not regular work. But if I got to Oregon, it wouldn't matter so much about him, then."

"You go back to Boston, Marty'll find you," I said.

She nodded.

"I don't want to go back to Boston," she said.

"He will not be forgiving of your little fling with Anthony," I said.

She shrugged.

"If you didn't go to Boston, where would you go, Oregon?"

"Oregon is no good now. He ruined it."

"You got to go somewhere," I said.

"What's the difference if I haven't got any money anyway?"

I reached into my right-hand pants pocket and took out Julius's money and handed it to her.

"Should be about five thousand."

"I can't pay you back."

"Why should you be different," I said. "You want to go to Oregon?"

"No. Not now."

"You got family anywhere?"

"I don't want to see them," she said, "and they don't want to see me."

"Makes it nice and even. How about L.A. You ever been to L.A.?"

"No."

"Time you went," I said.

I got up and made some phone calls leaning against the bar in the living room, staring out the window at the un-erupting volcano. Hawk leaned back on the couch with his feet up on the coffee table, his eyes half closed, as if he were asleep. I knew he wasn't. When I got through I came back and sat on the couch beside her.

"Okay," I said. "You're on the five P.M. Southwest flight to L.A. Gets in at six-oh-two. Hawk and I will take you to the airport, put you on the plane. In L.A. a guy named Chollo will meet you at the gate. He'll carry a sign that says CHOLLO on it."

"Chollo?"

"Yeah. There's also a cop in L.A. named Samuelson. I'll write it down for you. You need cop help, you call him. He'll know who you are."

"What's this Chollo guy going to do with me?"

"Look out for you," I said. "You can trust him."

She nodded.

"So you want to pack some stuff?"

She nodded.

"Maybe one shoulder bag, so we can move right along?"

"Yes, that will be okay."

She didn't move. Hawk opened his eyes slowly and smiled at Bibi.

"Come on," he said. "I'll help you."

"Pack?"

"Sure."

"You can't help me pack."

"No?"

"God no."

"We better get going then," he said.

She stood and we went up to her room and stood around while she packed.

"You thought of a name yet for that mouse you got on your cheekbone?" Hawk said.

"I thought I'd wait and let it pick its own name when it's older."

"Marty give you that?"

"Yeah."

"Neither one of us looking too good today," Hawk said.

Bibi came out of the bedroom with her suitcase, and stood quietly near the door.

"Okay," I said.

"What about the hotel bill?" Bibi said.

"We'll let Anthony worry about that," I said.

Hawk went out first, then Bibi, then me. We let her carry her shoulder bag, because if we had to fight neither of us wanted to be carrying it when the fight started.

But there was no fight. We got into Lester's car out front and drove to the airport.

At the security gate, I handed Hawk my gun and went through with Bibi and walked her to the gate. Before she boarded she hesitated and looked at me.

"What are you going to do?" she said. "After I leave?"

"I was thinking we might get drunk," I said.

She nodded to herself and then she smiled and kissed me very carefully on the cheek and went on down the ramp. I stayed at the gate until the plane took off.

CHAPTER
29

THE PHONE RANG IN MY HOTEL ROOM AT 7:35. I WAS LYING IN bed awake, when it rang, planning out a full day of volcano watching.

"She never showed," Chollo said without preamble. "I waited three flights. With my sign. I don't know what she looks like. Nobody came up and spoke to me. So I went home, figured it was another gringo trick."

"Perfect," I said.

"Anytime you want me go stand around LAX again with a silly fucking sign, be sure and let me know," Chollo said.

"I'm not happy either," I said and hung up.

I got out of bed and stood at the window and looked out. Be hours before the volcano erupted. I called Susan but her machine was on which meant she was already downstairs in her office. I called Julius's room, but he'd checked out. I looked at the business card the little guy in the Panama hat had given me. It said Bernard J. Fortunato Investigator, Professional and Discreet. There was a phone number with a Vegas area code. I called it. No answer. So I called the cops. They're always there. I asked for Homicide, got Romero, and told him what I knew.

"Back in Boston," Romero said, when I was through, "when you were on the cops, did you keep losing your gun?"

"I've had better weeks," I said.

"I hope so," Romero said.

After I hung up I showered and shaved in the empty large hotel suite, making as big a deal out of it as I could. I called Hawk to see if he wanted breakfast. He did. I dressed carefully, and went down. Bob brought us coffee.

"Hey, Boston," he said. "You got yourself some kind of shiner."

"Any kind will do," I said.

Hawk drank some orange juice. I had decaf and a couple of bagels. Hawk had scrambled eggs with chives, coffee, and sourdough toast.

"What we going to do now?" Hawk said.

"You may as well go home."

He nodded. "You staying around?"

"Another day or so maybe, just make sure I haven't missed anything."

"Missed anything," Hawk said. "We missed every

fucking thing there was to miss out here. We lost Anthony, we lost Bibi. Shirley got killed. Julius fired us, and Marty Anaheim whacked you on the bazoo. Probably would have whacked me on the bazoo too, if I was there."

I drank some decaf.

"You know who I miss," I said. "I miss Pearl the Wonder Dog. She'd act like I was terrific if she were here. She'd think I was the balls."

"Sure," Hawk said, "me too."

After breakfast I said goodbye to Hawk and went to talk with my new friends in Vegas Homicide.

Romero was drinking coffee in his cubicle in the Homicide squad room. "After you called us," he said, "Cooper went over to the Grand. Talked with Mickey Holmes, the security guy over there. Used to work here. Bernard J. Fortunato checked out last night. There was no Martin Anaheim registered. Mickey says guy answering his description was with Bernard J. Fortunato yesterday when he checked out and no one's seen him since. Julius Ventura and party flew out on Delta at eight-fifteen this morning. To Boston, via DFW. So far we got no flight record on Anthony Meeker. We're still checking. He coulda paid cash, used another name. We're checking cash ticket purchases. Car rentals too."

"Would have had to use a card for a car."

"So I've heard," Romero said.

"You got anything new on Shirley Ventura?"

"Nothing that matters. Still raped and strangled. M.E. says she was slapped around some before she was killed."

"Any of her belongings show up?"

"No."

"You release the body?"

"Yep. Local funeral parlor is shipping it to Boston for them."

"What do you know about Bernard J. Fortunato?" I said.

"Never heard of him," Romero said. "He's in the phone book, no address. We'll get one from the phone company and check him out."

"He had a gun."

"I'll check him from that end too," Romero said. "You want to call me in a couple days, I'll let you know what I know."

"I'll probably go to Boston tomorrow," I said. "Any problem?"

"No. I can find you if I need you."

"You talk to LAPD about Bibi Anaheim?"

"Yeah. They never heard of her," Romero said. "Neither has anybody in Oregon. They do they'll let us know. You know anything about her? Maiden name? Where she grew up?"

I remembered the wry reference to marrying Marty after high school. *Fairhaven High, 1977.*

"No," I said and wasn't even sure exactly why I lied.

"Grand, just like everything else in the fucking case—nowhere to look and nothing to do."

Romero got up and got some more coffee from the coffeemaker in the squad room. He looked at me. I shook my head. He came back in with the coffee and sat back down at his desk and put one foot up on his open bottom drawer and tilted his chair back a little.

"Talked to a homicide guy in L.A. named Samuelson." He blew on the black surface of the coffee for a moment and then took a sip. "Says he knows you. Says hello."

"I screwed up a case with him once too," I said.

Romero shrugged and grinned at me.

"Shit happens," he said.

"Yeah," I said. "Quite often."

CHAPTER
30

I WAS IN MY OFFICE WITH MY FEET UP STUDYING THE WAY MY name looked backwards through the frosted glass window of my office door. The office had been shut up since I left for Vegas, and I opened the Berkeley Street window to dilute the accumulated closeness. Then I started studying the door again. The mail had been routine and easily disposed of. There were no phone calls.

Maybe SPENSER ought to be in script. A nice flowing script might make me seem lovable, and could contrast nicely with INVESTIGATIONS, which would be in a bold, no-nonsense sans serif. Maybe some sort of motto would be good. WE DON'T SOLVE ANYTHING BUT WE GIVE OUR FEE AWAY.

The door opened and Susan came in with a large canvas tote bag with the PBS logo on it.

"No patients?" I said.

"Teaching day," Susan said. "But you sounded so down when you called last night that I canceled class and came over to welcome you home. What happened to your cheek?"

"Line of duty," I said. "You think my name on the door would look good in script?"

"No."

"Nice bag," I said.

"Official Cambridge tote bag," she said.

She put the tote bag down on one of my empty client chairs and took a large thermos out of it. It was a tan and blue thing, the kind Dunkin' Donuts sells you with a starter fill of coffee. She put it on my desk.

"Decaf," she said.

"Thank God," I said.

A box of donuts came out next, and two plastic coffee cups and two pale pink linen napkins.

"You bought donuts?" I said.

"Yes."

"I wasn't aware you knew how."

"I don't. But I watched the other people in line."

I opened the box. Plain donuts. Perfect.

"Do you know how to eat a donut?" I said.

"I'll watch you on the first one," Susan said.

She opened the thermos and poured two cups of coffee into the plastic cups. I ate half a donut.

"Ugh," Susan said. "Is that how it's done?"

"Girls sometimes take smaller bites," I said.

"I certainly hope so," Susan said.

She picked up one of the donuts between her thumb and forefinger and broke off a crumb and put the rest of the donut back. She took a bite of the crumb. I ate the other half of my first donut and drank some coffee, and looked at her. She had on some kind of expensive white tee-shirt, and jeans that fit her well, and some low black cowboy boots with silver trim. I always felt as if I breathed more deeply when I was looking at her, as if I were taking in more oxygen, and doing it more easily, as if the air were clearer.

"Welcome home," Susan said.

"Yes," I said.

"It went badly," Susan said.

"Mostly," I said, "it didn't go at all."

"You found Anthony Meeker," Susan said.

I shrugged.

"You couldn't prevent Shirley's death," Susan said.

"No."

"You weren't able to find who killed her."

"No."

"But you accept that, don't you."

"You can't solve every case," I said.

"You still don't know what was going on between Anthony and Marty Anaheim."

"No."

"But you accept that too, don't you."

"Lot of stuff I don't know," I said.

"And Anthony?"

"No one hired me to protect him," I said. "No one hired me to keep him in Vegas."

"And Bibi?"

"Bibi never showed up in L.A."

"You think anything happened to her?"

"I don't know. Chollo didn't know what she looked like. She could have walked right on past him."

"Which she probably did," Susan said. "From what you've told me, she had very little reason to trust men."

I shrugged again and had some donut. Susan smiled.

"Not even you, Sweet Potato," she said.

"I know."

"It's what's bothering you though, isn't it."

"It's all bothering me," I said. "Hawk and I spent the last week or so wandering around Vegas without a clue."

"You found Anthony Meeker," Susan said. "That is what you were hired to do."

"And I don't know where he is now, and I don't know who killed Shirley, and I don't know what was going on between Anthony and Marty, and I don't know why Gino Fish was so interested, and I don't know whether Julius was involved, and I don't know where Bibi is, or what's going to happen to her. She showed no signs of being able to fend for herself."

"You can't help people that don't want you to help them," Susan said.

"Thanks, Doc."

"You are a grown-up," Susan said. "You know that as well as I do. We both do work that teaches us that lesson daily."

"True," I said.

We were quiet. I started on my third donut. Susan broke another microscopic fragment off her first one and ate some of it. The sound of the traffic floated up from Berkeley Street. Somewhere someone was making a hole in something hard. I could hear the faint sound of a jackhammer.

"What are you going to do now?" Susan said.

"There were a couple of things I back-burnered," I said, "while I went to Vegas. I'll see if I can resurrect one."

"Good to work," Susan said.

"Good to eat," I said.

"I'll always feed you," Susan said. "Didn't you get a large sum of money recently? From some insurance company?"

"Yeah. A percentage of what I saved them. More money than I deserve. Actually, more money than anyone deserves, except Michael Jordan."

"So I don't have to feed you. You can take a little time off and pursue your hobbies if you wish to."

"You mean the Vegas thing?"

"Money is freedom," Susan said.

"I could go talk with Gino Fish again, see if he can tell me anything he didn't tell me before."

"No harm in that."

"No. Unless Gino finds it annoying and tells Vinnie Morris to shoot me."

"Would he shoot you?" Susan said.

"Depends."

"Would you shoot him?"

"Depends."

"Everything does, I guess."

"Everything but you and me, donut girl."

"Present company, always excluded," she said. "This is going to bother you until you get some kind of closure on it."

"I suppose it might," I said.

"It will," Susan said. "I have a Ph.D. from Harvard."

"This is going to bother me," I said, "until I get some kind of closure on it."

Susan smiled.

"It's good to face the truth," she said. "Would it help if I sat on your lap?"

"It might," I said.

CHAPTER
31

HAWK AND I WENT TO SEE GINO FISH ON A RAW DAY WITH NO
sun and the wind coming hard off the Atlantic. Gino lived
in a big colonial house on the ocean side of Jerusalem
Road in Cohasset. There was a circular drive in front and a
lawn that sloped to the seawall behind. The house was
done in white cedar shingles which had silvered in the salt
air, the way they're supposed to. A very handsome young
man answered the door.

"Gino home?" I said.

"Who should I say is calling?"

"Spenser," I said. "He knows me."

"Certainly, sir, and the other gentleman?"

"Hawk."

"I'm Mr. Fish's personal assistant," the handsome young man said. "Is there something I could help you with?"

He was wearing what appeared to be a pale blue sweat suit, with a stand-up collar. The sweat suit looked like it was made of silk. It also looked like it had never known sweat.

"Just tell Gino we're here, and we want to tell him something about Marty."

"Mr. Anaheim?"

Neither Hawk nor I answered. The personal assistant still hesitated. Hawk and I still stood.

Finally the personal assistant said, "If you'll excuse me for a moment."

He closed the door.

Hawk looked at me.

"Personal assistant?"

I shrugged.

"That's what he said."

Hawk nodded. The front door opened again and the personal assistant was there.

"Mr. Fish is busy at the moment, but if you wish to wait, he'll see you as soon as he's through."

"We'll wait," I said.

"Please come this way then," the personal assistant said.

He led us to the right off the central entry hall into a room with a huge picture window that looked out at the ocean. He gestured gracefully at the rock maple chairs with red plaid cushions that stood on either side of a brick fireplace. Neither Hawk nor I sat.

"Mr. Fish will be with you as soon as he's free," the personal assistant said.

"Yes he will," I said.

The personal assistant frowned as if he were puzzled. Then he nodded politely and left the room. Hawk went and looked out the picture window at the harsh gray ocean ruffled white here and there at the tips of its waves by the onshore wind.

"Thing about getting a place with a great view," Hawk said, "is, after you moved in and looked at the great view for a few days, you get used to it and it ain't a great view anymore. It just what you look at out your window."

"You're a deep guy," I said.

"And sensitive," Hawk said. "Maybe I should host a talk show."

"Will you have me as a guest?" I said.

"'Course not."

Hawk continued to look at the ocean. The room where we waited was completely furnished in rock maple furniture with red plaid upholstery. Couch, four armchairs, two slipper rockers. There were a couple of Hingham buckets around to serve as ashtray stands, and there was a big red-toned braided rug on the floor. The fireplace had a large round eagle mirror over the mantel.

"I wonder who's Gino's decorator," I said.

"Molly Pitcher," Hawk said. "What was it we doing here?"

"Looking for Bibi."

"And why we think she be here?"

"We don't," I said. "But we don't know where else to start. So if we find out what was going on between Gino and Marty and Anthony and Julius, maybe we'll get an idea of where to look for Bibi."

"Or maybe we won't."

"Welcome to the world of detection," I said.

"And why we looking for Bibi?"

"Because we're worried about her."

"Of course we are," Hawk said.

The door opened and Gino came in with Vinnie Morris. He saw Hawk and nodded to him. Hawk made no response.

"I came to see you," Gino said. "Now you come to see me."

"Equipoise," I said.

Gino smiled with neither warmth nor humor, on and off.

"Geoffrey spoke of Marty Anaheim," he said.

"Geoffrey?"

"My assistant. He said you wanted to tell me something about Marty."

"I just told him that to get in," I said. "I don't know anything about Marty. Is he back from Las Vegas?"

"I didn't know he was in Las Vegas," Gino said. "I don't know if he's back. Marty worked for me for fifteen years. He does so no longer."

"Can you tell me why?"

"No."

"Do you know his wife? Bibi?"

"I'm afraid not," Gino said. "I require that my private life be my own. I treat others on the same basis."

"He used to beat her up."

"Beating people up is what Marty does," Gino said. "It is why I employed him so long."

"You implied last time I saw you that Marty might be stealing from you."

"Did I."

"Yeah. You know Anthony Meeker?"

"Who?"

"That's a mistake, Mr. Fish. Last time we talked you knew his name."

"It's a mistake of my age," Gino said. "I still think well, but I no longer remember well. Is Anthony Meeker Julius Ventura's son-in-law?"

"Yes, you implied last time that he might be stealing too."

Gino was sitting in one corner of the big rock maple couch. He had his legs crossed and his thin hands resting in his lap. I could see the dappling of age spots on the backs of them. He pursed his lips a little and stared for a moment out his big picture window at what probably seemed to him, his ocean. He raised his hands from his lap and put his fingertips together and tapped his lips for a moment. Then he pointed his fingertips at me.

"You think, Mr. Spenser, that I am being cute," Gino said. "It is not an unreasonable thought. I am capable of cuteness. Indeed there is very little that I am not capable of. But in this instance I know very little more than you do. There have been some financial irregularities in my business. It was Marty's responsibility to oversee all the financial transactions and to ensure that they were as alleged. These irregularities came inopportunely at a time when we were beginning to organize in contemplation of a merger. I came to you to see if you could shed any light on whether Marty was culpable. You didn't shed much, being primarily interested in getting me to shed some light on your interest. It was largely a waste of our time."

"But you fired Marty."

"No. Marty left."

"Did he give a reason?"

"None. He simply failed to show up for work one day, and I have not seen him since. You tell me he was in Las Vegas. He may still be there. Or he may be next door, I simply don't know."

"When did he take off?"

"Three, no, four days after I came to see you."

I did some quick calendaring in my head. That made it the same day we found Anthony. When I got more time I'd think about that.

"As far as I know, Mr. Fish, he came to Vegas and checked into the MGM Grand either under another name, or in a room rented for him by another guy. Tough little guy, big nose, wore a Panama hat all the time. Very quick with a gun."

"You saw him there?"

"Yes."

"And you were in Las Vegas . . . ?"

"Looking for Anthony Meeker."

"On behalf of his wife?"

"His wife and his father-in-law."

"Do you know why Marty was in Las Vegas?" Gino said.

"Anthony Meeker was there with Marty's wife."

Gino was very still. I waited. Gino looked at his ocean again.

"And Shirley Ventura was in Vegas as well," he said.

"You know about her."

"Yes. Do you have any knowledge of who killed her?"

"No. Cops are trying to act like it was a random act, but I don't think they believe it."

"Do you?"

"No. Whoever killed her made every effort to conceal her identity. Which means he thought he could be connected to her."

"Her husband?"

"Could be," I said, "though it doesn't seem his style."

"Marty would enjoy something like that," Gino said. "He was apparently in the area."

"It's his style, okay," I said. "And she had his hotel phone number on her person. But I don't see a motive."

Gino was silent.

"Do you?" I said.

Gino didn't answer. He looked at Vinnie.

"If he uncovers something detrimental to our interests, Vinnie, will he use it?"

"He might," Vinnie said. "He might not. Telling him not to won't make any difference."

"Can he be controlled?" Gino said.

"No."

"If we kill him?"

"Have to kill Hawk too," Vinnie said.

Gino nodded thoughtfully.

"Gentlemen," he said, "you see my situation. I want to know what you find out, but I don't want your investigation impinging on my business. Can we work out a financial solution?"

"What do you think we're investigating?"

Gino paused a moment and almost smiled a real smile for a moment.

"Put that way, I must admit I'm not sure."

"Don't feel bad," Hawk said. "We not sure either."

"Well, who is your client?"

"We have none," I said.

"Are you merely curious?" Gino said.

"We want to find Bibi Anaheim, see if she's all right."

Gino stared at me and then shifted his eyes slightly and stared at Hawk. Then back at me.

"That's preposterous," he said.

"We softhearted," Hawk said.

Gino looked at Vinnie.

"Am I to believe this, Vinnie?"

214

"Yeah."

"Well, then by all means find her," Gino said. "If I learn of her whereabouts I will tell you promptly."

"Might help if you'd tell us a little more about your business and Julius's," I said.

Gino stood up slowly, but easily, and started from the room.

"Vinnie will show you out," he said, and left.

We walked to the front door with Vinnie.

"Don't make a mistake about Gino," Vinnie said. "Just 'cause he talks like fucking William F. Buckley. He's got no more feelings than a crocodile."

"You know where Marty is?" I said.

"No."

"His wife?"

"Never met the wife. Don't know where she is."

"Know anything that Gino didn't tell us?"

Vinnie looked at me with surprise.

"Hey," he said, "I take his money."

"Yeah," I said, "you do. I apologize."

"Thank you," Vinnie said and held the door open.

Hawk and I departed.

CHAPTER
32

FAIRHAVEN IS ON THE OLD ROUTE 6 IN SOUTHEASTERN MASS-achusetts across the harbor from New Bedford. There's a long bridge that sets down on an island in mid-harbor and then continues on to Fairhaven. If you keep going on Route 6 through Mattapoisett and Marion and Wareham and Onset, after a while you're on Cape God.

The high school had been built during a time when people thought learning was important and the buildings in which it was supposed to take place reflected that view. There were a lot of libraries scattered around Massachu-setts that had been built during the same period and had the same British Imperial look. The high school, like so many of the libraries, had gotten a little shabbier, as if to reflect current attitudes.

There were a few teachers there who'd been there eighteen years ago, but no one remembered any student named Bibi. A tight-jawed English teacher told me that she tried to forget them as soon as they left her room. And the principal told me he only remembered the bad ones.

"Yearbooks?" I said.

"We keep them in here," the principal told me. "If we keep them in the library, the students will deface them."

"Students are great, aren't they?" I said.

The principal was a cautious man. He didn't commit himself on that. But, once he had assured himself that I wouldn't deface it, he gave me the 1977 Fairhaven High School yearbook, and allowed me to sit on a straight chair in the school secretary's office to read it. I found Bibi's picture easy enough. Except for the acquired scar tissue she still looked like seventeen-year-old Beatrice Costa had looked. *Most Congenial. Drama Club 2,3,4. Yearbook Staff 4. Newspaper 2,3,4. Cheerleader 3,4. Ambition: television news reporter. Quote, "Hey, Abbey, where's the party."* There was nothing there about marrying Marty Anaheim and getting her nose busted. I kept looking at the pictures until I found Abigail Olivetti, whose quote was, "Bibi and I . . ."

I read the yearbook through for another hour and found nothing else to help me. The school had no record of Beatrice Costa's address or Abigail Olivetti's. The secretary told me that in a way to indicate that the question was stupid.

"We are not running a clearinghouse here," she told me.

"Probably more of a warehouse," I said. "May I use your phone book?"

She handed it to me, and turned back to her desk work with an audible sigh. It was clear that I had no real understanding of her importance, and the pressing nature of her work. Not everyone can file detention slips.

There were seventeen Costas listed in Fairhaven, and one Olivetti. I wrote down the phone numbers and addresses and gave the phone book and the yearbook back to the secretary, and gave her my full-voltage smile. It was the smile that normally made them take off their glasses and let down their hair. I waited. Nothing happened. The woman was obviously frigid.

"Are you through here?" she said finally.

"No more pencils," I said. "No more books. No more teacher's dirty looks."

"Really!" she said.

As I left the building, classes were changing and the students were milling about in the halls. They seemed inconceivably young to me. Full of pretense, massively other oriented, ill formed, partial, angry, earnest, resentful, excited, frantic, depressed, hopeful, and scared. When she was this age, Beatrice Costa had pledged herself to Marty Anaheim and nothing after was ever the same.

I sat in my car with the motor running and looked at my lists of names. It made more sense to start with the one Olivetti than to work my way through all seventeen Costas. I dialed the number and a woman answered.

"My name is Spenser," I said. "I'm a detective trying

to locate a woman named Bibi Anaheim, whose maiden name was Bibi Costa."

"I remember Bibi," the woman said. "She's a friend of my daughter's."

"Your daughter is Abigail Olivetti?"

"Yes. Where did you get her name?"

"From the high school," I said. "Does your daughter still see Bibi?"

"Oh, I should think so, they've been best friends since they were little," the woman said.

"Does your daughter live in town?" I said.

"No, she's up in Needham."

"Mass?"

"Un huh. She's all grown up now of course. Married and kids and all. And she waited, thank God, until she was old enough."

"Who'd she marry?" I said.

"Carl Becker. He's got a big job with the phone company and they had to move up there. But she calls home every week, and sometimes the kids get on."

"Isn't that nice," I said. "Is she a housewife?"

"No, she works in a bank. I think it's too much, with the children and all, but she's very modern, I guess. Things are different now."

"Ain't it the truth," I said. "Can you give me her address and phone number? I'd like to get in touch with her."

"About Bibi Costa?"

"Yes."

"Is Bibi in some kind of trouble?"

"I don't know," I said. "She's missing and I'd like to find her."

"I don't think I should give out Abbey's number," the woman said.

"Well, just the address then."

"No, I think you should talk with my husband. You can call back tonight if you'd like to. He gets home about six."

"Thank you," I said. "That won't be necessary. Can you tell me if any of Bibi's family lives in town?"

"No, there was just Bibi and her mother. Her mother remarried and moved away years ago."

"You don't know where?"

"No."

"Do you remember who she married?"

"No."

"Well, thank you very much," I said, "for your time."

We hung up.

It goes that way a lot, conversation often dries up as they start thinking about how they don't actually know you, and don't quite know what you're up to. It's always wise to get as much as you can as soon as you can. If I couldn't find Abbey Becker in Needham, Massachusetts, I'd turn in my file of Dick Tracy Crimestopper tips. As I started back across the bridge toward New Bedford, I was calling information on my car phone.

CHAPTER
33

ABIGAIL BECKER LIVED ON SCHOOL STREET IN NEEDHAM IN A small gray shingled ranch house with white shutters and a bright blue door. There was a pink bicycle with hand brakes and gear shifts and low-slung handlebars leaning against the side of the house. I parked on the street near a hydrant across from the house and sat in the car with a large cup of decaf and two plain donuts. The street was lined with houses that looked like the Becker house, varying only in color and ornament. It was empty of life at 10:15 on an overcast Wednesday morning in the fall. Kids in school, parents at work. It was raining sporadically and it was dark enough so that the houses where someone was home showed lights in the windows.

Abigail's mother would certainly have called her and

ROBERT B. PARKER

told her about me. She would also have said that she
didn't tell me where Abigail lived, and maybe Abigail
would believe it. Though if I could find her mother, she
might figure that I could find her. I sat. The rain on my
windshield made the colors of the fall trees look like an
impressionist painting. I ate a donut and drank some coffee. I could see the house okay. The rain had little effect
on the side windows. I ate my second donut and finished
my decaf. There was no sign of life in the Becker house. I
got out of the car and walked to the front door. They had
kids in school. The parents worked. They'd hide a key
somewhere. I looked around for the best spot as I went up
the walk. There was a doormat, but that was so obvious
they probably wouldn't use it. On the front step I paused,
glanced around, and opened the mailbox. No. There were
windows on either side of the front door, and there were
shutters on either side of the windows. I ran a hand behind the shutter to the right of the door. No. I tried the
other one, and the key was there hanging on a loop of
string from a thumbtack in the back side of the shutter
frame. I rang the bell and waited. Nothing. I opened the
front door and went in. The house was empty. I could
feel the emptiness immediately. The living room was to
the right, the dining room to the left. They were both
furnished in cheap Danish modern. *Five piece living room
set now only $1100.* The dining room was walnut. The liv-
ing room was blond. In the living room, on the mantel
over the clean fireplace, were pictures of three young
girls, elementary-school age, maybe twelve, ten, and

eight. I went down the short center hall to the kitchen. Cereal bowls and plates with toast crumbs on them, coffee cups and juice glasses and cutlery were stacked in the sink. An empty milk carton sat on the kitchen table, and a jar of grape jelly with the cap still off stood on the table beside it.

Across the hall was a family room with a daybed in it, one of those kind on wheels which you can rent. It didn't look like it belonged there. Furniture had been pushed out of the way to make room for it. The bed was unmade. There was a small lavatory off the family room. There was a lip liner on the sink, and in the wastebasket several tissues with the kiss imprint that women leave when they blot their lipstick. There was no sign of clothing.

Upstairs there were four bedrooms, the beds unmade, clothing scattered on the floor. There were damp towels wadded on the floor of the bathroom, and a capless tube of toothpaste oozed some of its contents onto the sink top. Three of the bedrooms obviously belonged to the girls. The fourth was larger and appeared to be the master bedroom. There was a king-sized bed, unmade, and two closets. One was full of women's clothes, the other full of men's. A pair of white panty hose was draped over the foot of the bed. Some boxer shorts had been tossed toward the laundry basket in one of the closets and fallen considerably short. The house was a mess. I'd been in enough houses on short notice, or none, to know that houses were often a mess. There were three kids to get dressed and fed and off to school before their parents got ready for work. They'd pick up a little when they got home. They might clean on the weekend. They'd put everything in order before they had company. They were not expecting a burglar. I had broken and entered often enough in my life to be used to it. But I never liked it. I always felt sort of voyeuristic, peeping in on the personal clutter of people's privacy.

I went back downstairs and looked around in the family room again. There was a pale green plastic hair roller on the floor under the rollaway bed. There was an empty bottle of nail polish remover on top of the television set and a highball glass with a little water in the bottom. I smelled it. It smelled like bourbon. The water was probably melted ice. Someone, presumably a woman, had been staying in the room. But there were no clothes, no luggage. I went back up to the master bedroom and looked more carefully through the closet and the bureau. All the woman's clothes were size 12. They all seemed consistent in style. Susan would have been helpful here, but she had always had some kind of hang-up on breaking into people's homes and snooping in their closets.

I walked around the house again and saw nothing else that would help me so I went back out the front door, hung the key up behind the shutter, and walked toward my car. The rain was still coming down, making the still suburban street shine a glossy black. I turned up my collar as I walked.

In my car I started the motor and turned on the wipers, set the heater on low, and sat some more, looking at the house across the street. The houseguest could have been Bibi and she could have scooted when Abbey's mother told her a detective was looking for her. Perfect. Trying to find her may have made her harder to find. The universe was a recalcitrant bastard.

I had a west suburban directory in the car with me and I started calling banks on the car phone until I found one that employed Abigail Becker. She worked close to home, at a branch of DePaul Federal right here in Needham, downtown, maybe a mile from her house. I found her there, behind a desk on the customer side of the counter. The sign on the desk said she was Branch Manager. She was a biggish woman, but attractive enough with neat brown hair and blue eyes, and nice smile lines at the corner of her mouth. She didn't look like a lousy housekeeper. She had on a tan tweed suit which fit her well, and a dark brown blouse. That's why she hadn't worn the white panty hose. She would want tan to go with her outfit. She stood as I approached her desk. She would be about Bibi's age, which if they graduated '77, would make her thirty-six.

"May I help you, sir?"

"You Mrs. Becker?" I said.

"Yes, I'm the branch manager. How can I help."

I took out my wallet and showed her my license.

"My name is Spenser," I said. "I talked with your mother yesterday. I'm looking for Bibi Anaheim, formerly Bibi Costa."

"Mother told me you'd called her. I didn't realize she'd told you how to reach me."

"She didn't," I said. "Intentionally. But she mentioned your name and said you lived in Needham, and . . ." I shrugged modestly. "Elementary."

"Yes, of course, won't you sit down."

I sat.

"You and Bibi were high school friends."

"Yes, earlier than that. We were friends all through school."

"Do you still hear from her?"

"Not very much, I'm afraid. We exchange Christmas cards, really, very little more than that."

"You know where she is now?"

"Well, I gather she's not at home, in Medford?"

"No, would you have any idea where she might be?"

"No, I'm sorry. I don't."

"You've not heard from her?"

"No. Not in ages."

She shifted in her chair and crossed her legs. I was right. The panty hose were dark tan. The legs were good too.

"And you have no thoughts where I might find her?"

"No, I'm very sorry, but I really don't."

"Names of any friends she might have contacted?"

She shook her head slowly.

I stood and took one of my business cards out and gave it to her.

"Well, if you do hear from her, or you think of anything that might be useful in finding her, please give me a call."

"Of course," she said and stood and shook hands with me. "I'm sorry I couldn't be more helpful."

"Me too," I said and went back out into the rain with the collar of my trench coat turned up. In uniform. Driving back to Boston I thought about how she had not once asked why I was looking for Bibi or if she might be in trouble, or any of the questions she might have asked if she really hadn't talked with Bibi. Maybe if I laid low in the weeds for a while and didn't bother Abigail anymore, the houseguest, whoever she was, might assume the risk was over and come back.

CHAPTER
34

Hawk and I were in Bay Village, on the south end of Charles Street, approaching a couple of hookers.

"This is a pretty long end run ain't it?" Hawk said.

"You got a better idea?" I said.

"Could talk with Julius again."

"We can do that," I said. "But let's see if we can find out a little about what's going on down here in the trenches."

"That where we are?" Hawk said.

"Right here where the cash is earned," I said.

"Good evenin'," one of the hookers said. "I'm Wanda."

"Aren't you cold?" I said.

She had on a red sleeveless top and a white miniskirt and three-inch white heels.

"Got a sweater over in the doorway," she said. "You cops?"

"You ever see a cop dressed as good as me?" Hawk said.

"Some of the undercover Vice guys looking pretty fresh," Wanda said.

"We're not cops," I said. "We're looking for a missing woman."

"You think she hooking?" Wanda's friend asked. She had on black toreador pants and a huge blond wig.

"No, but it's a place to start," I said. "Who runs you?"

"We got us a pimp," Wanda said.

"Bet he don't think of it that way," Hawk said.

"What's his name?" I said.

"Chuckie. Either you gentlemen going to fuck one of us?"

"I don't think so," I said.

" 'Cause if you ain't you best be moving along. Chuckie don't like us, you know, ah, wasting time with people ain't customers."

"Where is Chuckie?"

"Around. Keeping an eye on things."

"So if we stay here for a while, Chuckie will show up and tell us to move along."

"That what he usually do," the blonde said. "But you two looking kind of big and quick."

"You think we'd scare him off?"

"Chuckie bad," the blonde said. "But there two of you . . ."

I nodded.

"Hawk," I said. "Why don't you sort of even the odds for Chuckie."

Hawk nodded.

"Ladies," he said, and started walking toward Park Square.

"You want Chuckie to hassle you?" Wanda said.

"I want to meet him," I said.

"Chuckie's pretty mean," Wanda said.

The blonde reached over and felt my bicep.

"Oh!" she said. "Maybe this be something."

Wanda felt my bicep too. The two women giggled.

"You know who Chuckie works for?" I said.

"Chuckie don't work," Wanda said. "We work."

"You know who Chuckie pays off?"

"Naw, man, don't know nothing 'bout that stuff."

A dark Pontiac Bonneville drove slowly along Charles Street, and slid into the curb beside us. A tall high-shouldered black man got out and walked around behind the car and stopped beside me. He had on a black and red leather warm-up jacket and a red do rag on his head. First Deion, now the world. His arms were a little too long for the jacket and his wrists where they showed below the cuffs were thick.

"You a police officer?" he said.

"No."

"Then you looking to have yourself some fun?"

"Nope, just passing the time of night with these ladies," I said.

"Well, sir, these ladies are mine, you know what I mean, and they working, so they don't really have no time to be passing."

"You Chuckie?" I said.

"You best move along," Chuckie said, " 'fore you get your white ass fucked up."

"Now, see, that's the trouble with you pimps," I said. "You got no judgment. You always play the race card too early."

The two hookers had moved back a little toward the doorway to watch. They were excited.

Chuckie raised his voice and moved very close to me.

"I don't want you bothering my whores," he said.

"Who runs prostitution these days, now that Tony's in jail?" I said.

"Don't know no Tony," Chuckie said.

"Tony Marcus," I said.

"Don't know nothing 'bout no Tony Marcus," Chuckie said. "Ain't gonna tell you again. Hit the road."

Chuckie had a gun on the right side of his belt, forward of his hip. I could see the hint of it under his jacket. I was trying to figure out how to push him hard enough to talk without pushing him so hard he went for the gun. Chuckie helped me figure it out. He put his left hand on my chest and gave me a shove.

"Move it," he said.

He was grand-standing a little in front of his whores, it was to be expected. But I hate being pushed. I hit Chuckie a left hook and turned my shoulder in and stepped in under his left arm and hit him a right uppercut, under his chin, close to the neck, where I was less likely to hurt my hand. He fell over on his back and I stepped beside him with my gun out and pointing straight down at the bridge of his nose. The whores were giggling nervously.

One of them said, "Whoa, Mister Chuckie."

Chuckie lay there, his bell still ringing, trying to get his eyes to focus. I waited. When he could hear me, I spoke to him pleasantly.

"There's a gun on your belt, right side. Take it out with the first two fingers of your right hand. Two fingers only. I see more than two and your brains will make a very small mess on the sidewalk."

Chuckie hesitated. I thumbed the hammer back. He twitched slightly. Had he been standing it would probably have been a jump, then he took the gun out.

"Slide it toward the gutter," I said. "Two fingers only."

He did and I stepped away from him and picked it up, and put it in my coat pocket. I uncocked my own gun and put it away.

"Now," I said, "what I was wondering was, who runs prostitution in town since Tony went to the house of blue lights?"

From flat on the sidewalk, Chuckie gave me an expressionless I'll-get-you-for-this stare. I gave him a gentle kick in the ribs.

"Tony still runs it," he said. "From the place."

"And who helps him on the outside?" I said.

"Tarone."

"Give me a full name."

"Tarone Jessup."

"Thank you."

I turned to the whores giggling in the doorway.

"Ladies," I said.

They giggled some more. Nervously, trying not to. Chuckie would probably beat them up if he thought they were laughing at him. I smiled at them.

Chuckie was sitting up now.

"Hey, man," he said. "You going to gimme back my gun?"

"No," I said.

"Piece cost me five hundred dollars, man," Chuckie said.

"Think of it as rent," I said, and kept on going.

CHAPTER
35

Hawk located Tarone Jessup the next day and we went to see him in the back room of a video arcade on Ruggles Street. The front room was full of black teenaged boys who stared at me as Hawk and I walked through the room. Tarone's door was open and we went in. There were three men in the room. One at the desk with his feet up, two sitting against the right-hand wall.

"You Tarone Jessup?" Hawk said to the guy at the desk.

"Un huh."

He was a thin jittery-looking guy with a sharp nose and oval black eyes like a bull terrier.

"I'm Hawk."

"Knew you were," Tarone said. "Who that with you, Casper the friendly ghost?"

The two guys against the wall laughed more loudly than the remark required.

"He do look kind of pale," Hawk said.

"He look like a honky motherfucker to me," Tarone said.

"Just think of me as color challenged," I said. "Who you been paying off to run your whores in Bay Village?"

Tarone was wearing a small brimless black cap and some sort of loose-fitting multicolored African tunic. Authentic.

"The honky cut right to the fucking chase, don't he?" Tarone said.

The two guys against the wall guffawed some more. One of them had the thickened features of a not too successful prize fighter. The other one, taller and younger, looked like a guy who might benefit from a few pops on the beezer.

"We looking for a woman," Hawk said. "We starting at the other end, so to speak, working back. You understand? Got nothing to do with you."

"You want a woman?" Tarone said. "I get you a woman, man. We got a lot of them."

He looked at the two guys on the wall. They thought he was funnier than a bucket of bullfrogs. The younger one was stamping his foot as he laughed.

Hawk looked at me. Then he leaned over Tarone's desk and spoke very softly to him.

"Tarone, you don't know me," Hawk said. "But you know about me. Don't you."

"Sure, I heard 'bout you."

"Anybody mention I enjoy being fucked with?"

Hawk's eyes were maybe six inches from Tarone's. Tarone looked quickly at his two pals. Then he looked back at Hawk. The two pals stood up, somewhat stiffly, against the wall. Hawk's eyes were steady on Tarone, barely breathing room between their faces.

"Be cool, Hawk," Tarone said. "I ain't fucking with you."

Hawk slowly straightened. He smiled pleasantly. But his eyes still held on Tarone's.

"Well, good," Hawk said. "That's nice. Who you paying off to run your whores in Bay Village?"

"Guy comes by, Anthony, collects a percentage every week."

"Anthony Meeker?" I said.

"Yeah."

"Who's he deliver it to," Hawk said.

"Mr. Ventura."

Hawk looked at me.

"How much?" I said.

"We give him five grand a week," Tarone said.

"Do any business with Gino Fish?" I said.

Tarone shook his head.

"Marty Anaheim?"

Tarone shook his head again.

"Pay off anybody else?"

"Just some Vice graft," Tarone said. "Nickels and dimes."

I nodded.

"Anything unusual about your deal with Ventura?"

"No. It's his turf. He got a right to tribute."

"Tribute," I said.

Tarone shrugged.

"What he calls it," Tarone said.

"And you don't deal with Gino Fish," I said.

"Not direct. He may have some deal going with Mr. Ventura. If he do, I don't know nothing about it."

"Thank you for your time, Tarone," I said.

I nodded at Hawk and we started for the door.

"Hey, Hawk," the young guy said. "You sure you tough as you think?"

Without speaking, Hawk turned and kicked him in the groin. The young guy doubled over and fell on the ground. And moaned. Hawk looked at the ex-fighter. The ex-fighter shook his head, and Hawk turned back to the door.

"Probably am," Hawk said.

CHAPTER
36

Dᴵxᴵᴱ Wᴀʟᴋᴇʀ ᴀɢʀᴇᴇᴅ ᴛᴏ ᴛᴀᴋᴇ ᴀ ʀɪᴅᴇ ᴡɪᴛʜ ᴍᴇ ʙᴇꜰᴏʀᴇ she went to work, and I picked her up outside The Starlight at about 4:30 on a Thursday afternoon. It was lousy weather, overcast and spitting rain. Dixie was wearing a yellow slicker jacket over jeans and a tee-shirt. To keep the rain off her head she was wearing a black baseball cap with her hair spilling out the adjustable opening in the back.

"Nice to see you dressed," I said.

"Thanks a lot."

"Be nice to see you undressed too," I said.

She smiled without much enthusiasm.

"That's better," she said. "Go back down to one-A. Anthony's place is out Eastern Ave."

"You know the address?"

"No, but I can find it. I went there enough."

"Good."

"Be the first time I went there with somebody sober."

"You or me?" I said.

"Both," she said. "I hope I can find it without a hand up my skirt."

"Well," I said, "if you can't . . ."

She smiled, more genuinely now.

"I'll let you know," she said.

Route 1A is narrow and residential as it runs through Lynn. The rain was annoying. It didn't wet the windshield enough to prevent the intermittent wiper blades from dragging, but if I shut the wipers off altogether, the water beaded up and made it hard to see. Timing is everything.

"You didn't find Anthony in Vegas?" Dixie said.

"Found him and lost him," I said. "His wife was killed."

"Really? By him?"

"Don't know," I said. "My guess is no."

"Yeah, he doesn't have the balls for it." she said.

We turned left onto Eastern Avenue and drove past solid wooden houses, mostly two-family, mostly white, with small lawns in front, and some trees along the street. It was about as residential as Lynn got.

Dixie said, "Slow down. It's along here someplace."

We slowed. Cars behind me honked their horns.

"We're holding up traffic," Dixie said.

"Take your time," I said.

More horns. One driver pulled out around me and raced past me, tires screeching. As he passed he gave me the finger.

"He thinks I'm number one," I said.

"There it is," Dixie said.

I pulled in by a hydrant in front of a white three-decker with dark green shutters and some scraggly lilac bushes along the driveway. The cars behind me gunned their engines in angry liberation as they passed me. I felt properly chastened.

"He's got a place on the second floor," Dixie said. "You go in the front door and there's a hallway with stairs. Place always smelled like kerosene to me."

"He own it or rent it?" I said.

"I don't know. He always called it his pad."

"Hell of a love nest," I said.

"See what I mean?" Dixie said. "What kind of a stiff has a romantic hideaway in a three-decker in Lynn?"

"You haven't heard from him since I talked with you last?" I said.

"No. I got no interest in him. He called me I'd hang up."

"If he does, find out where he is before you hang up," I said.

Dixie smiled again. It was sort of an awkward-looking smile, as if she hadn't had a lot of practice with it.

"You want I should do your job for you?" she said.

"Long as it gets done," I said.

I pulled the car out and circled the block so I was heading back down Eastern Avenue toward the water.

"You got time to eat before you go to work?" I said.

"Sure."

"Anyplace around here that won't poison you?"

"I don't know."

"Must be something in Swampscott," I said. "Along the water."

"I never eat around here."

"Where do you live?"

"Everett, I got a place there with my sister."

At the end of Eastern Avenue I turned left onto Humphrey Street and found a small place across from the beach. I parked in the town lot and got out and walked around to Dixie's side of the car. She sat still in the front seat and didn't get out. I opened the door. She still sat without moving.

"Care to dine?" I said.

She looked up at me and I realized she was crying.

"Or not," I said.

"You don't have to pay me off," she said, "just because I showed you where Anthony lived."

"I know," I said. "But I like your company."

"Are you going to expect anything after?"

"No."

Dixie sat staring straight ahead. She sniffed a little as she cried.

"It's been a long time," she said, "since anyone took me to dinner."

"Well, let's try it," I said. "If you like it we can do it again."

She nodded and got out of the car while I held the door. The food in the restaurant wasn't too good, but we had a pretty nice time.

CHAPTER
37

CHINATOWN IS CRAMMED INTO BOSTON A LITTLE BELOW THE combat zone, a little east of Bay Village, not very far from where South Station backs up the Fort Point Channel. Hawk and I were in a Chinese market on Hudson Street talking to Fast Eddie Lee, who controlled Chinatown. We had an interpreter with us, a Harvard graduate student named Mei Ling. Mei Ling sat next to Hawk, and when she wasn't translating, she looked at him.

"Mr. Lee says it is nice to see you again," Mei Ling told us.

"Tell Mr. Lee we are glad too," I said.

Fast Eddie nodded and spoke without taking his cigarette from his mouth.

"Mr. Lee says you behaved honorably in Port City two years ago," Mei Ling said.

"He too was honorable," I said.

Fast Eddie smiled gently. He was a solid squat old man with wispy white hair. His thick fingers were stained with nicotine, and his teeth were tarnished with it. He was head of the Kwan Chang tong. He looked like an Asian Santa Claus. And he was as merciless as a pit viper.

"I am again looking for a woman," I said. "To find her I need to ask some questions about the way business is done in Boston."

I waited while Mei Ling translated. Fast Eddie lit a new cigarette with the butt of the old one, dropped the old one into a tin can of water, and put the new one in the corner of his mouth.

"Do you do business with Julius Ventura?" I said.

Fast Eddie nodded before Mei Ling could translate.

"Do you do business with Gino Fish?"

Again Fast Eddie nodded.

"Do you know Marty Anaheim?"

Nod.

"Anthony Meeker."

Fast Eddie spoke to Mei Ling.

"Mr. Lee wants you to say the name again, slowly."

"Anthony Meeker."

Fast Eddie said, "Ah," and nodded.

"Tell me about them," I said.

Fast Eddie thought for a few moments. We waited quietly. An old woman with her hair tight to her head sat on a stool by the counter near the door in the front of the store. She too was smoking. There were no customers. A ceiling fan turned slowly above us and gently swirled the smoke from Fast Eddie's cigarette. A big late-summer horsefly looped furiously about the store without apparent purpose.

Fast Eddie watched the fly for a while and then began to speak. He paused periodically for Mei Ling to translate.

"Marty Anaheim is known to Mr. Lee only by reputation," Mei Ling translated. "He is Gino Fish's assassin. Julius and Gino and Mr. Lee do business. They have separate, ah, spheres of influence, but sometimes those spheres overlap and provisions must be made. Sometimes those provisions are . . ."

Mei Ling paused, trying for the right word.

"It is a Chinese expression," she said to me. "My pig, your pig . . ."

"Quid pro quo?" I said.

Mei Ling's smile was brilliant.

"Yes," she said. "Exactly. Sometimes the provisions are quid pro quo, but sometimes the overlap is not equal and then payments need to be made to keep the, ah, equilibrium."

"Who handles the payments?" I said.

Without waiting for Mei Ling, Fast Eddie said, "Antho-ny Mee-ker." He made it sound like a Chinese name.

"Both ways?" I said.

Fast Eddie looked at Mei Ling.

"I don't know quite what you are meaning, sir," Mei Ling said to me.

"Did Anthony transfer money among all three of them. Mr. Lee, Julius, and Gino?"

Mei Ling translated. Fast Eddie nodded as he spoke to Mei Ling.

"Yes, Anthony carried the money to and fro among them," Mei Ling said.

The horsefly cruised down from above the ceiling fan and made a run past Hawk. Hawk caught it in his left hand, and killed it.

"Did you have any problems with Gino or Julius?" I said.

Fast Eddie thought about this a little as he started a new cigarette and got rid of the old one. Then he spoke for a while to Mei Ling.

"Since Joseph Broz retired," she translated, "there have been four people running the business in the main part of Boston. There are the Irish groups in Somerville, and in Charlestown, who have their own following and their own territory but the territory is peripheral. And they do not cooperate with the rest. They have some influence in South Boston as well, but the rest—east of Springfield, and north of Providence, all of which belonged to Joseph Broz—now belongs to Julius and Gino, and Tony Marcus and to Mr. Lee."

Fast Eddie took in a deep lungful of smoke and let it out slowly through his nose. He spoke again.

"The four of them are like large stones in a sack, Mr. Lee says. They grind at each other."

"Tell me more about that," I said.

More cigarette smoking, more gazing off into the middle distance while we waited. Then Fast Eddie spoke again and Mei Ling translated.

"When Mr. Broz was active the system ran smoothly. Then he went into his decline. Still there was some balance. Mr. Lee had the Chinese people, Mr. Marcus had the black people. And Mr. Fish and Mr. Ventura shared the rest. Their spheres were less clearly defined, and they had to cooperate more intimately to avoid conflict, which would not profit any of us. Thus their spheres became more like one cooperative sphere and the business balanced in three parts until Mr. Marcus went to prison. He has left a weak caretaker, which is wise, Mr. Lee says, because strong caretakers become owners. But that weakness invites others, and since Mr. Marcus went to prison there has been a shifting of the stones in the sack."

"People are trying to take over Tony's enterprise?" I said.

"There is a vacuum, people are being drawn into it."

"You?"

"No, Mr. Lee does not wish commerce with barbarians."

Mei Ling made a deprecating little smile at me and Hawk when she translated *barbarians*.

"Gino or Julius?" I said.

Fast Eddie shrugged.

"Both?"

Fast Eddie shrugged again.

"Anthony Meeker got anything to do with it?" I said.

Fast Eddie shrugged again.

"Inscrutable," I said.

Fast Eddie smiled. We sat.

"I do not think he will tell us anything else, sir," Mei Ling said to me.

Fast Eddie smiled widely.

"You cause mess," he said. "Send Tony Marcus to jail. Now you have to figure out mess. Good fun."

I stood and said, "Thanks for your help, Mr. Lee."

He smiled and nodded.

"Good fun," he said.

Hawk and Mei Ling both stood. Mei Ling put her arm through Hawk's and the three of us left the store.

CHAPTER
38

I WAS SITTING IN MY OFFICE WITH THE NEWSPAPER ON A RAINY day reading Tank McNamara when Shirley Ventura's driver came in, shaking the water off his trench coat.

He said, "I understand you're to talk with me?"

"Yeah."

He took off the trench coat and hung it on the coatrack behind the door, and took off his tweed cap and shook the water off it and hung it carefully on a different hook, so it wouldn't drip on the trench coat.

"Can I sit down?" he said.

I nodded toward one of the client chairs, and he sat in it. He was a big handsome kid with a lot of thick black hair. He had on a white collarless shirt buttoned to the neck and a wide black cashmere sport coat. He looked carefully around the room.

"Not a very fancy office," he said.

"Keeps the rain off," I said.

"You make much money?"

"Sometimes."

Jackie thought about that. I waited.

"People I know," Jackie said, "tell me you're a stand-up guy."

I nodded. Jackie looked around the room some more.

"You're still interested in Shirley?" he said.

"Yep."

"You know she was tight with Marty Anaheim?"

"No," I said.

"Yeah. I used to take her to see him."

"She had you take her?" I said.

"Yeah. She couldn't drive a car."

"You mean they wouldn't let her or she didn't know how?" I said.

"Both. I don't think her mother ever let her learn."

"Did she tell you she was seeing Marty?"

"Naw. She'd have me drive her to Copley Place. Say she was going to do some shopping, pick her up in an hour. But, you know, I don't work for her. I work for Julius. I'm not just a driver, I'm supposed to take care of her. Christ knows she can't take care, couldn't take care, of herself. You saw her in the restaurant that day. So I check her out. She goes into the center of the shopping area, near the elevators, where that waterfall thing is, and Marty's there, and they walk through the mall and talk for maybe half an hour, then she leaves and I take her home. This starts happening couple times a week before she went to Vegas. And I don't know what to do. I speak to her about it she'll go bananas, deny it, and get me fired. I tell Julius she cries to her mother and Momma's little girl would never do nothing wrong. So I'm out of a job and maybe Julius puts out paper on me."

"So you go along."

"Wouldn't you?"

I shrugged.

"I take her where she wants to go," Jackie said. "I keep an eye on where she is. I get her home in one piece. I'm doing what I can, you know?"

"I wonder why she didn't just take a cab?" I said.

Jackie laughed.

"Man, you don't get it, do you. She never did nothing on her own. The old lady is there all the time. The old lady has her way. Shirley stays home with her all day and plays dolly. She never left the house by herself. She never got a cab by herself. She probably don't know how."

"She and Anthony live with her parents?"

"Sure. Big house in Revere. Point of Pines. Shirley got a little suite of her own in the back. When she marries Anthony, he moves right in."

"So how come you're telling me this now."

"Since she got killed, it's bothering me. I hear Marty was in Vegas when it happened. I don't know if he killed her, but I been thinking. I'm thinking about what Marty was up to. Why is he shagging Shirley? You know? I mean, would you?"

I shook my head.

"Maybe love is blind," I said.

"Love? Marty Anaheim? Gimme a break. He's up to something, and the more I think about it the more I think it's maybe trouble for Julius."

"Maybe," I said.

"Well, I work for Julius. I worked for him since I was right out of the Marines, you know? He's been okay to me. You work for a guy you supposed to, you know, be on his side."

"I've heard that," I said.

Jackie started to speak and stopped.

"That a crack?" he said.

I shook my head.

"None intended," I said.

"Okay. But you see my problem. I can't tell Julius his daughter's shmoozing with Marty Anaheim. He can't hear it. The old lady can't hear it. She's walking around the house wearing a black veil and carrying a doll, for crissake."

"And you can't talk to the cops," I said.

"'Course not."

"So you came to me."

Jackie shrugged.

"Couldn't think of anybody else."

I nodded. Jackie was through. We both sat in silence

while the rain beaded on my office window and formed ropey little crystalline streams as it ran down the glass.

"Anybody in the outfit you can tell?" I said.

"No. Julius played it very close to his own chest," Jackie said. "Everybody just worked for him. We figured Anthony was going to be the number-two guy when he married Shirley, he wasn't such a fucking lightweight."

We were quiet some more.

Finally I said, "I don't know what I'll do with this, Jackie. Hell, I don't even know what it means. But sooner or later it will mean something and sooner or later I'll do something."

Jackie sat for a minute. Then he stood and put on his coat and hat. He looked at me for a moment and nodded and turned and went out without saying anything else.

I got up and stood at the window and looked down at the wet street and the cars going along with their wipers moving steadily back and forth. Diagonally across from me the grass around Louis' was still bright green and glistening under the early fall rain and somewhere in this great land was somebody who knew something about what was going on. But I didn't and I didn't know who did.

CHAPTER
39

THE SWEAT HAD SOAKED THROUGH SUSAN'S BLACK SPANDEX leotard and made a dark blotch in the small of her back. The muscles in her bare shoulders and back moved intricately as she did a set of rows on the Cybex machine.

"Don't bend back," I said. "Sit up straight. Use your arms."

"Are you sure I'm not just building up my arms?" she said.

"You're using mostly the lats," I said.

She finished the exercise and put her hand on her back a little above the hip bone.

"Right here," she said. "I need to get rid of this."

"Your hip?" I said.

"No, of course not. Right here, this disgusting roll of fat."

I couldn't see any sign of fat. But we'd had that argument before and I saw no reason to lose it again. We'd also had the discussion about the impossibility of spot reducing.

"Think of it as a beauty mark," I said.

We were in Susan's club surrounded by men and women, though more women, fighting age and weight. Many of them did not seem to be winning the fight, but none of them appeared ready to surrender. Susan's trainer was in Wellfleet with her boyfriend, almost certainly in sinful congress, and I had been enlisted to train Susan. Enlisted is probably not the right word. Drafted is probably the right word.

"Would the back machine help me?" Susan said.

"It'll strengthen your lower back," I said. "I doubt that it will reduce your vast corpulence."

"Show me how it works."

We worked on the back machine for a while. We did some lat pull downs. Susan declined the trunk twister.

"I've heard that people develop muscle there and their waist thickens."

"I doubt that," I said.

"I don't want to take the chance," Susan said.

"Of course you don't," I said.

"Let's work on the bicep thing-y," Susan said.

Women don't bulk up as easily as men, and they don't

define as easily, but Susan had visible muscles. She had as much back fat as Hakeem Olajuwon. She did three sets on the curl machine and went for a drink of water.

"Nice to see you drinking from the water fountain," I said, "instead of carrying your own personal bottle around."

"Woman of the people," Susan said. "Have you made any progress on Bibi Whatshername?"

"Anaheim," I said. "Is regress a word?"

"Yes, but probably not appropriate in this context."

"Well anyway, I'm accumulating information on the relationships among the players in the Boston mob scene, and I've learned that Shirley Ventura and Marty Anaheim were an item."

"Bibi's husband?"

"The same," I said.

"And how does that help you with Bibi?"

"It doesn't."

"But maybe it will," Susan said.

"But maybe it will."

"Do you have any idea how?"

"It's a little like you do, I think. You keep listening and nothing much makes any sense and you keep listening and you keep listening and then something appears—a pattern, an event, an evasion, a contradiction. Maybe just the small end of something you get hold of and begin to tug."

Susan bent over and took another drink of water and stood up with a few drops of it on her chin. She wiped it away with the back of her hand. She was wearing leather weight-lifting gloves, the kind without fingers. Her nails gleamed.

"Yes," she said. "Psychotherapy is like that. Though the hope is that it is the patient who sees the thing."

"All analogies are partial," I said. "Anyway, that's what I'm doing. I'm walking around and listening."

"And your goal is?"

"To find Bibi."

"And when you've found her?"

"See that she's all right."

"You are a very sentimental man," Susan said.

"My profession permits it," I said.

"Which is a reason you chose it," Susan said.

I shrugged.

"It takes a very tough guy to remain sentimental in this world," Susan said.

"My profession permits that too," I said.

"Which is, of course, another reason you chose it."

"I chose it because I heard it was a good way to meet lascivious Jewish shrinks," I said.

"Is that your specialty?"

"No," I said. "Lascivious Jewish women are my specialty. Shrinks are a subspecialty."

"And how many have you met?"

"Lascivious Jewish women?" I said. "Thousands. Shrinks? One."

"Had I been a lascivious Irish shrink, would you have loved me anyway?"

"The answer is yes," I said. "But I think you've just coined a tripartite oxymoron."

"Oy vay," Susan said. "Can the police help you find Bibi?"

"Vegas cops would like to talk with all three of them."

"Anthony's her husband, Bibi's his lover, and they both disappear after Shirley was killed. Who's the third one?"

"Marty. He was at the MGM Grand. She had the phone number for the Grand with her when she died."

"Will they keep you informed?" Susan said.

"I doubt it, but I'll call every once in a while."

"How about our police? Frank Belson owes you a pretty big favor."

"Quirk says he'll keep an eye on the wire for me."

"Not Frank?"

"I wouldn't ask Frank."

"Because he owes you a favor?"

"I wouldn't want him to think I'm collecting," I said.

Susan took another drink, and straightened and wiped her mouth, carefully so as not to smear her lipstick. She looked at me with her great dark eyes and smiled her wide-mouthed smile.

"Big boy," she said, "you are a piece of work."

"How nice of you to notice."

CHAPTER
40

Hawk came into my office on Monday afternoon, carrying a brown paper bag.

"He ain't in there," Hawk said, and put the bag on my desk while he took off his white leather trench coat and hung it on the rack.

"Anthony?"

"Yeah. Two women live there. And he ain't either one of them. They go to work every morning, come back every evening. After they left this morning I went in and looked around. Women only, no sign of anyone else."

Hawk took a sandwich and a twenty-four-ounce can of Foster's lager from the bag, folded the bag flat, and used it as a place mat.

"What kind of sandwich?" I said.

"Lobster, basil mayo, on sourdough bread."

"And you plan to eat all of it," I said.

"Un huh."

Hawk took a bite, and popped the top of the beer can while he chewed.

"Fine," I said, "I'll just suck on this paper clip for a while."

"How you doing in Needham?" Hawk said.

"The husband's got a daughter by his first marriage. She visits on weekends."

"So we oh for two."

"At best," I said.

"Nice detective work though, found Anthony's love nest, found Bibi's high school chum."

"Makes you proud," I said. "Doesn't it."

"Make a nice slogan," Hawk said. "Missing? Don't want to be found? Call Spenser. Your secret is safe with us."

"You haven't found anybody either," I said.

"Yeah," Hawk said. "But I got a lobster sandwich."

"Good point."

We were quiet while Hawk ate his sandwich, and drank his beer. When he was through he got up and washed his hands and face in the sink. Then he came back and sat down and put his feet up on my desk.

"So where are we," he said.

"I'm not sure," I said. "But I don't think we got a paddle."

"Well," Hawk said. "We know something."

"We know we don't know anything," I said.

"We listen to Fast Eddie Lee," Hawk said, "we know there seem to be a hostile takeover percolating."

"Okay, we know that."

"And it seem to have something to do with Anthony Meeker."

"But we don't know what," I said.

"Not yet," Hawk said.

"And we don't know where Anthony is," I said. "Nor what scam he and Marty were trying to run, nor what was going on between Marty and Shirley, nor what went wrong between them, nor who is going to take over what hostilely, nor who killed Shirley Ventura, nor whether Marty is after Bibi, nor where Bibi is."

"Okay," Hawk said, "so we don't know everything."

"I suppose you could say that."

"You talk to Julius since we left Vegas?"

"No."

"So we could do that," Hawk said.

"Well, aren't you perky," I said.

"I be even perkier, I knew exactly what the hell we trying to do. We looking for Bibi, or Anthony, or we trying to solve Shirley's murder, or we keeping tabs on the mob, or we trying to get even with Marty Anaheim for popping you in the kisser?"

"Yes," I said.

"Yes?"

"All of the above," I said. "I don't like somebody getting killed when they are sort of my client. I don't want

261

Marty to find Bibi and hurt her. I don't like losing Anthony. I don't like stuff going on and I can't figure it out. I'm trying to make sense out of this hairball."

"If there is a hostile takeover coming, we can sit tight and watch and after a while we'll find out," Hawk said.

"And maybe there'll be some fallout and we'll learn some other stuff."

"Maybe," Hawk said.

"And maybe Madonna will come into the office and moon us," I said.

"That ain't perky."

"Fuck perky."

CHAPTER
41

JULIUS LIVED IN A THREE-STORY STUCCO HOUSE WITH A FIVE-car garage and grates on the windows. He and I sat on high, hard, hand-carved mahogany chairs in his big ornate formal living room and looked out through the grated windows at the guest cottage, in the backyard, the big house in miniature. There was no grass in the backyard. It was covered with beige pea stone, ornamented with statuary.

"How's your wife?" I said.

"No good."

"Takes a while," I said.

Julius shook his head.

"She ain't going to get better," he said.

"I know a shrink."

"Shrinks are a bunch of fucking perverts," Julius said.

"Oh yeah," I said. "I forgot that."

"You know anything about where that fucking Anthony is?"

"No," I said. "But I'm still looking."

"You look all you want, long as you don't think I'm paying you."

"My own interest," I said.

"There's a hundred thousand out on him," Julius said. "You find him, you kill him, you get the hundred grand. Just like anybody else."

"Very fair," I said. "Did you know he and Marty Anaheim were running some kind of scam?"

"What kind of scam?"

"I don't know. Did you know your daughter and Marty were friends?"

Julius stared at me.

"Shirley?"

"Yeah."

He shook his head. "Not with Marty Anaheim."

"You any idea what that might be about?"

"You know this?"

"I got it on good authority."

"Who?"

I shook my head.

"Any thoughts?" I said.

Julius slumped back in his chair and stared at me.

"You want some fruit?" he said.

He made a listless gesture at a big pink and blue and white bowl on the coffee table. There was a large Technicolor picture of Shirley on the table near the fruit.

"No thanks."

"Her mother couldn't have no more kids," Julius said, "after her. Her womb was tipped or something."

He was staring out the window at the guest house. His voice rumbled up out of him, as if his mind were elsewhere and his voice was on its own.

"I had a business to run. Her mother was supposed to raise her."

He paused. There must have been other people in the big ugly house but there was no sound. Nothing moved. The house felt as if it had been closed up for a long time.

"She never let her out. Not even for school. One of the fucking nuns come in every day and teach her, and my wife would sit there the whole time. When she finally had to go to high school, my wife takes her in the morning, picks her up in the afternoon. She never learned to drive a car. Hell, she can't . . . couldn't . . . even ride a bicycle. She might fall off, get hurt."

We were quiet. I could smell the ripening scent of the apples and pears in the bowl on the coffee table.

"How'd she meet Anthony," I said.

"She knew him from high school. He used to come around, bring some videocassettes and him and Shirley and my wife would watch movies in here."

"The three of them."

"Yeah. My wife had to make sure he wasn't showing

her no bad movies. Make sure there was no sex going on. So they'd sit there and watch the movies and the thing is . . . it's a real funny thing, you feel like laughing . . . my wife gets to like this creep. The fucking head chicken gets to like the fucking fox. He's polite, you know, and he talks to my wife. Why not, what the fuck you going to talk to Shirley about. She's hardly ever been out of the fucking house. But my wife tells me he ain't a fucking hoodlum, except she don't say 'fucking,' like the hoodlums work for me. And he's going to marry Shirley and I'm going to give him a nice responsible job. And I say, then he'll be a hoodlum. But my wife don't pay no fucking attention. She's good at not paying no fucking attention. So I put him to work. He's collecting money for me on all of the out-of-turf accounts and paying off the people I gotta pay off to do business quiet in those places. I need somebody I can trust to do it."

"Why not pay off the people yourself?"

"Bookkeeping. I let Anthony collect, say, from bookies on Gino's turf and he pays Gino direct out of collections, and there's no money trail. Federal guys especially like to follow the money. The less tracks back to me, the easier everything works."

"And the easier it is to skim," I said.

"Why you want a trustworthy guy doing it," Julius said.

"Like Anthony."

Julius nodded slowly.

"Just like him," he said.

"You had any interest in moving in on Tony Marcus's business while he's in jail?"

Julius shrugged.

"You think about it," he said. "Tony's got some stiff named Tarone running his errands while he's in the place. Could knock him over easy."

"I met Tarone."

"I unnerstand Tony's problem," Julius said. "You don't want no hotshot running things while you're away, 'cause when you come back it might be his."

"Tony's in no danger there," I said.

"Other hand, you don't want some candy ass running things, anyone can walk in and take it away from him."

"Not easy being a crime lord," I said.

Julius ignored me. He liked talking about business.

"Used to be when Broz was younger, you go see him, you talk, he sorta decides what's gonna happen, everybody gets along, everybody makes money. Now, it's like, you know, an open city. So, yeah, we been looking over his operation. Gino probably has too. Fast Eddie Lee, I don't know. He ain't said. Fuckers never say much."

"Gotten to push and shove yet?"

"No, right now we're just appraising."

"Anthony have anything to do with the appraising?"

"Forget Anthony, I told you, there's a C-grand out on him. He don't matter anymore. He's already dead, he just don't know it yet."

"You think Shirley and Marty Anaheim might be connected to the appraising?"

267

"There ain't no Shirley and Marty Anaheim."

"I'm told there was."

"He's fucking lying," Julius said, his voice rumbling in his chest. "Give me his name."

I shook my head again.

"I find out who's saying that," Julius rumbled, "I'll kill him. Myself. Personally."

There didn't seem anywhere to go from there. I stood up.

"I'll go now," I said. "I'm sorry about your daughter."

"Yeah," Julius said.

"And I hope your wife can find some consolation."

Julius nodded. His head was forward a little. He seemed to have sunk deeper into his chair.

"She ain't going to," he said.

CHAPTER
42

On Thursday nights Susan ran a walk-in clinic at The Spence Health Center in Cambridge, and didn't get out until 9:00. Then she always drove over to my place to have dinner with me and spend the night. And always before we went to bed we walked Pearl the Wonder Dog together up the Commonwealth Avenue Mall. Which was what we were doing on this Thursday night, at about 11:30. It was definitely fall now. The leaves had turned, and where the streetlights made them bright they seemed almost artificial against the darkness. There was little traffic, the eleven o'clock news was over, and many of the brownstone and brick townhouses were dark. Susan held Pearl's leash. Pearl leaned firmly into her choke collar and made an occasional huffing sound.

"Ever wonder why she's in such a hurry?" I said. "She's not going anywhere."

"She likes to hurry," Susan said.

We crossed Dartmouth Street. Ahead of us at the Exeter Street crossing a car pulled up and two men got out and began to walk toward us. Behind us I heard a car slow and stop on Dartmouth Street. I glanced back; a man got out of the passenger side and began walking behind us.

I said to Susan, "Kiss me good night, and take Pearl and go right across the street here as if you were going home. When you're behind the parked cars crouch down and get the hell away from here."

"What is it?"

"Trouble, I think."

I turned her toward me and kissed her as if there were nothing else to do in the world. As I kissed her I took my gun out from under my coat.

I murmured against her mouth, "When I let you go, move. Don't hurry, but don't linger. Wave to me as you cross the street."

Susan didn't say another word. When we stopped kissing, she touched me on the face once, briefly, and headed across Commonwealth Avenue in the middle of the block; as she and Pearl squeezed between two parked cars she gave me a happy wave. When she reached the sidewalk, she turned and started back toward Arlington Street. The guys in front of me paid her no mind. I pretended to look after her. The guy behind me was walking casually, looking around like a late-night tourist. I palmed my gun, so that in the darkness no one could see that I was carrying it. It was the easy-to-carry little Smith & Wesson .38 chambered for five rounds. I always left the chamber empty under the hammer, so I had four. Usually that was enough, and would have to be again. After all, I had one more bullet than attackers. Though I would have, had I known the agenda, brought the Browning 9 mm which had thirteen in the magazine. To my right was a bench. I stopped and put my right foot up on it and pretended to tie my shoe. The two ahead of me were about thirty feet away. The guy behind me was a little closer. I saw one of the guys ahead of me move his hand and caught the flash of a stainless-steel handgun in the light that fused out from the streetlamps. A blued finish is better for being sneaky. I stepped suddenly up onto the bench and went over it and landed in a crouch behind it. There was a shot from in front and a bullet whanged off the cement leg of the bench. Across the street a car alarm began its siren call. I cocked my gun, took a breath, let it out, and drilled the guy with the stainless-steel hand-gun right in the middle of the chest. He made a huff, not unlike Pearl's huff, and fell over on his back. Another bullet plowed into the bench, hitting the wooden seat this time, and splinter-ing it. I cocked the .38, breathed out again, aimed for the middle of the mass which was coming at me on the run, and shot the guy behind me. He pitched forward, his mo-mentum overcoming the impact of the slug, and sprawled toward the bench on his face. I whirled toward the third guy, who should have been on top of me. He wasn't. He was running back down the mall toward Exeter Street. The car that had been idling on Dartmouth pulled away and disappeared toward the river, running a red light in the process. I stood, and turned sideways and shot at the running gunman. But the range was too great for the two-inch barrel. He opened the back door, dove in, and the car screamed away from the curb as the door closed behind him.

Behind me the car alarm was whooping and whining. I took some bullets from my coat pocket and reloaded while I looked for Susan. I saw her come out from behind a car with Pearl at the corner of Dartmouth Street. Pearl, gun-shy to the end, was trying to climb into Susan's lap. I put my gun away and knelt beside the man who'd followed me. He was a large man with a beard and a significant belly. He had no pulse. I moved to the front guy, beard-less and skinny. He was dead too. I couldn't think much anymore, but I could still shoot.

"You hit?" Susan said.

I put my arm around her.

"No," I said. "What's with the car alarm."

"I banged into every car along the street," Susan said. "One was bound to have a motion alarm."

"Smart," I said.

"I have a Ph.D. from Harvard."

"You didn't say stupid stuff when I told you to move," I said.

"You'd be worried about me and Pearl," Susan said. "I'd have been in the way."

Pearl weaseled her way in between us, and jumped up with her paws on my chest. I patted her head.

"They're dead?" Susan said. She didn't look at them.

"Yes."

"Who were they?" Susan said.

"I don't know."

In the distance, up Commonwealth Ave. from the Kenmore Square end, I could hear a siren above the racket of the car alarm. There were lights on in many of the windows that had been dark.

"You should take Pearl and go back to my place, otherwise they'll want to talk with you too, and it'll take half the night, and Pearl won't like it."

"No, you'll need a witness."

"Good point," I said.

"I'm glad you're not dead."

"That's so sweet," I said.

The first patrol car swung up over the curb at Dartmouth Street and drove down the middle of the mall toward us. The headlights lit the scene harshly and I could see the blood spreading out on the sidewalk around both the men I'd killed.

The patrol cops got out on each side of the squad car with guns drawn, hatless, keeping the open doors between me and them. Pearl barked at them. Susan shushed her. I put my hands on top of my head.

"Gun's on my right hip," I said. "You want me to take it out, or you want to come get it."

"Stay just like you are," the cop on the passenger side said. "And step away from the lady."

I did as I was told and the cop came out from behind the door with his gun leveled.

"Walk over here, put your hands on the roof."

I did as he told me. I backed away and spread my legs so that my weight rested on my hands and I couldn't move suddenly. The cop on the driver's side kept his gun on me over the roof, while his partner came and took my gun off my hip. He smelled it. Then he patted me down.

"Put your left hand behind your back," he said.

I did and he put a cuff on it.

"Now the other hand."

I had to straighten away from the car to do it. He finished cuffing me.

"You shoot them?" he said.

"Yes."

"With that thing?"

"Yeah."

When the cuffs were on his partner went to the two bodies and felt for pulses.

"They dead?" the first cop said.

"Yeah, both of them."

His partner was young and muscular with his uniform shirt tailored and his hair cut very short. I could hear more sirens in the distance, coming from both ends of

Commonwealth and at least one coming down Dart-mouth.

"Why'd you shoot them?" the first cop said.

"They tried to shoot me."

"You know who they are?"

"No."

"You see this, lady?"

"Yes," Susan said. "I'm with him. We were walking Pearl when these two men and another one came at us and tried to kill him."

"Pearl's the dog?"

"Yes."

"Where's the other shooter?"

"He got away in a waiting car," Susan said.

The first cop stepped away from me. He was older than his partner with longish gray hair, wearing the kind of translucent eyeglasses that they used to issue in the army.

"Three guys come to shoot you, two of them get killed and the third one runs away," the older cop said. "Don't usually happen that way."

"It was exciting," I said.

"I'll bet it was," he said. "You got a permit for the piece?"

"Yes."

"ID?"

"Yes, in my wallet, left hip pocket."

He took out my wallet, found my licenses: gun, private, and driver's. He studied them. He looked at my ID picture in the car headlights and then looked at me carefully.

Then he put everything back in my wallet and slipped the wallet into my back pocket. A second patrol car came down the mall from Exeter Street, a third one pulled in behind the first one from Dartmouth Street, and Frank Belson got out of an unmarked car parked on Dartmouth Street and walked up the mall toward us. The scene was now lit like an opera set. Belson spoke to the older of the first two cops.

"I was in the area. Whaddya got, Chick?"

"Guy shot two guys, claims self-defense, girlfriend's a witness."

Belson looked at me.

"Oh shit," he said.

Then he looked at Susan and Pearl and walked over and patted Pearl's head.

"Excuse my language," he said to Susan.

"I will not," she said. "It's fucking disgusting."

Belson nodded and grinned at her and turned.

Chick said, "You know him, Frank?"

"Yeah."

"He's a private detective."

"I know. You can take the cuffs off."

"He shot two guys," Chick said.

"You got him under arrest?"

"No."

"You gonna arrest him?"

"I'll leave that up to you."

"Take off the cuffs."

Chick unlocked the cuffs, and put them back in their

little case on his belt. I resisted the temptation to rub my wrists, too trite. Susan and Pearl came over to stand beside me. I put an arm around her shoulder. Belson turned to the other detective who had walked down behind him.

"You better get Quirk," he said.

The dick nodded and headed back to the car. Belson turned toward Chick and his partner.

"You should probably have your hats on when Quirk gets here," he said.

Both cops obviously agreed. They headed for the squad car, and one of the late-arriving cops went back to the car for his hat too.

Belson turned, finally, to me, and folded his arms, took a big inhale and let it out.

"Okay," Belson said, "tell me about it."

CHAPTER
43

I WAS HAVING DINNER AT THE CAPITAL GRILL WITH HAWK AND Susan.

"You let one get away?" Hawk said.

"Plus the drivers of the two getaway cars, whom you, of course, would have run down on foot."

"And bitten their heads off," Hawk said.

The waiter arrived with drinks.

"Merlot," he said as he put the glass of wine in front of Susan.

She said, "Thank you, John."

I had beer, Hawk had a glass of champagne.

"And you didn't get no license plate numbers?"

"Of course not," I said. "If I had I might have been able to learn something."

"So you don't know who they were?" Hawk said.

"Actually, I do," I said. "Belson called me. They were a couple of Russians, with long names."

"Russians?" Susan said. "From Russia?"

"Yeah, via New York. Since the demise of the evil empire, the Russian mob has developed a base in New York. OCU told Belson they're moving into Boston now."

"OCU?" Susan said.

"Organized Crime Unit," I said.

"So why are they trying to shoot you?" Susan said.

"I don't know."

"We been talking to a lot of organized crime types lately," Hawk said. "One of them could have hired some help."

"Why?"

"We getting too close to the merger plans?"

"If there are any merger plans."

"Fast Eddie say there are."

"What he said was that the rocks were bumping up against each other or something like that."

"He meant there were merger plans," Hawk said.

"If there are, and we're so close, how come we don't know it?" I said.

"'Cause we stupid," Hawk said.

"Oh," I said. "That's why."

John brought us two steaks and the cold seafood platter. He put the seafood in front of Susan.

"Isn't it a lot?" she said.

"We can help," I said.

"We can't solve nothing," Hawk said, "but we good eaters."

Susan speared a clam, dipped the end of it in cocktail sauce, bit off the sauced corner, and chewed it thoughtfully.

"What I can't figure out," she said after she'd swallowed, "is how you start out looking for Bibi Anaheim and end up in a shootout with some Russian gangsters."

"We can't figure that out either," I said. "Steak's good. You want a bite?"

Susan shook her head.

"Do you think they'll try again?"

"Got no way to know," I said.

"Except that whoever wanted you dead didn't get what they wanted," Susan said.

"Except that," I said.

"Aren't you worried about it?"

I shrugged.

"What kind of gun are you carrying tonight?" Susan said.

"Browning," I said.

"The one that's heavier and more uncomfortable to carry, but it will shoot a lot of bullets before you have to reload."

"Thirteen in the clip, one in the chamber."

Susan nodded slowly while she looked at me.

"What do you think?" she said to Hawk.

"Think I'll stick around," Hawk said.

"That would make me feel better," Susan said.

"Make anyone feel better," Hawk said.

Susan smiled and ate the rest of her clam.

"I can't eat all of this," she said. "Maybe the baby would like some."

"You going to give it to the dog?" Hawk said.

"She's a good eater too," Susan said.

CHAPTER
44

HAWK HAD ON A DARK BLUE SERGE SUIT AND A COLLARLESS white linen shirt. His shaved head gleamed. His black ankle boots gleamed at the other end. He had one of my office chairs tipped back against the wall to my left, and he was sitting in it reading a book called *Remembering Denny,* by Calvin Trillin. I was at my desk trying to learn how to say "you'll never get me, you dirty rat," in Russian.

"You got a plan yet?" Hawk said without looking up from his book.

"We could hide in here with the door locked, sleep in shifts."

"I thought of that," Hawk said.

The phone rang.

"Be nice if we could figure out which anthill we stepped in," I said.

"Yeah, be great, we could call them names while we sleeping in shifts."

"We know who they are, we might know what to do."

The phone rang again.

"Be a nice change," Hawk said.

I nodded and picked up the phone.

"Da?" I said.

"I want to speak to Spenser," a voice said.

"Speaking," I said.

"You was working out in Vegas in September," the voice said.

"Yeah."

"With a big black guy, bald head?"

"Actually he's not bald, he shaves his head."

"Same difference," he said. "My name is Bernard J. Fortunato, you remember me?"

I slid my desk drawer open and looked at the business card I had put there more than a month ago. It said Bernard J. Fortunato. Investigator, Professional and Discreet.

"Yeah," I said. "Little guy with a Panama hat and a short Colt."

"I'm compact," he said.

"Sure," I said. "That's what I meant to say, compact guy with a Panama hat and a compact Colt."

"You still interested in a broad named Bibi Anaheim?" he said.

"What makes you think I'm interested?" I said.

"I don't think. I know," Fortunato said.

"Okay, how do you know it?"

"Because I pay fucking attention," Fortunato said. "I look, I ask questions. You still interested in her or not."

"Yeah, I am."

"She's back in Vegas," Fortunato said.

"Now?"

"Right now," he said.

"Where?"

"She's staying at the Debbie Reynolds Hotel and Casino."

"You've seen her?"

"Yeah."

"And you recognized her?"

"I told you. I pay attention. It's my business."

"You tell her husband?" I said.

"No."

"I thought you worked for him."

"I did. He hired me to keep an eye out in Vegas for a guy named Anthony Meeker. Said if I spotted you, you might lead me to him. Told me where to pick you up."

"Which you did."

"Right."

"And we did."

"Right," Fortunato said. "Then I kept an eye on him until Anaheim showed up in person."

"And you rented him a hotel room in your name."

"Yeah, and he stiffed me on it, and he stiffed me on the

job," Fortunato said. "And after he popped you one on the kisser, I figure you and him ain't pals so I'm telling you what I seen."

"To get even?"

"You interested or no?"

"Interested," I said. "You want to work for me?"

"I'm in business."

"Good, keep an eye on Bibi Anaheim until I get there. If she leaves follow her."

"Expenses?"

"Guaranteed," I said.

"Even if she goes to like, Paris?"

"Even then," I said.

"You want to know what I charge?"

"No."

"I ain't getting burned again. I give you the numbers you wire money to my account today. I don't get it today, I drop the broad like a bad habit."

"Spenser's the name, cash is the game, where you want it sent?"

He told me the amount and how to send it. Lucky I was bucks up.

CHAPTER
45

JOE BROZ STILL KEPT AN OFFICE IN THE FINANCIAL DISTRICT with an executive-level view of the harbor. There were still a couple of hard cases lounging around in the outer office, working on their relaxed tough guy look. And Joe himself still had a little left of the old theatricality. But this time when I went into his white office he was an old man. The changes weren't so much physical as attitudinal. As if he had decided to be old. He had arranged himself in front of the big picture window behind his desk, his back to the door, a dark form without detail against the bright morning light that came through the eastward-looking window. When I came in he didn't move while I closed the door behind me and walked to a chair and sat down in front of his desk. I waited for a while. Finally, Joe turned slowly from the window to look at me. He had on a dark blue suit, a dark blue shirt, and a powder blue tie. He should have been flipping a silver dollar.

He said, "How long I known you, Spenser?"

"Long time," I said.

"You got a smart mouth. You think you're God's gift to the fucking universe. And you been a pain in my ass since I knew you."

"Nice of you to remember, Joe."

"I shoulda put you in the ground a long time ago."

"But you didn't," I said.

"Half the people I know are dead and most of the others are gone, and you keep showing up."

"Good to be able to count on something, isn't it?"

Broz walked stiffly from the window and lowered himself gingerly into the chair behind his desk. He put the palms of his hands carefully together and rested his chin lightly against his fingertips. He took in some air and let it out slowly through his nose.

"Whaddya want?" he said.

"Some Russians tried to kill me last night."

"Good for them."

"Depends how you look at it," I said. "Two of them are dead."

Broz shrugged. "I know you're good," he said. "Never said you weren't good."

"I got no fight with any Russians," I said. "Somebody sent them."

Broz kept looking at me with his clasped hands under

his chin. He had a powder blue show hankie in his breast pocket. It matched the tie perfectly.

"And there's some, ah, realignment, maybe, going on in the rackets in town. There's something happening with Gino Fish and Julius Ventura. I hear the Russians are trying to move some people up from New York."

Broz nodded silently.

"Thought you might be able to tell me a little something."

Broz didn't move. He didn't say anything. Looking past him through the big window all I could see was sky and the kind of light you get over water. I waited. Joe unclasped his hands and rested them on the dark walnut arms of his leather chair and tilted the chair back slowly.

"You want a drink?" he said.

"Little early in the day for me."

Joe nodded.

"Early, late, don't make much difference to me anymore. I don't sleep much and when I do, I don't know I'm sleeping unless I have a dream. I eat when I'm hungry. I drink when I want to."

He stood and moved slowly to the ebony bar with the blue leather padding in the corner of the room where so many years ago a guy named Phil had made me a bourbon and water, with a dash of bitters. Things hadn't worked out between me and Phil. I had to kill him a couple of weeks later. He took some ice from a silver ice bucket and put it in a lowball glass and poured some Wild Turkey over it. He carried the drink carefully back to his desk and

6966

put it down and sat carefully back down in his chair. Then he picked up the drink and looked at it and took a sip and put it down carefully. He looked at me for a moment and then shifted his eyes so that he was staring past me.

"I know I owe you," Broz said. "You don't say anything about that, and I notice that you don't. But you coulda killed my kid, when was it? Three years ago?"

"More like five," I said.

"Five years ago. You coulda killed him, and you'da been justified."

He picked up his drink and had another sip, put the glass down carefully without spilling any, and looked at it absently.

"Kid's out of the business," Broz said. He could have been talking to himself for all the notice he seemed to take of me. "Set him up in a nice tavern out in Pittsfield. Wasn't cut out for the business. And Vinnie's gone."

"He's with Gino now," I said, just to remind him I was there.

"You know Gino's a fairy?"

I didn't answer. Broz didn't care.

Broz shook his head. "When I got Gerry settled in the tavern I was gonna pass the business on to Vinnie."

He drank some more Wild Turkey.

"I was gonna retire," he said. "I was gonna give the business to the kid and Vinnie coulda helped him, but it didn't work out. My wife's dead. I got nothing much going on at home, I got nothing to do, so I figure I may as well work some more. Tony Marcus is away, and his deal is up for grabs, and Gino and Julius are starting to move in 'cause they think I'm over the hill, you know? And I'm thinking about all this and one day this Russian comes in to see me from New York, and he says they'd like to get an operation going up here, and I tell him there's no room for anybody else, and he says they want to join my crew and get rid of Gino and Julius and take over the Marcus operation and they want me to run the whole deal."

Broz smiled a little and tasted a little more of his Wild Turkey.

"And I ask the Russki what his people get out of it? And he says they don't know the territory up here, they want to get set up and sort of ease in, and all they want from me, when I die, they get the business."

"What about Fast Eddie Lee?" I said.

"I asked him that. He says they don't do business with Chinks. Says they leave Fast Eddie alone, long as he leaves us alone."

"You believe that?" I said.

"They think Fast Eddie's too tough a nut for them right now, they figure they get everything else and isolate Fast Eddie and then when they're ready they move on him. Be what I'd do."

I nodded. We sat quietly. Me looking at Broz. Broz looking past me. Broz was taking a lot of time to get there. But I had time. The plane to Vegas didn't leave until 4:05 in the afternoon.

"I told him no," Broz said. "I told him there wasn't much outfit left, certainly not enough to take on a partner. He says they bring in new business as they expand. I tell him I don't want to expand. I got no heart for it anymore. I tell him I don't care what happens to the outfit after I die. They can have it as well as anybody else. But, I told him, if anybody makes a move on my outfit while I'm still around I will chew them up and spit them into the harbor like mackerel chum. He says okay would I consider acting as a kind of consultant for them, being as how I know my way around this city. I say if the price is right I got no problem giving them advice. So the price is right and we make that deal. They leave my crew alone, they can consult me on whatever else they want to do."

"An elder statesman," I said.

"So they ask me who they should start with. I tell them Tony Marcus. He's in the place. Stooge is running the operation."

"They say they don't want to do that because it would make Gino and Julius suspicious. And it might push them together and the Russkies might have to fight them both before they want to. They want to take them out one at a time, and I say in that case start with Julius. And they say why? And I tell them that Gino's got Marty Anaheim running number two, and Julius got that asshole son-in-law."

"He's not number two for Julius," I said.

"No, but he's waiting around to take over, you don't get a good number-two man, you know what I mean. I know, I lost Vinnie 'cause of the kid."

"So, did they?"

Broz did a big elaborate shrug.

"I'm a consultant, they call me when they need me."

"How would they go about it?"

Again the flamboyant shrug. "Don't know."

"How would you go about it?"

"Make a deal with Gino. Then after he helps me drop Julius, make a deal with Tony Marcus's stooge to drop Gino. When I got that done, I could pick the stooge off at leisure. Then Fast Eddie could have the Chinks, and I'd have everything else."

"You think they'll leave you in place?" I said.

"I got no place no more," Broz said. "They got no reason to fuck with me."

"So why did they hit me?"

"Don't know," Broz said.

He leaned forward in his chair and picked up the phone and dialed.

"Broz, lemme talk to Vic . . . Broz, couple your people tried to hit a guy named Spenser. How come? . . . Yeah, I know he did. He's sitting here with me in my office . . . yeah? . . . yeah? . . . no he ain't my friend but I owe him something and I pay my debts . . . yeah . . . who asked you to do it? . . . yeah . . . I don't know, maybe it's personal. Can you lay off Spenser this time around? I only owe him this one, next time you can blow him into caviar, you wanna . . . Okay? Okay."

He hung up the phone.

"Marty Anaheim asked them to hit you."

"So it looks like they did what you'd have done."

"Looks like," Broz said.

"Except that Marty's not with Gino anymore."

"No he ain't."

"But he probably was," I said, "when the scuffle started."

"Probably."

Broz was obvious in his disinterest.

"You know why Marty left Gino?" I said.

"No."

Broz drank the rest of his Wild Turkey.

"You can have Marty," Broz said. "Nobody will give a fuck. But stay away from me and the Russkies."

"I'm looking for Bibi Anaheim," I said.

Broz stood carefully and walked carefully to the bar. He poured more Wild Turkey over ice and turned, leaning against the bar the way he always had.

"What I told you is between you and me."

"Sure," I said.

"Your word?"

"My word."

"Your word's good," Broz said. "We even now?"

"I don't know, Joe, I never said we weren't."

"No," Broz said, "you never did."

CHAPTER
46

"Y̶OU FIGURE MARTY WANTED TO BOP YOU 'CAUSE YOU KEEP poking at this thing?" Hawk said.

"Yeah," I said.

We were 33,000 feet above western Pennsylvania in the first-class compartment (neither Hawk nor I fit well in coach) on our way to Dallas to catch a flight to Las Vegas. I had survived the takeoff again. My tray table was down. I had a scotch and soda and the cabin crew was moving along the aisle serving food.

"Don't seem too smart," Hawk said. "We was poking, but we wasn't getting anywhere. 'Cept the rocks jivin' in the bag. And what he think we going to do 'bout that anyway."

"We might tell Julius," I said.

The food service was moving closer to us. The food is almost always hideous on an airplane and I can never wait for it to get there.

"You think Julius don't know?" Hawk said.

"Might not know the details."

"And we do?"

"Marty doesn't know what we know," I said. "He only knows we're pecking at it and we won't go away."

"So how come he don't hit me?"

"Maybe figured with me gone, you'd back off. Maybe figured he'd get you next."

Hawk sipped some champagne and thought about it.

"Nobody ever say Marty is smart," Hawk said. "But even he got to figure killing you going to stir things up more than they calm things down."

"Maybe it wasn't the mob takeover stuff," I said.

A stewardess with big blond hair put a tray of food on my table. Her name tag read CHERYL. I took a bite. Hawk looked over as I chewed.

"What'd you get?" he said.

"Might be chicken," I said. "How about you?"

"They steamed the steak, just right," Hawk said. "You think he don't want you to find Bibi?"

"Yeah."

"Why?"

"Because I think he killed Shirley Ventura. And Bibi knows it, or knows enough to let us figure it out."

Hawk chewed silently and swallowed.

"You ever wonder why they don't just serve you couple

nice sandwiches on an airplane," he said. " 'Stead of trying to microwave you a five-course meal that tastes like a boiled Dixie cup?"

"Often," I said.

Hawk drank his champagne.

"Anytime somebody get killed and Marty in the area, it's a decent bet he done it," Hawk said.

"Plus they had something going," I said. "She used to meet with him regularly. And she had the phone number of his hotel in Vegas when she was killed."

"Plus he had something going with her old man."

"Which might have had something to do with the mob realignment that was developing."

"Maybe Bibi will know something," Hawk said. Cabin attendant Cheryl came by.

"Did you enjoy your meal, sir?" she said to Hawk.

"Horse died hard," Hawk said.

Cheryl smiled. "More champagne?"

"Be a fool not to," Hawk said.

Cheryl produced a bottle at once and filled Hawk's glass.

"I'll keep it chilled for you up front," she said.

Hawk nodded gently.

"Be nice if you did," he said.

"And I'll check back regularly," she said.

As she walked away there was a little extra something in the way her hips moved, I thought.

"You think Cheryl's in love with you?" I said.

"Yes," Hawk said.

We survived the landing in Dallas. Cheryl gave Hawk a small slip of paper as we were getting off. He smiled at her and slipped it into his shirt pocket. Hawk and I killed an hour very dead strolling around DFW, and then got a plane to Vegas.

"Did I see Cheryl slip you her phone number?" I said to Hawk when we were airborne and I was able to get my teeth unclenched.

Hawk took the folded paper out of his shirt pocket and looked at it.

"Full name, address, and phone number."

"Does it say 'For a good time call Cheryl'?"

"'Course not, you think she forward or something."

"She based in Boston?" I said.

"Dallas," Hawk said.

"Too bad."

Hawk shrugged.

"Maybe stop off on my way back," he said.

"Be a fool not to," I said. "Lester going to pick us up?"

"Yeah," Hawk said. "'Less we crash and burn, killing all on board."

"Of course unless that," I said.

I ordered a scotch and soda from a senior stewardess with a deep whisky voice. She was heavyish with gray hair, and green-rimmed half glasses hanging from a lavender cord around her neck. Hawk ordered champagne and she tramped off to get both drinks.

"Maybe she'll give you a note too," I said to Hawk.

"Be for you if she does," he said.

When I finished my drink, I leaned my seat back and closed my eyes and didn't sleep, just as I never sleep on an airplane, while I speculated on the most sensible way to exit when the plane crashed on landing. At ten minutes to eight Pacific time we banked languidly over a frenzy of neon in the middle of the velvet blackness, and at one minute to eight Pacific time we eased onto the tarmac at McCarran and taxied gently to the gate. Made it again. Lester was waiting for us and at twenty to nine we were sitting at the bar in the Debbie Reynolds Hotel and Casino waiting to talk with Bernard J. Fortunato.

CHAPTER
47

THE DEBBIE REYNOLDS HOTEL WAS DEFINITELY MORE GLAM-orous than Sears Roebuck. There was a small lobby with a few slots and a coffee shop/bar where we were. Across the way a gift shop specialized in Debbie memorabilia. There were life-sized posters, framed pictures, cassettes of her movies, sweatshirts with Debbie's picture, many copies of her book, tapes of Debbie singing, key chains, hats, mugs, and no doubt much more. The bartender told us that Debbie came out every night after her show and talked to her fans right here and signed autographs.

"We wrap this up quick," Hawk said, "before her show ends, we can come here and meet her."

"Get a picture of us with her," I said, "to bring back to Lee Farrell."

Bernard J. Fortunato came into the bar and sat on a stool next to me. He was still wearing his Panama hat, and a pink and white necktie. He had a toothpick in his mouth.

"How you doing," he said.

He looked appraisingly at Hawk.

I introduced them.

"You as good as you look?" Fortunato said.

Hawk smiled.

"Or as bad," he said.

Fortunato nodded, and turned to me.

"She's still here. She went up to her room maybe an hour ago, hasn't come down. Room five twenty-one, I already duked the desk clerk."

"There a back way out of here?" I said.

"She either gotta come through the lobby," Fortunato said, "or use the fire stairs that dump out in the alley at the end of the building nearest the Strip."

I pointed.

"That end?" I said.

"Yeah."

I looked at Hawk, he nodded and left the bar.

"Where's the house phone?" I said.

"Lobby, near the desk."

I paid the bartender and Bernard and I walked to the lobby. There was a small reception desk there and some phones to the right. A guy in a short-sleeved blue and white striped shirt sat behind the desk smoking a cigarette without taking it out of his mouth. Now and then he leaned away from the counter and flicked the accumulating ash into a receptacle I couldn't see. Or maybe onto the floor.

"How much you duke him?" I said to Fortunato.

"I give him a C," Fortunato said. "It'll be on the bill."

There was a rack of Las Vegas guide magazines, advertising on their covers celebrations of infinite scope built around superstars of colossal magnitude, whom I, in my ignorance, had not always heard of. On the other hand, I had heard of Debbie Reynolds.

"Call Bibi," I said. "Tell her who you are, that you work for Marty, and you want to see her in the lobby right now."

"And she scoots down the back stairs and your pal grabs her in the alley."

I nodded. Bernard picked up the phone and spoke into it. He listened and spoke again.

"You don't know me, but my name's Fortunato and I work for Marty Anaheim."

He paused, listening.

"Yeah, you do," he said. "He's your husband."

He listened, moving the toothpick from one corner of his mouth to the other.

"Have it any way you want," he said. "I'm in the lobby. I want to see you. I can come up or you can come down."

He winked at me.

"No, no, sis, those are the choices, you come down or I come up."

He listened, nodding slightly.

"Okay, but I don't see you in fifteen, I'm knocking on your door."

Then he hung it up, and grinned at me.

"I guess she wants a head start," Bernard said. "Says she was in the shower, has to get dressed, be down in fifteen minutes."

"Might be true," I said.

"Sure. I got a tenner says she'll be in here with the schwartza in less than three minutes."

"His name's Hawk," I said.

"No offense. Hell, I call myself the mini guinea."

I looked at my watch. We waited. A group of people who must have gotten off a tour bus from Kansas trouped in through the front door. They turned right and followed their tour guide down the corridor toward the ballroom where Debbie's next show was gathering momentum. As they cleared the lobby, Hawk walked in the front door with his hand gently on Bibi Anaheim's arm. It was two minutes and thirty-four seconds from the time Fortunato called.

"You owe me ten," Fortunato said.

"I didn't bet," I said.

CHAPTER
48

I PAID BERNARD J. FORTUNATO OFF, IN CASH, ON THE SPOT, expenses included. He folded it up without counting it and slid it into his right-hand pants pocket.

"You don't want to count it?" I said.

"Naw, my line of work you can't tell the difference between who you can trust, and who you can't . . . time to find another line of work."

Bernard tipped his hat forward a little lower over the bridge of his nose and we left him getting a drink at the bar in the hotel lobby. Probably waiting for Debbie.

It was about 11:30 and Convention Center Drive was the road less traveled at this time of night in Vegas. Hawk and Bibi and I were nearly the only people on the street, as we walked west toward the Strip in the neon-tinged late-night twilight, which was about as dark as it gets in Vegas. If Bibi was glad to see us, she had mastered her emotions completely. She had not spoken since Hawk had brought her into the lobby. And as she walked between us she seemed to be dwindling inside her silence, as if eventually it would become so thick we couldn't find her.

"Told her we ain't working for Marty," Hawk said.

I nodded.

"We've been looking very hard for you," I said.

She gave no indication that she'd heard me.

"Mostly we were worried about you. You've had a lousy life for quite a while."

We got to the Strip and turned left, heading south toward The Mirage. On the Strip the dry desert night was full of people and cars and lights, thick with the smell of exhaust fumes and cigarette smoke, and deodorant spray and hair spray and mixed drinks and cologne and desperation. There was a lot of energy on the Strip but it was feverish, the kind of energy that makes you sleepless, that makes you drive too fast, and chain-smoke, and drink heavy. The Strip was choked with people in dogged search of fun, looking for the promise of Vegas that had brought them all from Keokuk and Presque Isle and North Platte. It wasn't like it was supposed to be. It wasn't the adventure of a lifetime, but it had to be. You couldn't admit that it wasn't. You'd come too far, expected too much, planned too long. If you stayed up later, played harder, gambled bigger, looked longer, saw another show, had another drink, stretched out a little further . . .

"I was in Fairhaven High School a few days ago," I said to Bibi. "Nice-looking old building. Looks like a real high school, doesn't it."

She didn't respond. As we walked through the crowd, people would occasionally stare covertly at Hawk.

"I met your friend Abigail," I said.

Nothing.

"Abigail Olivetti," I said. "Hey, Abbey, where's the party?"

Bibi was silent.

"Almost twenty years ago," I said.

Bibi started to cry. Nothing dramatic, just some tears silently on her face. She made no move to wipe them away.

"Seems a long way back, doesn't it?" I said.

She nodded.

"Didn't work out so good," I said.

She shook her head.

"We might be able to make it work better," I said.

She stopped walking and stood crying in the middle of the sidewalk in front of the Desert Inn. I put my arm around her shoulder. She stiffened and turned stiffly toward me and stood stiffly against me so she could cry on my chest. Hawk appeared to pay no attention, but I noticed he had moved in front of us so that he shielded her with his body and people couldn't see her crying.

We stood like that for a while and finally she stopped crying, though she made no visible effort to do so, and pulled stiffly away from my chest. She seemed no longer in concealment, as if the crying had revealed her and she had nothing left to hide.

"I met Marty my senior year," she said. "Everybody was scared of him but me."

We began to walk again. The sidewalk was crowded but people seemed to give us room. When you walked with Hawk you never got jostled.

"Where'd you go when you got to L.A.?" I said.

"I had a friend in Oceanside, Dianne Lalli, I went to see her."

"From high school?"

"Yes. I don't have any friends after high school. Did you really see Abbey?"

"Yes, she's married, three kids, lives in Needham, works in a bank."

"What's her husband do?"

"Works for the telephone company."

Bibi nodded gently. "Mine don't," she said.

"You stay with Dianne Lalli all this time?"

"No, her husband didn't like me staying there. I went up to Portland for a little while, then I came here."

"Why here?"

"Anthony."

"You think he's here?"

"I know he's here. He's got an answering service. It was how we used to get in touch, you know, when he couldn't call me at Marty's house, and I couldn't call him at Shirley's."

"And you called it."

"And he called me back. From here. The Mirage. He said I should come and join him."

"After he run out on you that way," Hawk said, "wouldn't think you'd want him back."

"I don't. It's why I'm staying where I'm staying," Bibi said. "He's crazy. He's got to finish what he started. He's got to lose everything."

"He know you're here?"

"Not yet."

"So why'd you come?" I said.

"The money he took was ours."

"Where'd you get it?" I said.

"He skimmed it from Gino and Julius," Bibi said. "For us. It was for us to start a new life."

"Whose idea was that?"

Bibi almost laughed.

"The new life was mine. The funny thing is the skimming idea was Shirley's. She got him to start holding out on Julius, said even if her father caught him he wouldn't do anything, because he was her husband."

"She wanted to get out of the house?"

"Guess so," Bibi said. "Away from her mother, Anthony says."

"Was supposed to be a new life for her too," I said. "How'd Gino get involved."

"New lives are hard," Bibi said, "aren't they. Anthony liked the deal. He figures he's doing Julius. He may as well do Gino. Only this time he got caught."

"By Marty," I said.

She looked surprised.

"How'd you know," Bibi said.

"I'm a trained detective," I said. "And instead of blowing the whistle, Marty cut himself in."

"Yes."

"And he became Anthony's partner, which is how you met Anthony."

"Yes."

She spoke so easily and without affect that it was hard to realize that she was telling me most of what I'd been trying to find out since Julius and Shirley came to hire me.

"And Marty met Shirley," I said.

"Marty knew Shirley?"

"Yeah," I said. "They used to meet regularly."

"Was he sleeping with her?"

"I don't think so."

"Lucky for her," Bibi said.

"Was the deal more than just money?"

"I don't know, it might have been."

"Was Marty happy being number two for Gino?"

"No. He said Gino was a pansy, and he hated taking orders from him."

I looked at Hawk.

"He using Anthony as his inside man in Julius's outfit," Hawk said.

"While he was funding a war chest," I said.

Hawk nodded slowly.

"Could be," he said.

"And then, as luck would have it," I said, "here came the Russians."

"Marty a *glasnost* guy," Hawk said.

"I don't know anything about Russians," Bibi said.

"No reason you should," I said to Bibi.

"And since they all in on this scam together, he takes up with Shirley," Hawk said. "To keep track of Anthony, like he used Anthony to keep track of Julius."

"What I like is how Marty thought he was running Anthony," I said. "Only he wasn't. Anthony got enough money to get away from Shirley and he took off with Marty's war chest. And Marty's wife."

"And Marty left with Shirley rolling around loose on the deck worried about her man," Hawk said.

"So he had to kill her when she showed up out here," I said. "Because she knew what was going on, or enough of it to cause him trouble."

"And gonna have to kill her," Hawk said, nodding at Bibi, "and he gonna have to kill Anthony."

"If we're right," I said.

"We might be," Hawk said.

"Yeah," I said. "We're due."

"I don't follow what you're saying," Bibi said. "Did he kill Shirley?"

"I like him for it," I said. "It makes some sense."

"I don't know why."

"If we're right," I said, "Marty's trying to run the

whole mob scene in Boston. You don't have to know why we think so, just remember the part about how he has to kill you too."

"That's not news," Bibi said. "He'd have killed me anyway, one way or another. In some ways he already has."

I nodded.

"I don't know if I can ever love anybody again. I don't know if I can ever be with a man again."

"That can be fixed," I said. "First though we got to fix this."

"I'm going to get my money back before Anthony loses it," Bibi said. "It's mine, and, in God's truth, I got nothing else to care about."

"Care about yourself," I said.

"Getting my money back is the best I can do," Bibi said.

"How you going to get the money?" Hawk said. "If there's any left."

"Whatever he has left, I want," Bibi said. "However I can get it. He took everything I ever had."

"Like your style," Hawk said as if he were thinking out loud.

"Want some help?" I said.

"I don't want any help from any men," she said. "Even you. I know you're a good man. Both of you are good men. But I have to stay clear of men for a while."

"Help is help," I said. "Regardless of the source."

"I never met a man that cared about me. I know you

do, but I can't react to it, you know? Not now anyway. And even you are trying to use me to nab Anthony."

"I want to make sense out of Shirley Ventura's murder and I want to see to it that you don't get hurt," I said. "When you went to Portland, how'd you get there?"

"Train."

"How'd you pay for the ticket."

"I had mon . . ." She paused as she remembered. "Okay, you gave me money and I ran away on you. I know. But you need to understand. I've been exploited all my life by men. I'm not able to trust you. I have to do what I can do by myself. I got a right."

"Affirmative action," Hawk murmured.

"I never been on my own before. I married Marty when I was seventeen to get out of the house. Didn't work out. Fifteen years later I took up with Anthony to get away from Marty. That didn't work out, either. I been looking for men to take care of me all my life, and I don't want to do it anymore."

"Why were you in such a hurry to get out of the house?"

"My old man was an asshole."

"And so were his replacements," I said.

Bibi stared at me for a moment.

"Well, that's over," she said finally. "No more assholes."

"So much for us," Hawk murmured.

"Must be kind of scary," I said. "On your own all at once."

"Yeah, it is, but no scarier than my life has been. I know you want to help me, and as much as I can, I appreciate it. I'm grateful. I am. But damnit I can't depend on a man, even you."

"It's a good thing to change," I said. "But it's kind of hard to do alone. And it's kind of hard to do all at once."

"This is the first step. Don't you get it? I can't turn to you. I want to. For God's sake I'm scared to death Marty will find me. But I simply cannot."

I looked at Hawk.

"I don't think I'm winning this conversation," I said.

"'Pears not."

"Okay," I said. "You want to go back to your hotel?"

Bibi was quiet for a bit, looking at me.

"Yeah," she said, "I do."

"Would you prefer to walk back alone?"

She took a deep inhale.

"Yes," she said. "I would."

"You know if Marty can find you, he'll kill you. Anthony too, I think, if he had the balls."

"He doesn't," Bibi said.

"Can never be sure," I said.

Bibi looked at me grimly with her lips clamped shut.

"Okay," I said and made a be-my-guest gesture with my hand and stepped aside. Bibi began slowly to walk back along Las Vegas Boulevard toward Convention Center Drive. After a few steps she turned.

"I get some money," she said, "I'll pay you back."

"Sure," I said.

She went a few more steps back along the empty street. Again she stopped and turned.

"I appreciate what you've done, both of you."

"Glad to help," I said.

CHAPTER
49

SHE KEPT WALKING. HAWK AND I WATCHED HER AS SHE WENT past the Desert Inn and turned right onto Convention Center Drive.

"We spend weeks looking for her," Hawk said. "And a lot of dough. And we fly three thousand miles and when we find her she gives you a speech and you let her walk."

"Always had a soft spot for feminism," I said.

"Of course," Hawk said. "Me too. Wouldn't be correct, I suppose, if we sort of kept an eye on her while we having it?"

"Paternalistic and exploitive," I said.

"What if she don't spot us?" Hawk said.

"Then it's fine," I said.

The rest of the way back to The Mirage, Hawk and I

had a lengthy discussion as to who would tail Bibi in the morning and who would sleep in. My argument was that early rising was in his genes from all those ancestral generations of chopping cotton before the dew had faded. He felt that this was a racist stereotype. He decried racial stereotyping, and explained to me that I was a white-bread paddy with a plantation mentality. I argued that, being of Irish descent, I had no mentality at all, plantation or otherwise. And he insisted that no one was too stupid to be a bigot. He had me there, but I didn't admit it and when we got to The Mirage we stopped in the lobby and flipped a coin and he lost.

As it turned out the argument was aimless, because forty-five minutes after I got to my room the phone rang and it was Bibi.

"I'm in the lobby," she said. "Marty's here."

She sounded out of breath.

"In the lobby?"

"No, I saw him in the lobby of my hotel when I came back from walking with you."

"He see you?"

"No, I ran all the way here."

"Room ten twenty-four," I said. "Come up."

I had my pants on, and a pair of loafers, when she rang my doorbell. Being a careful person I picked up my gun before I opened the door, but she was alone.

"Lock it," she said when she came in. Her breath was still coming heavy, and her face was flushed.

"I ran all the way here," she said. "Put the chain on."

I pulled the spread up over the unmade bed. When I'm not with Susan I don't need a suite. The room was all there was. No view of the volcano.

"Sit down," I said. "Want a drink?"

She shook her head. She continued to stand.

"Was Marty alone?" I said.

"The little man was there, that was with you tonight. I saw him through the door and never went in. There might have been other men too. The minute I saw Marty I turned and ran."

"Bernard J. Fortunato," I said.

"The little man that was with you?"

"Yeah," I said. "Looks like he sold you twice."

She had her arms folded and she walked back and forth in the small room, staying away from the window though we were on the tenth floor.

"You mean he called Marty?"

"I'll bet," I said. "Double the profit, double the fun."

"I'm scared."

"Don't blame you."

"I don't know what to do."

"Stay here," I said. "That's the first thing. Don't take off on me."

"I feel so stupid after all that stuff I said tonight about men."

"What you said made sense," I said. "You're just not quite ready to do it all without help. Nobody does it all without help. And this is my kind of help."

She stared at me.

"Without your shirt on . . . I didn't realize. You're a big man, aren't you."

"Yeah, and you don't need to slip into the admiring-woman disguise," I said. "I'll help you regardless."

"I wasn't . . . maybe I was. But Marty is a huge man, and he's so vicious. Nobody can stop Marty."

"Hawk and I will stop him," I said. "You're going to be fine."

"Will you kill him?"

"We'll see," I said.

"Kill him," she said.

Her voice was soft and flat, and earnest.

"You have to kill him," she said. "It's the only way."

"We'll play it as it lays," I said.

"If you kill him," she said, "I'll do anything you want me to do."

"No charge," I said. "Either way. I'll go to Hawk's room and you can sleep here."

She shook her head.

"I can't be alone," she said.

"Okay. I'll put the mattress on the floor. One of us can sleep on it and one on the box spring."

"That's very nice of you."

"Yeah. And listen. The way you were talking earlier was the right way. There's things some people can do and other things other people can do, and if you need help, it doesn't mean you're dependent. So don't be dependent. Stay with no-more-assholes."

She nodded, still clenched inside her folded arms, still

avoiding the tenth-story window. I unmade the bed, dragged the mattress onto the floor, folded the spread over to serve as padding on the box spring, found an extra blanket in the closet, put a pillow on the mattress, and left a pillow on the box spring.

"Your choice," I said.

"I can't just lie down and go to sleep," she said.

"You can do whatever you like," I said. "All I want to know is when you do lie down, where you wish to lie."

"I don't have any pajamas."

"Me either," I said.

She still stood, hugging herself, looking like she didn't know what to do. I looked at the box spring. It was probably less comfortable than the mattress.

"The bathroom's there. Use anything you find in there. I got a big day tomorrow, wrestling with Marty and such, and I need my rest."

I took off my shoes and put them side by side on the closet shelf, a habit ingrained in me by Pearl the Wonder Dog, who saw them as chew toys. I took off my pants, and hung them neatly on a hanger in the closet. I put the gun on the bed table beside me and, ever the gracious host, jumped on the box spring and went to sleep in my shorts. I don't know what Bibi did before retiring.

CHAPTER
50

THE MORNING WAS A LITTLE MORE INTIMATE THAN EITHER of us would have wished, but we got through it and by nine o'clock were downstairs breakfasting with Hawk and Bob the waiter. Hawk of course showed no surprise when Bibi and I sat down with him. And when I explained the situation he seemed pleased.

"You check on Anthony?" I said to Hawk.

"Yeah, my friend say he's here. Room fourteen-fifteen. Comped."

"How nice for him," I said.

Bob the waiter came by and poured me some decaf.

"Hey, Boston," he said. "Come back to visit your money?"

We ordered breakfast and lingered over it while we

pondered the situation. Actually Hawk and I did most of the pondering. And Bibi drank a lot of tea. But, by ten of eleven, we had pondered up a course of action. Hawk left before we did. I signed the check, left a big tip for Bob because he remembered me, went back up to my room with Bibi, and called Bernard J. Fortunato as soon as I got there.

"I need to talk with Marty Anaheim," I said.

"So why you calling me?"

"Because you know where he is," I said.

"What makes you think so?"

"Cut the crap, Bernie. You double-dipped. You sold her to me, then you sold her to Marty. He's in town I want to see him. You know where he is."

"Gotta make a living," Bernie said. "Whaddya want to see him about."

"Save a lot of trouble, you tell me where he is," I said.

"Save a lot of trouble for you," Bernie said. "Whaddya want?"

"I got his wife, and Anthony Meeker with me, we need to make a deal."

"Say I tell him that and he wants to see you, where you want to do it."

"Vacant lot," I said, "off the Strip, halfway between The Mirage and the MGM Grand, back of a boarded-up Greek restaurant, you know it?"

"Where they found the dead broad?" Bernie said.

"Yeah."

"What if he don't like that spot?"

320

"Then the hell with him," I said.

"I'll get back to you."

"You know where I am?"

"Yeah, sure, you're at The Mirage. What am I, stupid?"

"And Marty's probably at the Grand," I said. "People tend to go back to the same hotel."

"Even if he is you don't know what name."

"Why would he use a fake one?" I said.

"Beats me," Bernie said, and hung up.

In ten minutes Bernie called back.

"Marty'll be there at one," he said.

"Okay," I said.

I hung up the phone and said to Bibi, "Come on, let's collect Anthony."

She looked at her watch.

"He may still be in bed."

"Okay, we'll start there. You knock on his door, and stand where he can see you through the peephole. When you hear him start to take the chain bolt off, step out of the way."

"What are you going to do?" Bibi said.

"Reason with him."

We went up four floors from my room and found 1415 at the other end of the corridor. I stood against the wall to one side of the door, the side the doorknob was on. Bibi rang the bell. There was no movement. She rang it again. A voice said something indistinguishable. Then silence. Then the voice again. Still indistinguishable. Then the sound of the chain being removed. Bibi stepped to the other side of the door, and when it opened, I rolled off the wall and stepped through it, and hit him with a left hook and he staggered back into the room and sat abruptly on the bed. I took Bibi's arm and pulled her with me into the room, and shut the door.

Anthony's eyes shifted toward the night table and I took a long step past him and picked up a .380 Colt off the table and put it in my coat pocket.

"What the fuck are you doing?" Anthony said.

"Solving this case," I said.

"What case?"

"This one," I said.

"I don't know what you're talking about," he said. "Why the fuck'd you hit me?"

"Get your attention," I said.

He was wearing his bathrobe and the right side of his jaw where I'd punched him was beginning to puff.

"Put some clothes on." I said. "We're going out."

"What are you, nuts? You can't come in here and order me around, for crissake."

"That's what the punch was for," I said. "To remind you that I can come in here and order you around. Get dressed."

"Bibi, honey, this is crazy, what's going on?"

"You have to do what he says, Anthony."

I gave him a light pat on the cheek.

"Move it, Anthony, any reason to pop you again is a good reason."

Anthony said "For crissake" again but he went to the

back of a chair where his pants were, turned his back modestly, took off the robe, and slipped into the pants. When he went to the bathroom, I went with him and watched him splash water on his face and comb his hair, and came back with him while he took a clean white-on-white shirt out of the top bureau drawer and put it on. He buttoned the shirt up and turned back the cuffs and tucked the tail inside his stretch waistband. There were no belt loops on his pants.

"Where we going?" he said.

He was putting on his wristwatch.

"We're having a meeting with Marty Anaheim."

He froze. His mouth opened but he didn't speak. His eyes shifted to Bibi. She nodded.

"He'll kill me," Anthony said and his voice was scratchy. "He'll kill Bibi too."

"No," I said. "He won't."

"Yeah, he will, you don't know. He will kill me."

"I won't let him," I said. "Come on, we need to get going."

"Why don't we call the cops?" he said. "They can take care of Marty, can't they?"

"Cops think you killed your wife," I said. "And they got no reason to look for Marty. You want to give them a ringy ding?"

"Why do you need me?" Anthony said. "I'm on a good roll at the blackjack tables. Today I was going to bust 'em. I got no problem with Marty. Bibi can go with you. Hell, she's his wife."

I hit him again, not too hard. He bumped against the wall but didn't go down.

"That's why," I said.

"Jesus man, stop it. I'll go. Okay? Fine. No problem."

He straightened from the wall, rubbing the lump where'd I'd hit him twice.

"Can I have my gun back?"

"No."

We were silent down the corridor and in the elevator. He could of course make a dash in the casino and probably succeed, but it would bring the cops. And the cops thought he killed his wife. Outside the bright desert air hinted faintly of carbon monoxide as we walked down the Strip.

"It's fucking hot, man," Anthony said. "We gotta walk? How come we can't ride."

"Shut up," I explained.

"Where's Hawk? Shouldn't he be with us? You think you can go up against Marty alone?"

"Marty won't be alone," Bibi said. "He's never alone. There'll be three, four others with him."

"Got that covered," I said.

We got to the defunct Greek restaurant about five to one. There was plywood over the plate glass windows, and on the front door as well. Someone had sprayed *Julio Caesar Chavez* on the front door plywood in swirling black. We went around behind the building. It was as deserted as it had been when I was there last, looking at Shirley Ventura's dead eyes in the bright sunlight. Beside

324

me Anthony was making little whimpering sounds. Bibi was swallowing audibly. There was the sound of birds though I didn't see any, and the sound of cars going seventy-five on Interstate 15 maybe a hundred yards away, beyond the wire fence that enclosed the empty back lot. The wire was woven with weeds and grass that had formed a nearly solid mat along the fence. There were colonies of the same weeds scattered sparsely over the lot. Our feet crunched loudly on the gravel surface. Fifty feet beyond the restaurant was a corrugated metal utility building. Deep into the back corner of the lot were several cars gutted and partly disassembled, looking like discorporating carcasses.

"Place has Marty written all over it, hasn't it?" I said.

Neither of them answered. So much for small talk.

CHAPTER
51

WE WAITED. THE NEAR MIDDAY SUN BAKED DOWN ON THE gravel lot. A big maroon rental car crunched into the gravel area in front of the restaurant. It stopped out of sight. I could hear the doors open and close and then the crunch of footsteps and Marty Anaheim came around the corner of the restaurant wearing a white linen suit over a black tank top. With him was a fat Mexican in a flowered shirt and a funny small hat. Bibi was stone silent beside me. Anthony was moaning softly.

"Marty, you stylish bastard," I said. "Love your tank."

Marty and the Mexican kept walking straight toward us, without saying a word. This was calculated to make me feel faint. It wasn't working with me, but it seemed effective with Anthony. Finally they stopped about two feet away. The Mexican moved a little ways to my right. He had small eyes and they had no expression in them.

"Who's this," I said and nodded at the Mexican, "a loaner from the local guys?"

Marty ignored me. He stared straight at Bibi.

"When this is over, little girl, you're coming with me."

She didn't say anything. Marty looked at Anthony.

"And you're dead," he said.

Then he turned his attention, almost as if it were an afterthought, to me.

"Okay, asshole," Marty said. "Whaddya want?"

"I want to wrap this whole deal up, Marty."

"What deal?"

"The deal where you steal from Gino and kill Julius's daughter, and get into bed with the Russians in Boston, and have them try to whack me, and . . . you know, that deal."

Marty never blinked.

"And what are these two shit birds doing here?" he said.

"I knew you were looking for them," I said. "I brought them so you'd come."

"My God," Bibi said, "you used us for bait."

Marty really looked at her for the first time.

"Hard world, ain't it, baby."

Bibi didn't answer. I could feel the weight of the sun on my back.

"So what's your deal?" Marty said to me.

"I'll get to the deal in a minute," I said. "But I need a couple answers."

"You need a lot of things, asshole."

"It started," I said, "with Anthony here, skimming a little off the accounts he serviced for Gino. And you caught him, because Anthony's dumber than a rake handle, but instead of closing him down, you turned him, had him skimming from Gino and Julius and splitting the dough with you."

Marty nodded slightly. The small dry wind drifted across the lot and made a feeble attempt at ruffling Marty's hair.

"And while you had him in pocket, you had him spy on Julius."

"Not just him," Marty said. "Julius's daughter. She was a dumb quiff but she was smarter than Anthony."

"And when Anthony took off on you both, you became allies. Which is how you knew we were looking for him out here."

Marty shook his head in disbelief.

"She wanted him back, for crissake."

"And you wanted him dead, and she knew it. So she came out here to make sure you didn't hurt him."

Marty laughed. There was no pleasure in the laugh, only scorn. Scorn might be the only thing Marty had ever really felt.

"And you killed her," I said. "You beat her up and raped her and strangled her and dumped her body with no ID right over there."

Marty shrugged.

"You got some kind a question you're asking or do you just like to flap your face?"

"Did you beat her up and rape her just to throw the cops off, or was it recreational?" I said.

"That your question?"

"One of them," I said.

Marty grinned. It was an expression as scornful as the laugh had sounded.

"Both," he said.

"What I figured," I said.

"Got any other questions?"

"How come you set the Russians on me?"

"What makes you think it was me."

"Joe Broz told me."

For a moment Marty was startled. It was a brief slip and then he got the scorn back in place.

"So?"

"So, why?"

"Why do you think? You're all over my business. You're looking into Asshole Anthony, and you're looking for Bibi, and you're talking to the niggers, Gino and Julius and Fast Eddie. You're in the way. And you don't even fucking know what you're in the way of. A cheap fucking nickel-and-dime goddamned gumshoe poking around into something he couldn't understand if he found it, for crissake."

"Something really big, huh?"

"Bigger than you could handle, cheapie."

"Taking over the town, huh?"

"For starters, cheapie, just for starters."

"Today, Boston," I said. "Tomorrow the world."

"You think it's funny?"

"So far," I said, "all you've had to do is run Anthony and your wife, and you're oh for two on that. The Russians would feed you through a compactor an hour after you all took over."

"You think so?"

"Doesn't matter," I said. "I'm not going to let it happen anyway."

"You?" Marty laughed again. It sounded like claws on a tin roof. "Spenser, you fucking kill me, you know it. You going to stop me. You, asshole? You just delivered me the three people on the fucking planet I want to kill most."

"Killing isn't comparative," I said. "I think you mean the three people you most want to kill."

Marty ignored me.

"And you don't even know what you've fucking walked into, for crissake."

"Marty, you're not saying you set us up?" I said.

"Asshole!"

"You don't mean you sent some people down here ahead of time," I said.

Marty frowned slightly.

"I'm shocked," I said. "Shocked."

The Mexican didn't move, but I could sense a tightness in him that hadn't been there before.

Without taking his eyes off me, Marty yelled, "Paulie."

The door to the utility shed opened and two guys came out. One of them was leaning heavily on the other one. There was blood on his face. Hawk came out of the shed behind them. He held a big stainless-steel finish .44 Magnum loosely at his side, the barrel pointed aimlessly at the ground.

"One over behind the fence," Hawk said. "In the weeds."

His teeth flashed very white as he grinned at the Mexican.

"*Hasta la vista*," he said.

"Deceit breeds deceit," I said to Marty. "Hawk came down here, before I called you."

Beside me Anthony said, "Shoot him. You got to shoot him quick while you have the chance."

Nobody paid any attention to him.

The Mexican's small eyes shifted from Hawk to Marty to me and back to Hawk. He gave Marty one more brief sidelong glance and then turned without a word and walked back toward the street. Marty looked after him for a moment. Beside me I felt Anthony start to take a step, and I put my hand out and gripped his arm. I shook my head. He froze.

"Hard to get good help out here," I said.

Marty shifted his gaze back at me. He glanced at Hawk standing behind the two gunmen. In the background I heard the rental car start up and the gravel scatter as it drove away.

"Okay," Marty said. "This is the way I like it, anyway. It's down to you and me, ain't it."

"Appears so," I said.

"You got a deal, or what?"

"Couple things," I said.

"Like what?"

I said to Bibi, "This guy used to beat you up?"

"Yes," she said.

Her voice was so soft and flat it was almost inaudible.

I said to Marty, "You killed my client, Shirley."

"Yeah?"

"Yeah," I said and hit him a short left hook that landed under his right eye.

Beside me I heard Bibi gasp.

I hit him the same left hook again and a straight left on the nose. Blood started. Marty clubbed at me with his right. I took the hit mostly on the left shoulder and upper arm, but even so it rocked me and my arm hurt. I circled him a little, moving toward his left, and popped in the straight left on his nose again. He bulled inside the punch and grabbed me around the waist and lifted me in the air. I brought both fists simultaneously together on each side of his head, just in front of his ears. He grunted and staggered, still holding onto me, and turned his hip and slammed me onto the ground. I landed on my back and as he came down on top of me I doubled my knee and he fell on it, and slid sideways, to my right, while I rolled sideways to my left, and onto my feet. He scrambled onto his hands and knees and started to lunge at me and I kicked him in the head. It knocked him sideways and he went back down, landing on his right side, scrabbling away from me even as he landed. I waited. I could hear somebody's breath rasping in and out, and realized it was mine. Sweat was soaking my shirt and running down my face and arms. My hands were slippery with it, and Marty's blood. The desert seemed to have focused down to Marty and me. He got to his feet. I hit him again the straight left. He grabbed at my arm and missed, and I came in over his left shoulder with an overhand right that caught him under the left eye. I saw his knees buckle. He was still fighting but he was pawing at me. I slapped his left hand away and rolled in a right cross with all of me behind it and he went down. I waited. He got up and rushed in low at me, his head down. I kneed him in the face and he fell forward, trying to hang onto my legs as he went down. I stepped away from him and waited. He lay for a minute facedown on the hot gravel, and then he pushed himself up slowly like a man doing his hundredth pushup. I waited. He got his knees under him. Then his feet. Then he stood. Upright, but wobbly. His left eye was closed. Blood ran down his face and the front of his shirt was covered with it. I waited. He took a step toward me and pitched forward and lay motionless, facedown on the ground. Nobody moved. Nobody said anything. The traffic went slowly by on the Strip and more distantly, and much faster, behind us, on Route 15. Bibi stepped over next to Marty and quite deliberately kicked him in the side of the head. Then she turned and looked at me.

"You used me," she said, "as bait."

"Some," I said. "But you make a nice witness, too. You heard him say he killed Shirley."

"You better kill him," Anthony said. "While we got the chance. You wouldn't get in trouble. We'd all say it was self-defense."

I looked at him without saying anything. He turned toward Hawk.

"Do it," Anthony said. "Do it now, nobody'll say anything. Shoot those two guys too, if you're worried."

Hawk looked silently at Anthony for a minute and then looked at me.

"Old Marty didn't quit," Hawk said. "I'll give him that."

"Even if I was just a witness," Bibi said. The soft flat voice was shaking a little. "You still used me. You think it was right to use me?"

"It was necessary," I said. "And it worked. Sometimes I have to settle for that."

"You shouldn't have used me," she said.

CHAPTER
52

It was November and while it hadn't snowed yet, it was cold out. Susan and I were sitting with Pearl the Wonder Dog between us on the couch in front of a fire in the kitchen of the nearly finished house we'd been working on in Concord. We had been sitting side by side, on the couch, with the potential for necking, but Pearl had weaseled herself in between us and the necking remained potential.

"The DNA match between Marty and the sperm he left in Shirley sort of settled it for him," I said.

"Were the police grateful?" Susan said.

"For cops," I said. "Romero let Bibi walk without a word."

"How about Anthony Meeker."

"The little bastard," I said. "He caused the whole damned mess in the first place. Starting with when he married Shirley to get at Julius's money."

"But they haven't got a crime they can convict him of?"

Pearl leaned heavily against me, and gave me a wide rough wet lap on my cheek.

"She loves her daddy," Susan said.

"She also loves where the gravel scrape is healing," I said. "No. He hasn't done anything they can catch him for. But Romero said they could hold him a few days as a material witness before they turned him loose. And I took the liberty of letting Julius know where he is."

Susan sat back a little and looked at me.

"God, sometimes even I forget how hard a man you are."

"He married an emotional cripple and exploited her and got her killed," I said. "He left Bibi broke in Vegas and took off with the money that was supposed to be their start-over cash."

Pearl gave me another lap.

"Besides," I said, "I like dogs."

"So did Hitler," Susan said.

I eased Pearl away from me and got up. Pearl immediately transferred her weight to Susan. I put a couple more logs in the fireplace and went to the stove and opened the oven. There were yellow eye beans baking in an old-fashioned brown and tan pot. I put a pan of corn bread batter in to bake beside them. Then I got some Iron

Horse champagne out of the refrigerator and two glasses and brought them back to the couch.

"What about the mob takeover business in Boston?" Susan said.

"Don't know," I said. "Read that Tarone Jessup got killed, and a couple weeks later I read that two Russian immigrants from New York got dumped on Blue Hill Ave. Probably means that Tony Marcus has got to risk a tougher caretaker until he gets out."

"Do you think the Russians can do it?"

"They've got to form an alliance," I said, "with Julius, or Gino, or Fast Eddie Lee. After the fiasco with Marty, I don't think it's going to happen."

"What's going to happen to Marty?"

"Once they get wind of his connection with the Russians, I think platoons of feds will head for Nevada to see what kind of deal they can make with him to help them with the Russians."

"Would it be bad if the Russians succeeded? If they, what? Took over organized crime in Boston."

I shrugged. "Too big an issue for me," I said. "I work on a smaller scale."

"Who killed Shirley Ventura," Susan said.

"Yeah."

"How to save Bibi Anaheim."

"She's gone back to using her maiden name," I said. "Costa."

"Have you ever thought about what would have happened if you and Hawk had failed."

"Yeah."

"She was right," Susan said. "You did use her."

"I know."

"Even though it was in her best interest."

"I know."

"You should have found another way."

"I know."

"If you had it to do over again you'd do the same thing," Susan said. "Wouldn't you?"

"Yeah."

Susan smiled at me and drank some of her champagne. Incredibly, Pearl had found a way to lie down and stretch out fully on the couch between us. This left us less room than one would have hoped for, at opposite ends of the couch. The fire had fully involved the new logs I'd put on, and the flicker of it on the dark windows made the room seem nearly antic. I tasted my champagne. It was very cold, as it should be, and the bite of it was clean on the back of my mouth.

"You don't always do the right thing," Susan said.

"True," I said.

"But you get as close as you can," she said.

The fireplace hissed as sap boiled out one end of a log. The log settled a little deeper into the flames.

"What are we having with the beans and corn bread?"

"I got four venison chops," I said. "They've been marinating in red wine and rosemary."

"Dessert?"

"Bread pudding with whisky sauce."

"God," Susan said. "I won't be able to walk."

"How about other activity."

"Anything prone is fine," Susan said.

"My feelings exactly."

"Good," Susan said. "What happened to Bibi."

"She said she was going back to Fairhaven," I said.

"With her old name," Susan said. "Starting over."

"Who was it who said there are no second acts in American life," I said.

"I don't know," Susan said. "But he or she was wrong. You might recall that we're in act two ourselves."

"I remember."

"She's been abused. She needs help," Susan said.

"I suggested that. She said she wasn't interested. I gave her your phone number anyway, and said you might be useful."

"If she calls, I can get her a referral down there," Susan said. "I'm too tied to you to help her myself."

"Good to know," I said.

"She may not call," Susan said.

I shrugged.

"She isn't able to know yet," Susan said, "how much you helped her. She's got too much history weighing on her, and all she remembers is you used her to get Marty."

"I know," I said.

"She may know some day," Susan said.

"Doesn't matter," I said.

Susan got up and walked around the couch. Pearl immediately expanded into the vacant area. Susan sat on the arm of the couch next to me and put her arm around my shoulder and laid her cheek against the top of my head.

"Yes, it does," she said.

Robert B. Parker is the author of more than fifty books. He lived in Boston. Visit the author's website at www.robertbparker.net.

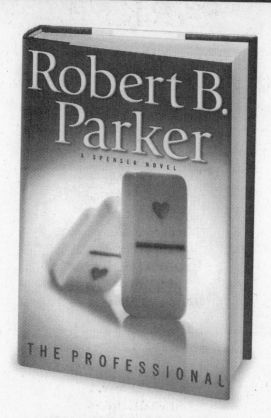

A Jesse Stone Novel from
New York Times Bestselling Author

Robert B. Parker

STRANGER IN PARADISE

An Apache hit man arrives in Paradise to find
a missing girl and snuff out her mother. But
his conscience is getting the best of him. If he
doesn't make the hit, he'll pay for it. So might
Jesse Stone, who's been enlisted to protect
them all.

penguin.com